THE LAST AVAILABLE

SEAN R. FRAZIER

ALSO BY SEAN R. FRAZIER

The Call of Chaos (The Forgotten Years Book 1)

The Coming Storm (The Forgotten Years Book 2)

Descent into Madness (The Forgotten Years Book 3)

Ascent into Light (The Forgotten Years Book 4)

Mage Breaker (Mage Breaker Saga Book 1)

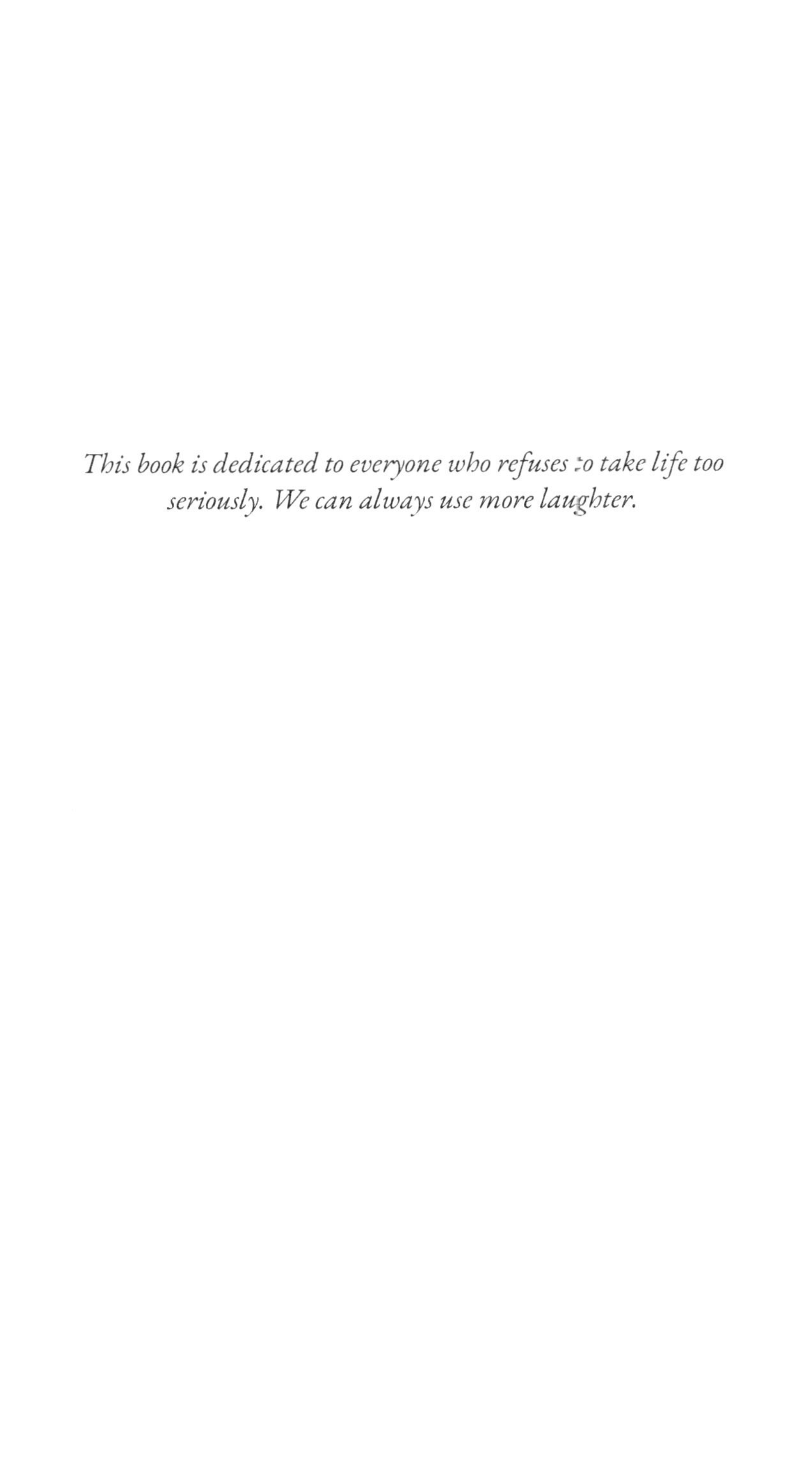

This book is dedicated to everyone who refuses to take life too seriously. We can always use more laughter.

1

ur tale begins at the Inn of the Scorned Woman which, as luck would have it, sat directly across the street from the Forgetful Husband Tavern. From the juxtaposition, you would think the two establishments were somehow related but, ironically enough, they were not. At least, that's what I've been told. I am not the utmost authority on such matters, but one does wonder.

The air was hot and balmy that night—typical of a summer evening in Ralph's Keep. It was a town well accustomed to both sizzling summer nights and frigid winter days. Being nestled smack dab in the middle of the Realm, the town was also very familiar to travelers like the one who entered the inn's taproom.

He was a large hulk of a man who had a bit of trouble fitting through the front door. But then, he wasn't really a man at all. He was an orc! Throg Axehammer was his name, and he removed his horned helmet as he sat at a large, circular table in the corner of the mostly deserted common room.

He grunted and picked his green teeth with a dagger, glaring around the room through squinty eyes and a pensive frown on his face. Throg was certainly not an individual you would want to cross ... or double cross ... or even triple cross, if such a thing was possible.

On his back he carried a hefty, dual-bladed battle axe. His armor consisted mostly of animal hides with bits of metal haphazardly jutting out here and there. There was not a hair on the green beast's head, and it was doubtful there was much of a brain there, either.

It was late—almost closing time—and only one man was working at the bar. His name was Jaco Wingsgood and he owned the place. A large man himself, he was quite well built for someone who worked behind a counter most days. He scratched his bald head and picked up several glasses as he walked into the kitchen.

Throg stroked his bare chin and stared at the table. I wondered if he perhaps wanted a drink—it probably wasn't wise to keep an orc waiting. To my surprise, he patiently sat, picking his nose and examining the room. For a moment he looked less imposing and more ... bored. Soon enough, however, the front door opened, and another man entered. He looked around briefly and then, without a word, he sat across the table from the orc. Most people wouldn't intentionally put themselves in such danger, so I suspected this was another expected guest.

He was clad in brown breeches and a bright blue tabard that was littered with the symbols of many different deities. On his left hip hung a long, slender sword and he carried a shield. He removed his shiny, winged helm and straightened his brown, shoulder-length hair.

This man must have been Brutus TheKind. He fit the description, anyway. The fact that his armor was shiny and his garb was immaculate confirmed my suspicions and I was beginning to wonder if this man was just that dangerous or if he had never seen combat at all. Whether "TheKind" was truly his last name was up for debate as was whether he followed that namesake.

Throg looked Brutus over as the man inspected the fingernails on his right hand, obviously not paying attention to the orc, the orc's glare, or the drool dripping from the brute's fangs. Instead, he occupied himself by admiring his own visage reflected quite accurately in his shield. I couldn't tell if there was tension in the air or just mutual malaise and discomfort.

Soon after, a raven-haired woman entered the common room. Clad in chain armor that desperately tried to cover only the most sensitive areas of a lady, she carried numerous weapons. I noticed a longsword, a great sword, a short sword, and some kind of large stick. There were several more on her person, but I couldn't determine what they were.

Her name was Pylara Wondercleave—a vicious female warrior with a reputation for her combat prowess—she loved to kill, and everyone knew it. Of course, all this killing mostly involved vermin and small animals. But she was apparently the best at it—a true professional. I wasn't sure if she had some kind of a vendetta against them or if that was the only work that she could find around these parts. Either way, I would not want to be a squirrel right now. Rumor had it, if you looked into her brown eyes for too long, you died.

Possibly because she would stab you while you gazed at her.

She sat next to Brutus and propped her feet up on the table. I snickered a little when I noticed that Brutus' hair was much better kept than her own.

"Nice armor," he snickered, "or lack thereof."

"You can stop staring now," she snarled. I could see her grip on the massive tree branch tightening.

I sipped my mead, letting the faint tastes of apple and roses wash over my tongue, waiting for the next individual to arrive and hoping these people didn't kill each other. I did not have to wait long ... for someone else to arrive of course. This wouldn't be much of a tale if they all died in the first chapter, right?

The door soon opened and Liandra Firefang sheepishly poked her head into the room, her red eyes scanning everything. After looking around, she seemed satisfied and slowly crept in. The group at the table all stared at her as she sat near Brutus. Her blond hair fell at haphazard, uneven lengths—some of it even sticking straight up— and the ends were singed.

The group remained silent, eyeballing one another with suspicion. It looked as though they were all waiting on someone else to either start the conversation ... or a fight. To say the situation was tense would have been ... well, I don't even know. Either they were busy sizing up one another or they were preoccupied with their own business. There were serious trust issues, here, as well as hygiene problems.

And then the halfling entered. The door flew wide, colliding with the wall and creating a sudden noise that jolted everyone out of their serenity.

"Hail!" he shouted, entering the room and slamming the door behind him. "Devinon Nimblefingers has arrived. I know you've all been waiting patiently, so we are now free get started!"

He was taller than your average halfling—probably about four feet two inches which technically made him a two-thirdling but that's neither here nor there. His brown hair was combed over to the right and was just long enough to partially obscure his blue eyes. He hurried over to the table, which now was rather full, and pulled a chair from another table, dragging it across the floor and making a terrible noise.

Throg grunted but, otherwise, nobody seemed fazed at all.

They were cool, calculating adventurers who were ready for anything. At least, they thought they were. I hoped they were.

And, finally, the musician appeared in the doorway. I recognized him as Liam Suavenair, the great flute-player. And, by "great", I mean that he knew which end was the business end of the instrument. He wasn't terrible, but he certainly had a long way to go. No, his real talent was supposedly singing. It was a shame that he insisted on trying to play the flute instead. But I heard he could play a mean rendition of "Hot Cross Buns."

"Hello, everyone!" he shouted, flourishing his cloak. It wasn't clear if he was somehow trying to make a grander entrance than Devinon, but it looked as though he were trying. His brown hair was in a long ponytail and his green eyes had a piercing intensity that seemed to make everyone want to be his friend. The colorful patterns on his tunic and breeches made my eyes hurt and he proudly displayed them as he sat next to Devinon who looked like he wanted to vomit.

That was all of them. They looked about as awkward as a dog with one wing. I decided to let them sit in silence and stew, hoping to glean something—anything—from their actions. At the very least, I hoped to get a read on how qualified they were for the job. And maybe, just maybe, they might bond.

"Hungry," Throg grunted, dropping a dagger loudly on the table.

"Perhaps something from the kitchen?" Brutus gazed around the room, obviously looking for a serving maid. When he found none, he shrugged and gave up.

I had already taken the liberty of ordering food and was waiting for Jaco to return. The surefire way to get people to come to a meeting was to let everyone stuff their faces. That provided the added benefit of improving everyone's mood with a full stomach. And you couldn't just serve appetizers. Few believed appetizers made a meeting worth it.

Also, there was less talking and arguing with full mouths.

Thankfully, as if on cue, Jaco emerged from the kitchens with two trays piled high with food—fresh cheeses, bread, steaming meats, and several mugs of ale. How he carried it all, I have no idea, but that's not important.

"I hope you lot are hungry," Jaco laughed, setting the trays down in the center of the table with some plates and utensils. The group said nothing and, instead, eyed him suspiciously. Several moments of silence went by as he stared back at them, obviously nervous and unsure how to act. Eventually, he slowly backed away and disappeared into the kitchens.

And the group continued to eye one another with great scrutiny. Nobody made a move to be the first to eat. At first, I found this behavior charming and admired their suspicions— it always paid to be cautious—but, honestly, it began to annoy me as I continued to observe them. There was cautious and then there was paranoid, and they were quickly moving into the latter. I began to have doubts, but they were the only option at this point.

"Well, then," Liam piped up, reaching for a leg of lamb. Everyone immediately turned and stared at him. You would've thought he'd just produced a dead puppy from his backpack, ripped it open, and ate it right in front of everyone. "Well, I am certainly not about to let all this tasty-looking food go to waste. If you guys won't eat it, then I will."

"That's fine with me," Devinon Nimblefingers replied, "we'll all just watch and see what happens."

"What you mean?" asked Throg. "Food look tasty."

"He means," Liandra interrupted, "that the food could be poisoned. We'll let the minstrel take the first bite and, if he kicks over, then we know not to eat it."

"Poisoned?" Liam laughed. "Who would want to poison

us? Besides, there's always a chance that, even if it *is* poisoned, I could resist it. Then you would never know, would you?"

Just a hunch," Devinon said.

"Why would anyone want to poison us?" Liam asked.

"I don't know," Devinon retorted. "I mean, you've only been here a few minutes and I'm already seriously considering it."

"That's preposterous!" Liam shouted.

"I gotta say, I'm with him," Brutus agreed. "Those colors you're wearing are pretty obnoxious and making me ill. Poisoning you might be the best course of action."

"Enough!" Liandra shouted, slamming her dainty hands on the table. She promptly rubbed them and winced ... and I'm not sure, but she may have apologized to them.

"Look," Devinon continued, "we don't even know why we're here. He looked around the room. Though I mostly had my back turned to the group I could almost feel his gaze wash over me. I decided to try to defuse the tension.

"*I* am why you're here," I said, turning around and finishing my mead. I set the goblet down on the counter and approached the table. "I have assembled you here in this fine establishment."

"And who the Hells are you?" Devinon's blue eyes looked me up and down. The rest of the group was not so scrutinizing. Throg looked downright vacuous.

"Who I am is not important right now."

"Why not?" Pylara asked.

"Because," I replied. This was going nowhere fast, but I knew what adventurers liked so it wouldn't be difficult to change the subject. "Treasure."

"Because, treasure?" Devinon's eyes lit up and a grin crossed his face. "I like the sound of that.

"I am not interested in treasure," Brutus argued. "Worldly

possessions are not important to a follower of Gamchakara, Deity of Faith."

"Well, then, you can keep your faith and I'll keep the treasure!"

"Ha ha, just kidding. I totally want treasure."

"You don't get *all* the treasure," Pylara demanded. "You keep your sticky fingers off of my share or you'll pull back a stump!"

"Pfft, you don't scare me," Devinon laughed, reclining in his chair. "I've got a higher Dex score than you."

"A what? Make sense, kid!" Pylara glared at Devinon, obviously confused.

"Never mind. And I'm not a kid!"

I cleared my throat to get their attention which stopped the banter.

"The food is not poisoned," I said. "If you'd like, I could eat some of it first. It looks delicious." I took a deep sniff of the air. "And it smells even better."

Throg dropped a bone on the table and burped loudly. Everyone's gaze shifted to him.

"Throg hungry, didn't want to wait." He tore a loaf of bread in half and shoved it into his mouth while everyone watched.

"Well, that's proof enough for me." Liandra gathered some food on her plate and began to eat.

Everyone else followed suit and soon, it seemed that the general attitude was improving. Had I told the group that I mixed a friendship potion in with the food they probably would have freaked out. I lacked the patience to try and get everyone to be comfortable with one another in such a short amount of time so I took a shortcut. It wasn't the first time I had done something like this, and it certainly wouldn't be the last.

Not that I enjoy tampering with food, I simply hoped to stave off a world-ending event.

"So," I continued, "as I was saying, my name is Gerald Maltarand, and I am happy to see that you have answered my summons. For I have an important quest that requires a party of trusty, stout adventurers to complete, and I'm hopeful you are those adventurers."

Everyone suspiciously eyed one another, nobody daring to speak. They sat this way for several moments and, as I observed them, I began to have my doubts. Sure, I could have assembled more seasoned adventurers, but they came at a higher price and their larger egos often got in the way. Besides that, they often took longer to get things done, usually preoccupied with telling stories of their greatness or of how they royally screwed up. And don't even get me started on the theater quotes ... bringing up obscure, supposedly humorous lines from plays and stories. No, I needed new blood for this.

"I can see," I continued, "that you are all excited about this opportunity, so I will elaborate." I paused a moment to make sure everyone was paying attention. It was crucial that they know what they were getting into—not for their safety, but so they could actually complete the task. "A dark force is overtaking the land and I have gathered you all here to help me stop it."

The group remained quiet. They sat in silence. If they could, they would've *drowned* in silence. I was beginning to wonder what I had gotten myself into.

"Again?" Devinon finally said. "What the Hells? Didn't we *just* get done with a major crisis, like, last month? What was it called again?" Devinon paused, lost in thought.

"The 'Ender', I believe it was," Liam replied.

"Yes!" Devinon laughed. "Right. The Ender. So what in the fifteen-or-so Hells is so damned important this time? Can't we just be left alone for once?"

"Probably something so dire and dangerous," Liandra mumbled, "that we are the only people who can stop it, right?" She stared at her plate, carefully waving her hands over her food until it started to smolder and, eventually, burst into flame, startling Liam and Brutus. "Doesn't that sound about right?"

"Obviously," Devinon responded, dripping with sarcasm.

"Be that as it may," Brutus interrupted, "we should hear the man out. He has, at least, paid for our dinner." He paused a moment, about to take another bite. "You *did* pay for our dinner, right? Because I'm a little light on coin this ... um ... lifetime."

"The priest is right," Devinon added. "Besides, there's probably a fat reward and Papa needs a new ... everything."

"Rewards aren't everything, you know," Brutus replied. "The goddess of goodwill—

"Bah!" Devinon shouted. "Shut your godhole."

"I was being sarcastic," Brutus laughed, "obviously, rewards are everything!"

"You're supposed to use a sarcastic voice then."

"But that's part of the sarcasm, isn't it? Like, if I overly emphasize the sarcasm, then it's not really sarcasm."

"What does that even mean?" Devinon laughed. "Sarcasm is *always* sarcasm. For example, if I tell you 'I love that tunic!' I'll say it in a different tone. Otherwise, you might think I really *do* like it and, well, that would be a fashion nightmare."

"Wait," Brutus interrupted. "You don't like my tunic?"

"Of course I do!"

"Wait a minute ..."

"The child is correct," Liandra interrupted. The sleeve of her robes had somehow caught fire. She extinguished the flames, though her food was still burning. "We should like to get paid, of course."

"Still not a kid," Devinon growled.

"Loot!" Throg slammed his fist on the table, shaking everyone's dishes.

"I think we should look at the bigger picture—something much bigger than just loot," Pylara said. "*Loads of loot!*"

Even Liam appeared to perk up when treasure was discussed. Frankly, it surprised me that Brutus cared about payment but he also didn't seem to be completely on the level when it came to his faith. Normally this would make things problematic but questionable morals made for flexibility and, sometimes, you just had to do what needed to be done. Most priests had sticks up their butts anyway.

"What we do?" Throg asked, his mouth full of food. Half of it dropped back onto his plate. If I didn't know better, I would've sworn that he'd been eating the exact same chunk of bread this whole time. Maybe if he stopped missing his mouth …

"Yes," Liandra began to clarify. "What is it you would like us to do?" She finally snuffed the flames from her food and began to eat it. What once was a cut of beef now resembled coal, though she appeared to enjoy it.

Liam alternated between playing his flute and humming a tune nobody recognized or cared for.

"It's dangerous," I said. There was no point in sugar-coating it. "The world hangs in the balance."

"As always," Pylara added.

"A new evil has descended upon the land," I continued, "evil like nothing the world has ever seen before."

"Has the world *heard* evil like this before?" Devinon giggled. "Or smelled it?"

"Ew!" Throg held his nose. "I no like smelly evil!"

They continued for several minutes, joking about various aspects of evil. As I waited for them to get bored, I briefly considered if this ended in a total party kill, it wouldn't necessarily be a terrible thing. But I *needed* them. The *world* needed them ... fart jokes and all.

Once they were finally done, I continued.

"To the north," I sighed, "there is a land called 'The Fel—"

"The Smell?" Devinon joked, holding his nose. "Sounds gross!"

"You mean The Gel?" Throg laughed, spitting food everywhere. He was the only one laughing at his joke, in fact. The rest of the party stared at him in relative silence until he was done, which was a good three or four minutes. It's always best not to interrupt a laughing orc ... or an orc doing anything for that matter.

"So, anyway," I sighed again, "They have been stricken with a plague. People are falling mysteriously ill, livestock is dying, and crops are withering away."

"It sounds to me," Liam interjected, flipping the hair out of his eyes, "that they require a healer and some water. Staying hydrated is key, as is remaining limber and flexible, but not so much in this case."

"It goes far beyond that," I replied. "Evil has descended upon them."

"What this evil?" Throg demanded, slamming his fist on the table. Though he tried to hide it, I could see a grimace pass over his face. His fist had come down on his knife, which he quickly pulled out.

"Nobody knows," I said.

"But it needs an ass-whoopin'!" Devinon laughed, punching the air. "Just line up all the evils and we'll take 'em all down!"

"Yeah, like dominos!" Brutus added.

"No not like dominos," Devinon argued. "Like those things you can set up and topple just one and they all eventually fall."

"Those are dominos, fool," Liandra retorted.

"No they're not."

"Pretty sure they are," Pylara continued.

Even Throg seemed to agree.

"So," Liandra said in her usual, quiet tone, "you want us to travel north to a place we've never been to confront an evil we know nothing about?"

"That sums it up nicely," I said. "But there is a whole lot more to it than that."

"Oh?" Brutus perked up. He was sincere and appeared to be ready to go at that very moment.

"Indeed. Before you confront evil, you must prepare yourselves. It's a grueling, dangerous path you will tread, and you must be ready.

"Bring it on," Devinon cheered. "I'll stab that path in the ass!"

"The first step in your quest is," I paused a moment to make sure they were all listening. "You must go to Alexander's Book Emporium and bring me a copy of 'A Brief History of the Entire World'."

2

Well, sonofa—" Devinon Nimblefingers was obviously upset. The morning sun warmed his face and forced him to squint his eyes.

"What problem, kid?" Throg Axehammer scanned the area ahead, ready to have his axe in hand at the first sight of danger.

"It's an errand quest," Devinon replied. "A godsdamned errand quest."

"A what?" Liam was only barely paying attention. More than anything, he appeared to be ogling every woman he saw.

"An errand quest—seriously, you guys are clueless!" Devinon ground his teeth in frustration and balled his fists. "We're supposed to save the world … by getting this dude a book? Why can't his lazy ass get the book himself if it's so important? We've got better things to do."

"This important," Throg stoically replied. He sniffed the air and grunted his approval. "If Gerald say so, then it so."

"He didn't even give us coin to buy it!" Devinon dug his fingernails into his palms. "What has this got to do with saving the world from an all-powerful evil? Gerald's just being lazy."

"And cheap!" Brutus added.

"Yeah, and cheap. We need less reading and more world-saving."

"I think bookstores are fabulous!" Liandra did not appear to be paying much attention to the actual conversation at hand. Instead, she was daydreaming about all the books in the store to read, page through, and possibly set on fire.

"We have plenty of coin, I'm sure," Liam laughed as he flicked the strands of soft, brown hair from his face. "Why, I alone have a hundred gold coins on me right now!"

"Not for long," Devinon muttered quietly, grinning ear to ear. He began imagining all the different ways he could get at the bard's coin purse. He was relatively certain it wouldn't be much of a challenge no matter which method he used. Suddenly, this worthless grind quest didn't seem to annoy him as much, but the bard still did.

"Fine," he grumbled, "let's go get this damned book already. It doesn't even sound exciting—A Brief History of the Entire World. I bet the ending sucks."

When they reached their destination—Alexander's Book Emporium—they stopped outside. It was a simple, one-story building with two large windows showcasing a plethora of tomes for the perusal of its patrons. Pylara peered in through one of the windows to see that the shop was moderately busy. It appeared this particular store was quite popular and—

"Enough already," Devinon growled.

"Enough what?" Throg replied.

"Enough ... um ..." Devinon stammered. "Enough exposition already."

"I have no idea what the kid is talking about," Pylara replied, impatiently. "Can he just shut up already?"

"First of all," Devinon growled. He walked up very close to her. It was difficult to appear imposing when your adversary was at least two feet taller than you. "I am *not* a kid. Second—"

Liam opened the door to the shop, with Brutus close behind, and was about to enter when Devinon, forced to remove his gaze from Pylara, grabbed them both and tried his best to stop them. They seemed to barely notice at first but eventually stopped.

"What's your hesitation, child?" Brutus asked. "Do you sense danger inside?"

"We haven't determined how we're getting the book yet," the halfling whispered. "We need a plan. We're adventurers, and adventurers need to be prepared. We can't just *walk* in there and grab it!"

"Of course, we're not," Brutus laughed. "We're going to *buy* it! That's what one does at a bookshop."

Throg pushed his way past his companions and stormed into the store, followed by Pylara, Liandra and, eventually, the rest of the party.

"We're going to *buy* it," Devinon grumbled, mocking Brutus. "Where's the fun in that?" He, quite reluctantly, followed his companions into the bookstore. Though the shop looked orderly and clean it smelled moldy and damp.

Everyone else must have smelled it too. Throg even went so far as to pinch his nose. It's not something most people have seen before—an orc repulsed by a smell—considering they often use the rotting corpses of their fallen enemies as trophies ... and eat them from time to time. Though it was odd to see, none of the patrons paid Throg any mind—largely because making fun of an orc in any fashion often nominated you to be an immediate (and unwilling) blood donor.

"So," Throg started, trying to speak while holding his nose. "Where ib dis book?"

"What?" Liam asked.

"Where ib de book?" Throg repeated, anger seeping into his voice.

"Many apologies, good orc," Brutus added, "but I cannot understand you."

"Book! Book! Where book?" Throg stomped his feet in frustration, causing many patrons to stop and stare. A few even ducked behind bookshelves to hide as several books tumbled from their shelves.

"Oh!" Liam snickered, "the *book*! Why didn't you say so!"

"I suggest we fan out and try to find it," Pylara said. "Keep your eyes open for—"

"Danger?" Brutus asked, raising his shield.

"Books," Pylara sighed.

"We're splitting up the party?" Liam replied. "I think that's a bad idea. You *never* split up the party! There could be danger at every turn!"

"In a book shop?" Liandra asked, wrinkling her face in disbelief. "I think we'll be fine."

Unfortunately for Liam, everyone had already begun to scatter, searching the shelves for "A Brief History of the Entire World." Well, that is, everyone except Liandra, who stationed herself in front of one of the shelves and began poring through several books at once. She pulled out at least ten books and piled them on the floor in front of her. Liam briefly considered asking Liandra to search with him but thought better of it. Instead, he nervously inspected the shelves and stacks alone, quietly whistling a tune off-key.

Throg eventually got used to the smell which meant he could now use both hands to search, which was a futile effort since he couldn't read to begin with, but he occupied himself looking at illustrations. Brutus became distracted and ended up wasting time reading a book about lizard religions. Despite exhaustive efforts, Pylara, Liam, and Liandra came up empty-handed, unable to locate the proper tome.

Everyone searched a few minutes longer but, once it was

apparent there was no more progress to be made, Throg approached the shopkeeper.

He was an older gentleman—possibly having seen fifty summers—sitting at a small table. His spectacles nearly slid off the end of his long, slender nose as he focused on the papers before him. After running a hand over his graying beard he wrote something, crossed it out, and then wrote something else, appearing not to notice the hulking orc looming over him.

Throg waited patiently, looking nervously around the shop and fidgeting. Several times he started to speak but stopped himself and remained quiet, not wanting to disturb this man's deep thoughts. He tried to whistle but failed miserably and resorted to humming. Whistling wasn't a skill he was good at—probably because it didn't involve killing something.

"So, if these 'Threads' can channel power," the man muttered to himself, "then ..." He trailed off, writing some more.

Throg tried to reach an itch on his back which was, quite inconveniently, located behind his axe. He squirmed and stretched but couldn't properly get at it. Frustrated, he pulled his axe off and feverishly scratched his back. In the process, however, he lost his grip on his weapon and it slammed down upon the table in front of the shopkeeper, who jumped out of his chair and stared upward, suddenly noticing the orc. Throg began to panic which made the shopkeeper panic.

"Book," Throg said. "I need book."

"Wh ... whatever you want," the man stammered, shaking. "Just ... just don't hurt me. You can have any book in here, okay?"

"No hurt," Throg replied. He picked up his axe to put it back on his back, but this apparently scared the man even more. "Book ... Brief history something something."

The man didn't appear to hear Throg as he backed away slowly, shaking uncontrollably. Throg, now with his axe safely affixed to his back, tried to reassure the man that no harm would come to him, but his efforts only worsened the situation. He held his hands up in front of him, palms out and tried to explain to the shopkeeper who panicked even more, now hyperventilating and sweating.

"A Brief History of the Entire World," Liandra said, suddenly appearing beside Throg and keeping her voice calm and reassuring. She stepped in front of the orc and flourished her red robes. Pylara and Brutus stepped in behind her. Devinon and Liam, however, were nowhere to be seen. "And possibly some of the books on this short list I've compiled.

Her "short list" consisted of several large pieces of parchment.

"Oh," the man sighed, obviously relieved that he was not dying today. He took a moment to calm himself and wipe away the sweat from, well, everywhere. "Well, then. I only keep one copy around most of the time—on account of the book's cost and size, that is. Also, it reads like a grocery list and nobody ever asks for it." He leaned in closer to the group. "It's not light reading and the writing is rather dull," he whispered. "Plus, the end is predictable and uninspired."

"I knew it!" Devinon shouted, triumphantly, seemingly appearing out of nowhere.

"Sounds ... fun," Brutus quipped.

"Let me go in the back and get it for you." The shopkeeper disappeared through a curtain behind him, leaving the five companions to wait awkwardly.

"This is possibly the worst quest ..." Liandra trailed off. She twirled a finger through her smoldering hair and rolled her eyes. "We have better things to do."

"But do we, though?" Brutus asked.

"I definitely do," Devinon sighed.

"It must be important," Brutus reassured him. "Otherwise, Gerald would not have asked us to do it."

"I hope we're rewarded," Pylara added.

"I like her thinking," Devinon agreed. "Loot makes even the dullest quest worth it."

The man reemerged empty-handed from behind the curtain with a worried look on his face.

"I, uh," he stuttered. "I seem to be out of that particular book. "But I've plenty of other—"

"No," Throg interrupted. "Need *that* book."

"The fate of the world depends on it," Brutus added. "We simply *must* have it. If you cannot provide it, you have doomed us all!"

"Doomed ... doomed us all to what? Illiteracy?" The shopkeeper paused and scratched his chin. "Well," he continued, adjusting his spectacles, "you could try the book shop over in Dindledon. It's only about a day's ride—"

"Ew," Pylara snorted. "Hells no. Too many halflings."

"Yeah," Brutus agreed. "I don't want to sound insensitive but ... yeah, too many hygiene-challenged halflings walking around in bare feet and food stains on their clothes."

The party all stopped and stared at Brutus, completely surprised.

"What? My goddess finds them to be unsavory little vermin."

Everyone stood in awkward, uncomfortable silence, completely unsure of what to say. In fact, nobody was sure that they actually disagreed with Brutus. The shopkeeper looked just as nervous as the rest of them felt.

"So, then," Brutus declared, breaking the silence. "I guess we're out of luck today. We shall find an alternative. You guys fetch the bard. I'll wait outside." With a flourish of his cloak, he made his heroic exit from the book shop.

3

ell," Pylara said as she exited the bookstore, "the bard's dead."

In her arms, she held Lam's brutally devastated corpse. Her face showed sadness but also disappointment and exasperation ... and maybe a little boredom.

The rest of the party stood in the street, speechless, unsure of what to say for several moments.

"What?" Devinon shrieked. Brutus held out his palm into which Devinon reluctantly placed five gold coins. After being counted, the coins quickly disappeared into Brutus' coin purse. "When the Hells did that happen?"

"I believe you owe me *ten*," Brutus said.

"Fine." Devinon fished out five more gold coins and dropped them into the cleric's hand.

The rest of the party looked uneasily at the transaction, but nobody said a word.

"What are you looking at?" Devinon asked, staring back at the group while Brutus fidgeted. "Come on, guys, he's a *bard*. Or he *was* a bard. They suck! They never survive! This one merely expired sooner than I anticipated. That's a mistake I won't make again." He glared at Brutus. "I have to admit, though, he's really good at exceeding expectations."

"I told you he'd die during the first quest," Brutus laughed. "Bards never live long."

"What kind of god do you follow, anyway, cleric?" Liandra asked.

"Baranarf, of course," Brutus replied. "He's the god of chance. Some say that he's the god of luck, but they're mistaken—misguided, even. This was obviously not luck."

"Not for me, anyway," Devinon mumbled.

"Wait," Liandra interrupted, "I thought you were a patron of Selana, goddess of frothy ale."

"That was yesterday," Brutus laughed. "Specifically, yesterday evening."

"I found him under a pile of books," Pylara said, still holding the bard's remains and looking quite uneasy.

"So, I guess it *is* true, then," Devinon giggled but everyone else looked confused. "The pen really *is* mightier than the sword?" Still, nobody laughed. "Really? Nobody? Are you all devoid of humor? Have you no ability to laugh? Did you not find that funny?"

"No," Throg replied tersely.

"Well," Liandra said, smirking. "Perhaps a little."

"You are all terrible people," Pylara growled. "Also, he's heavier than he looks. Can we please go somewhere? Eventually, I'd like to set him down."

"I never pay attention to encumbrance," Brutus quipped. "House rules."

"Well, aren't you the lucky one?" Pylara shifted the corpse on her shoulder. "I don't have that luxury, apparently."

"I honestly thought he'd live longer," Devinon groused, kicking at a rock on the ground. "Defeated by literature is a terrible way to die."

"Where we go?" Throg asked. Sadness was an odd emotion to find in an orc, but it was the best way to describe the look on his face. Though, if I'm being honest, it could have been hunger or gas.

"Back to the inn, I suppose," Pylara replied. "Not only did Liam die, but we failed. Gerald gave us the simplest of tasks and we failed miserably." They stepped into the street to begin the sullen walk back to the inn. "How are we supposed to save the world when we can't even retrieve a simple book?"

"Oh, give me a break," Devinon snorted. "A book wasn't going to save the world. Besides, everyone says it's boring. How is a boring book going to help save the world? This is absolutely the most meaningless errand quest ever! Gerald's just lazy and couldn't be bothered."

"Regardless," Pylara replied, "we failed—it was the most basic task, and we failed."

"Well," Devinon laughed, "maybe *you guys* failed." He produced a rather hefty book from his tiny backpack and held it up. "If you think that musician is heavy, you should lug *this* garbage around."

"That's the book!" Brutus gasped. "But if you had it all this time, why did we—"

"Because I *didn't* have it all this time, orc brain."

"Hey!" Throg yelled.

"No offense." Devinon was quick to respond, lest he share Liam's fate at the meaty hands of Throg. It was never wise to piss off an orc with your words—but it was so difficult to tell when they really understood words at all. "Anyway, this piece of crap isn't worth the 10 coppers it would have cost. While you guys were busy looking through the shelves and talking with that moldy shopkeeper, I was busy doing actual *work*."

"Stealing," Liandra replied.

"Acquiring. And since it wasn't easy to find, yes, I had to *work* to locate it."

"We should go back and pay for the book," Pylara said.

"And tell him what?" Devinon laughed. "How do you explain that to the shopkeeper? 'Oh hi. We're sorry but this book somehow jumped into our backpack and we'd like to pay for it now.' Besides, you see what that bookstore did to Liam. That place is a death trap! This lousy book is fair payment for the bard's death. He owed us that."

Brutus snickered, trying to keep it quiet but failing.

Throg grunted. Whether it was his way of laughing or a sign of disapproval, nobody could tell. He started down the street and the rest of the party followed as Devinon lagged behind, grumbling to himself.

"This had better be worth it," he mumbled. "I lost 10 coins on this quest."

"I thought you said you didn't pay for it," Pylara rebutted.

"I didn't. But I'm sure Sir Brutus Holyroller over there will enjoy my ten coins."

Brutus grinned. There was no doubt he would, indeed, enjoy Devinon's ten coins.

"It was an awful bet," Devinon continued. "It wasn't fair."

"You are a terrible holy man," Pylara growled, scolding Brutus.

"I am a priest, milady, not a paladin. There are many fundamental differences, not the least important of which is that I have a sense of humor and, also, better fashion sense."

When the party returned to the Inn of the Scorned Woman, the tap room was packed to the walls and there was nowhere for them to sit. Awkwardly standing in the doorway and holding a corpse, they looked around for Gerald but couldn't find him anywhere.

"Oh, screw this," Pylara growled as she slammed Liam's body down on the familiar round table—the very table they were sitting at when this quest began. The current patrons—merchants, from the looks of them—gasped in horror and two of them nearly fell out of their chairs. "Get out," she growled.

For a moment, nobody moved. The merchants froze, fear written on their faces. Then, as if it was a coordinated effort, they all jumped to their feet, gathered their things, and hurried out the door as the party watched.

"Nice," Devinon chuckled. "I guess it helps to have a dead guy you can slam down on a table. Maybe we should keep him around for a while. It might make things easier. Think of him as a tool except, now that he's dead, he's a useful tool!"

Nobody spoke.

"What I'm saying is, he's always been a tool but now—"

Pylara glared at Devinon.

"Right," he said, nearly choking on his words. "Or not."

"If you feel the need to explain the joke," Brutus said, "then it probably wasn't funny."

Devinon rolled his eyes. "Or you're hanging around a group of stiffs who don't understand humor. But, whatever."

"Can we just sit down and pretend this never happened?" Liandra asked.

"Pretend what never happened?" Devinon replied.

"All of it."

They wasted no time getting comfortable. Soon enough, a serving maid approached and cleaned off the previous group's dishes. The party waited patiently until, finally, Devinon spoke up.

"Could we get a round of ale for everyone, please? And something to eat—whatever you've got for breakfast. Oh, also, the priest has decided to pay for us all. He's very generous, you know. He's a follower of gbskdjsdf, goddess of generosity or something!"

Devinon grinned at Brutus who glared back but remained silent. That would take some of the sting out of the lost bet, but he had a feeling this was far from over.

"So," Liandra said, "where in the fifteen-or-so Hells is Gerald? I would think he'd want to have his book."

"Good question. Maybe his to-be-read pile is already overflowing, and he doesn't care as much as we thought he did?" Brutus chuckled, staring at the bard's body which still lay on the table. "Could we, uh … you know, maybe remove the ex-bard from the table?"

"Have a little respect for the dead!" Pylara scolded. "We lost a companion today!" She dragged Liam's body off the table and dropped it on the floor where it landed with a thud.

Devinon showed particular interest, leaning around the table to get a better look at the corpse. He eyed it with great curiosity.

"No, Devinon," Liandra said. "You cannot loot the body."

"Why not? He's not gonna need his stuff anymore!"

"Kid have point," Throg grunted, picking at his teeth with a fingernail—or claw, or whatever was on an orc's fingers.

"We don't loot the bodies of friends," Pylara added.

"Was he *truly* a friend?" Devinon continued, still inspecting the dead bard. "I mean, we really barely knew him. And maybe he *wants* us to have his gear! Perhaps he's an equipment donor."

"If *you* died, would you want us to have your stuff?" Liandra inquired, glowering at the halfling.

"Hells no," he replied instantly, apparently not needing even a fleeting moment to think about his answer. "You would have to pry my stuff from my cold, dead hands! And if you took it, I would haunt your asses all day and night—especially in the jakes while you're trying to poop!"

"That's what I thought," Pylara sneered.

"Yeah, but with Liam here, it's different."

"How exactly is this situation different?" asked Brutus, who appeared far too amused at the situation.

"Because he's not me. Also, I'm not planning on dying."

"How you know that?" Throg scratched his head, looking thoroughly confused. To his credit, he was paying more attention to his axe than he was to his companions. And he, too, kept staring down at Liam's corpse.

"Because."

"Because, why?" Pylara continued.

"Because I leveled and got a cool new ability that pretty much guarantees I'm not going to die. Wanna see?"

"I don't understand." Pylara looked more frustrated than anything else. She sighed and dismissed Devinon with a wave of her hand. At the same moment, the serving maid returned with a tray of tankards, each one filled with ale. Behind her was another serving maid with a tray overflowing with food. Once the food and drink were dispensed, the group fell silent as they feasted.

"Fine," Devinon muttered quietly, his mouth full, "but it's a really neat ability."

Shortly after the edible carnage began, I entered the taproom from the stairs, having come down from various activities in my room several floors up. I was eager for their return and, more importantly, to get my hands on the book they had retrieved for me. But, yes, I also had a sizeable to-be-read pile that was collecting dust because that's what they're for. I promised myself I would read them all and acquiring new books was just part of the process.

"Oh, there he is!" Brutus shouted through his full mouth. He pointed at me as I approached their table and sat.

"So," I started, "why exactly is there a deceased minstrel on the floor?"

"Well, where else are you supposed to store one?" Devinon asked.

"Devinon didn't want him on the table," Pylara answered.

"No," I continued. "I mean, what happened to him?"

"Oh!" Devinon laughed. "Well, I guess you could say that the pen is mightier than the sword?"

"I'm ... not sure I understand."

"Damn it." Devinon looked defeated. "Does nobody find that joke funny?"

"He was crushed to death under a pile of books like a tiny, weak little bug," Pylara interjected, her words muffled by food. "Unfortunate and sad, but still tiny and weak."

"For what it's worth," Devinon continued, barely able to suppress his raucous laughter. "He fought valiantly and defeated many tomes this day! I guess there were just too many of them." He feigned a sad sniff and returned to his breakfast.

"It is sad," Pylara said, in between bites, "but he was obviously unfit for—"

"Literature?" Brutus cackled. Devinon nearly spit out his food as he, too, laughed. Even Throg chuckled, though I'm not sure he understood the joke. In fact, he may have been thinking about something else entirely. Honestly, I was intensely curious, but doubtful, as to whether they had even been able to procure the book. Furthermore, I was dubious as to whether they had even found the bookstore, let alone the book.

I was, in fact, surprised they found their way back to the inn at all.

As if she read my mind, Liandra produced the thick tome from underneath the table and set it down, moving various dishes and assorted bits of food out of the way.

"Most excellent!" I said, barely able to contain my excitement. "You've done superbly, and I thank you. This will be a fine addition to my bookshelf! Hopefully I will get around to reading it soon."

"Wait," Liandra interrupted. "You sent us on a shopping run?"

"For a book you're not even going to read?" Pylara added.

"Well, yeah," I replied, flipping through the book's pages. It appeared in good condition. "Have you any idea how much Tomedash charges for delivery?"

"I thought this was somehow important," Brutus added. "You know, saving the world and all."

"He has a point," Devinon added.

"Thank you," Brutus replied.

"No, I mean Gerald. Tomedash is ridiculously expensive—they add all kinds of fees. They'll even charge you for a prologue!"

"Pfft," Devinon scoffed, "nobody reads prologues anyway."

"We thought this quest was of the utmost importance," Pylara whined.

"I told you." Devinon stood angrily, which may have somehow made him shorter. "Grind quest, people. Did you not listen?" He paused and a grin crossed his face. "Wait ... ding!"

The rest of the party looked confused, sitting in silence. Except Throg, of course. He was still eating and making a mess, I might add.

"You ... what?" Pylara asked.

"I leveled again! Yay! I got more health and a couple of neat abilities!"

"I'm not sure I understand," Brutus said, scratching his head.

"Seriously? Am I adventuring with a bunch of noobs?"

"Watch tongue, kid!" Throg rose, shaking the table and knocking a cup onto the floor. He had his axe in hand and snarled at Devinon. "I no boob!"

"Wait," Devinon stammered, half-afraid and half-confused. "No ... not *boob*. I didn't call you a boob. I called you a *noob*. Sheesh."

"What that mean?"

"It, uh, means … it's a compliment. Sure. I mean … of all words, you take offense at that? Does the word 'boob' mean something terrible in orcish?"

"Don't know. Don't speak orcish." Throg sat back down and tore into a piece of bread.

"You're an orc," Brutus said, "but you don't speak orcish?"

Throg ignored him, more interested in his meal.

"Anyway," I cleared my throat and continued. "I thank you all for fetching this excellent book for me. Your reward is ten gold and this fantastic feast. Also, I have another quest for you if you are up for it." I dropped ten gold coins on the table, ready to explain their next heroic endeavor.

Everything else I said after was lost since the five of them were busy distributing the money. Devinon insisted that he should get more than everyone else, but nobody was convinced. In the end, they each got two gold coins. I was surprised at how long it took them to figure it out. For a moment, I was sure they would resort to a physical confrontation.

"So, what's this other quest?" Liandra finally asked as she moved bits of food around on her plate.

"Old Mr. Wendingham's basement is infested with rats, it seems. He needs someone to get rid of them."

"Why can't he take care of his own damned rat problem?" Liandra inquired. The look on her face said it all—she wanted nothing to do with rats.

"Because he's an NPC," I said. "They don't take care of their own problems."

I was met with blank stares from all of them. This was normal for Throg, who probably wasn't even paying attention anyway.

"Have you never heard of a non-player char—look, do you want the job or not?"

"Fine," Brutus sighed. "I'm in. But we need to bring the bard back to life for this one."

"Why's that?" Liandra asked.

"So, the rats can all chew on him while we take them out, of course." Brutus fist bumped Devinon who laughed, spitting his ale out in a fine mist.

"I mean," Devinon interrupted, "in this instance, it doesn't really matter if he's alive. Rats aren't picky."

"I'll see what I can do," I sighed. "Be ready tomorrow morning."

4

When the rest of the party arrived, Devinon was waiting for them. Sitting on a chunk of wood by the front door, he appeared to be either sleeping or bored.

"Kid," Throg grunted, nudging Devinon's leg with his boot.

"Hey, now," Devinon mumbled, opening his eyes and squinting in the sunlight. "You ruined a perfect dream I was having."

"Oh?" Pylara inquired, obviously feigning interest. "And what dream was that?"

"The dream where we weren't embarking on another lousy, insignificant quest!" Devinon growled through clenched teeth.

"Oh, I'm sorry," Liandra retorted. "Is something like this beneath you?"

"Yes, actually. When there's no treasure to be had, it's beneath me. Have you seen this dump? We're not getting paid one gold piece for this job." Devinon stood and stretched, yawning what appeared to be an exaggerated yawn. "We'd be doing the city a favor if we just burned it down and called it good."

He had a point. The domicile outside of which they'd gathered was nothing special. In fact, it was far below special. It appeared to be held together by rope and luck, with emphasis on the luck. Devinon would've been surprised if anyone actually inhabited such a dilapidated wreck.

Which meant it was the perfect set-up for nefarious deeds. Possibly a front for something far worse that lurked below the surface—like that piece of candy that *looks* scrumptious but, when you bite into it, is filled with that nasty, peanut butter-flavored crap that—oh, I apologize. I'm getting ahead of myself. But, for the record, that stuff is trash.

"Let's get this over with," Brutus said, apparently in agreement with Devinon. "I would prefer to get as few rat droppings on me as possible. I just washed this tabard."

"You guys," Liandra pleaded, reaching for the handle and slowly opening the door. "This is important. Someone obviously needs our help and—oh dear gods it smells like rotten goblin piss in there!"

The odor was pungent and immediate, and it assaulted their noses the moment Liandra pushed open the front door. Everyone gagged and held their breath, trying not to retch as they let the room air out.

Except Throg.

"Smell like home," he said, breathing deeply and sighing.

Liam nudged Throg forward. "Well, then, you should have no problem. Go on in, my good man ... orc ... man-orc!" He produced his flute and held it aloft. "I shall remain out here and inspire you all with music!"

"Oh, *that's* what you call that noise?" Pylara asked.

"You simply don't appreciate the finer things. With you, it's apparently all swords and ... tree branches . . and killing. I am much more civilized than that. But I can help everyone more than you know!"

"When the Hells did you stop being a corpse?" Devinon inquired.

"Last night, my good child."

"How did that happen?" Liandra asked.

"Magic, I suppose. I'm just a musician and I know not of such things, but it moves the story along and that's all that matters!"

"Whatever," Pylara snorted. "Out of my way. We've got rats to kill." She brushed past everyone and entered the house, wielding her hefty tree branch in her right hand. She looked a little too eager.

Devinon shrugged and followed behind Pylara. Everyone else filed in behind him, still reluctant and trying not to gag.

Immediately, several chittering rats leapt at them. Pylara clobbered one with her branch while the remaining three bounced harmlessly off her. She smashed another, then another as she laughed, reveling in their collective demise.

The rest of the party, who once stood at the ready, relaxed a bit as they watched the proud warrior destroy their foes with zealous bloodlust.

A rat bit her leg, trying to sink its teeth into her boot. She squashed it underfoot and kicked the carcass into a wall. Several more rats' lives were snuffed out with one swing of her branch and, just like that, the fight was over.

"Well, that was easy!" Devinon laughed. "Mostly because I didn't have to do anything."

"I don't think that's all of them," Liam said, entering the room. "And rats don't usually attack like that."

"Yodeler right," Throg agreed. Liam shot the orc a sideways glance.

"Maybe they're diseased? Rabid?" Liandra offered, kicking a rat corpse with her boot. "Normally, rats would scurry away at the first sign of danger and try to hide, but those vermin were aggressive."

"Could be," Brutus responded, lowering his longsword. He still held his shield aloft, as if to warn any further enemies. "But you don't sound so sure about that."

"I'm not." Liandra looked around the room that was now littered with rat corpses. She waded through the bodies to a doorway on the opposite wall and peered in. "There is something more ... sinister at work, here. I can feel it."

"How do you know this?" Brutus stood next to Liandra and peered into the room. It was a bedroom, but instead of one or two beds, the entire room was rats' nests

Liandra pointed into the room. "Because of that," she said. In the center of the tangled mess of rats' garbage was a nest much larger than the rest. "There's at least one more left, and it's huge."

"There's a joke, here, about a messy bed," Brutus muttered, "or about making your bed or something."

Throg made a strange sound, like maybe a squeal or a wheeze or something. The entire party turned and looked at him. He appeared visibly shaken.

"What's wrong, Throg?" Brutus asked.

"Nothing wrong. Just surprised—rat *big*!"

"Are you afraid, Throg?" Devinon joked, sifting through rat bodies. "Afraid of rats? Are they gonna get'cha?"

"Shut up! *You* afraid of rats!"

"Big rats die just like little rats," Pylara growled. "Their skulls are no more difficult to smash and grind into dust."

The room fell silent for a moment.

"Well," Brutus said, "that's ... a disturbing and unpleasant image. So, Devinon, what is it you're doing, exactly?"

"Duh. I'm looting the bodies."

"Of *rats*?" Brutus had a disgusted look on his face, as if he had just been forced to watch orcish erotic theater which, as terrible as it sounds, can actually be quite enjoyable—once you get past the blood and fire and axes. Rumor has it they use *real* elves to slaughter during the performance. Oh, but I digress. "Rats don't have any loot," he continued. "They're rats. What loot could they possibly have? Turds and teeth?"

"So, anyway," Liandra finally said. "At the very least, there is one more very large rat, and maybe more smaller rats."

Throg squealed again.

"What in the fifteen-or-so Hells is it with you?" Devinon asked.

Throg sighed and his shoulders drooped. "When Throg young, rats kill Throg's brother Brog."

"That's awful!" Brutus said.

"That's terrible," Liandra agreed.

"That's hilarious!" Devinon laughed. Everyone in the party glared at him, except for Throg who was staring at the ground, shuffling rat poop around with his foot. "What? I mean, come on! Big tough orc taken out by *rats*? You don't find that funny? Rats ... and an orc ... you know what? Never mind."

"You're an evil kid," Pylara spat.

"More like chaotic asshole," Liandra added.

Liam chuckled. "Now *that's* funny!"

"Found three coppers!" Devinon exclaimed, looting a rat and pocketing the coins.

Pylara put a hand on the orc's shoulder. "I'm so sorry, Throg," she said, soothing him. "How long ago was this? How old was Brog?"

"Last year. Was twenty-seven" Throg mumbled sadly, at which point, even Pylara had a difficult time holding in the laughter.

"Anyone need a short sword?" Devinon asked, holding up a blade. "This rat had one."

"Right," Liandra said, her voice dripping with impatience.

"Can we get on with our quest so we can leave this dump and get paid?"

"The lady is correct!" Liam stepped up to the doorway and looked at the room. "Let's get this over with! We should search all rooms and kill whatever moves! Also, by "we," I mean "you guys." I shall inspire you by singing a song ... from over there, where it's safe." Liam pointed to the corner of the corpse-laden room. "Also, if whatever moves is us, I suggest letting it live."

"Fine," Liandra sighed. Or was it a growl? It was difficult to be sure. But the one thing that was painfully apparent, was that she was both irritated and impatient. And probably a little hungry. Maybe gassy. Her hair smoldered with white-hot embers.

"This rat was wearing a necklace!" Devinon shouted, stuffing the jewels into a pocket.

With that, the party went about searching the house for clues or rats or *anything* that would allow them to leave such a putrid domicile, for the whole place stank of wet cat and week-old cheese.

And dead rat. Of course, dead rat. It obviously smelled like dead rat.

"Anyone need a leather jerkin?" Devinon asked. "This rat was wearing one."

The house wasn't large, and it took little time to find a few stragglers and eliminate them, but the party didn't encounter a larger rodent during their search, which left them perplexed. Though, to be fair, most everything had that effect on them.

"Oh, hey!" Devinon shouted. "This rat was carrying a ... uh, rat corpse. Wow, that's just wrong, that is. Still, I like his style! I wonder if there's a rat carrying a minstrel corpse!"

Liam continued his song from the main room until the party congregated to plot their next move. Devinon was last to return, carrying an armload of various objects which he plopped down in front of them all.

"You found all of *this* by looting rats?" Liandra asked, obviously surprised.

"Yep." Devinon sifted through the pile with a dagger, displaying his newly acquired bounty. "I mean, most of it. A few rats were carrying food—chicken, curry, and the like—but I draw the line at that. Rats aren't known for their culinary skills."

Throg swallowed a mouthful of chicken and discreetly dropped the bone on the ground behind his back. "Yeah ... gross. Not eat that."

"This is all junk," Pylara said, using her tree branch to move the pile around.

"Well, yeah," Devinon replied, putting his dagger away. "I kept all the good stuff. But you guys can certainly have anything you want from this garbage."

"So, what now?" Brutus asked, leaning against a table. He yawned, then sighed.

"We should camp," Liam suggested.

"Camp?" Liandra laughed. "It's, like, still morning and we have a quest to finish!"

"And we can continue it after we've camped! I have taken several injuries from which I wish to recover."

"Injuries?" Pylara scoffed. She grabbed Liam's jaw and inspected his face, then his head, then she looked the rest of him over. "Injuries from what?"

"I don't wish to discuss it," Liam said. "But I feel as if I am near death."

"Near death!" Liandra laughed. "You look fine to me. How could you possibly know that you're near death?"

"He probably began with low health," Devinon scoffed.

"I would say," Liam explained, "that if I had ... oh, ten health points, that I am down to probably two or three."

"That's ridiculous!" Devinon argued. He squinted at Liam, looking him over. "I'd say four or five. Besides, I find it highly unlikely you started with ten. I could believe five and an argument could be made for six."

"I have no idea what you two are on about." Brutus stood up from the table. "But if the bard is injured, perhaps we should bed down for the night."

"It's still morning!" Liandra growled.

"Right, morning. We'll bed down for the morning."

"It's been precisely fifteen minutes since we started this quest," Pylara growled.

"But you're a priest," Liandra argued. "Can't you just pray to ... someone and cast a healing spell so we can get on with this?" She sounded angry and, in fact, her hair was glowing even brighter than before.

"Well, uh," Brutus stammered. He shifted his weight from one foot to the other and fidgeted. "The thing about that is ... I didn't prepare any healing spells for today."

"What?" Pylara didn't sound particularly pleased, either. "You're a priest! That's what you do!"

"I mean ... rats? Why would we need healing spells to fight rats? Spells to cure diseases, sure, but healing spells? We can handle rats. Well, most of us, anyway."

"Well," Devinon agreed, "he's got a good point."

"But we have a bard in the party! He's a living (for now), breathing (also, for now) excuse for healing spells!" Pylara countered. "He literally *attracts* damage!"

"She *also* has a good point," Devinon chuckled.

"Ah, yes," Brutus smirked. "I *did* forget that fact. But, also, I didn't really care."

"Fine!" Liandra growled some more. With as much as this woman growled, you'd think she might be a werewolf or something. Hmm ... now that I think about it, that's not too far out of the realm of possibility and might warrant further investigation. But that's for another time. "We'll rest and, Brutus, you can prepare some *useful* spells this time."

"Who take first watch?" Throg asked.

"Throg," Devinon replied, trying to be careful with his words. It was never wise to upset an orc, or to use words an orc didn't understand, which was virtually all words, ever. "We're in a house. I don't think we'll encounter anything random or any monsters that might be wandering."

Throg looked confused but didn't press the issue. Instead, he broke a chair into pieces and piled them neatly as the rest of the party watched, confused.

"Throg," Devinon once again spoke up. "Are you ... building a fire?"

"Throg build fire."

"Again, we're in a house. It's not dark outside, as is apparent from the sunlight shining through the windows. It's not even cold!"

Throg paused, his face riddled with confusion.

"What the kid is trying to say," Pylara continued, "is that we don't need a fire. We need neither warmth nor light."

"Nor protection," Brutus added.

"I'd feel safer with a fire," Liam interjected.

"Shut up," several of them shouted, in unison.

5

t was early the next morning when everyone awoke to the sound of a terrified orc, screaming as if he'd just seen two halflings procreating which, admittedly, would turn the stomachs of even the stoutest of adventurers. Everyone immediately jumped to their feet, weapons drawn. But a quick look around revealed no danger. Throg, in fact, was still asleep.

"Wait," Devinon said, nudging Throg with his boot. "The orc's having a nightmare?"

"It appears that way, yes," Brutus snickered, obviously trying not to laugh too hard. Joking at an orc's expense was often the last thing one did, even if said orc was asleep.

"Hey!" Devinon shouted, now kicking Throg. "Wake up! We're surrounded by rats, and we need your help!"

"Don't do that," Liandra scolded. "That's mean. Besides, he's probably dreaming about rats right now." She couldn't keep a straight face and stifled a laugh as she retreated to a corner to regain her composure.

Throg woke violently and awkwardly jumped to his feet, breathing heavily with his mighty fists balled tightly. He looked around him, growling and, for a moment, everyone thought he might go berserk and paint the walls with their blood—a deadly but vast improvement over the current, bland wall color.

"Whoa there, big guy," Pylara said, cautiously moving toward him with her right hand outstretched. "It was just a nightmare. The rats are all dead, remember?"

The tension passed quickly as Throg relaxed, obviously embarrassed. "Hate rats," he grumbled, spitting on a rodent corpse.

"How did you know he was dreaming about rats?" Brutus whispered, handing over a gold coin to Devinon.

"Lucky guess," Devinon laughed, gladly taking the coin which disappeared in a pocket. "At this rate, you'll be broke before we're through."

"Wait," Liandra interrupted, looking confused. "It's morning again. We slept that long?"

"I guess so," Brutus replied, slipping his helm onto his head. "Did we all get enough rest?"

"Indeed!" Liam exclaimed. "I feel much better now!"

"Well," Devinon added. "I guess that's all that's important, right? A well-rested musician."

"Correct, my boy!" Liam clapped him on the back.

"I was being sarcastic."

"Don't know the meaning of the word! Anyway, shall we continue our noble quest?"

"Yes, let's!" Brutus grabbed his shield and held it aloft. At first, it looked as though he were courageously about to enter a heroic battle but, upon further scrutiny, it was obvious that he was either inspecting it for damage or admiring his reflection.

Throg reluctantly stood, holding his axe in trembling hands. He said nothing and, likewise, nobody spoke to him. He may have had fears, but he could still make you wish you hadn't crossed him. Probably. I mean, unless you were a rat, apparently.

"So," Pylara said, once everyone was standing and ready to go. "What's our plan? You know, now that we're all standing here and geared up to take on some rodents."

Liandra looked around the room, squinting as if she were scrutinizing every rat corpse. "Devinon, why don't you search around and look for any doors or passages we might have missed."

"Because I don't want to sift through bloody, chunky rat corpses and guts. That's why."

They all glared at him except Brutus who was still gazing into his shield, this time inspecting his teeth.

"But you did *just* that very thing yesterday," Pylara scowled.

"There was treasure involved then."

"Can you just be useful for once?" Liandra asked.

"Fine, but Brutus is coming with me to help."

"Help with *what*?" Brutus gasped, stepping back.

"You can help me move rat chunks. You've got a sword and all I've got is daggers. Besides, we wouldn't want the minstrel to get injured so he can't come along."

"But I just polished this sword! What about Throg?"

Throg cringed and looked away.

"Okay, then," Brutus continued, "what about Pylara?"

"Because what we really don't need is *smaller* rat chunks and more blood!"

"I will destroy their tiny corpses and squash them into goo!" Pylara yelled. "Then I will turn that goo into goo!"

"Devinon winced, looking as if he was about to gag. "Okay, gross."

"Alright, I see your point," Brutus agreed. "What about Liandra? She could help?"

"So now you want *burning* bloody rat chunks? Come on, holy guy. Time to get your weapon dirty. I hope your deity today is the god of not getting rabies."

Devinon grabbed Brutus' arm and, even though the priest struggled, dragged him around the house, displacing dead rats, junk, and debris in an attempt to find the giant rat that that they knew must lurk somewhere nearby. It was at this time that the rest of the party decided it would be best to sift through all the recovered loot while Devinon and Brutus waded through the fields of their fallen enemies.

"Does anyone need a shield?" Pylara laughed, holding aloft a dented, pewter dinner plate. "Looks like it's sized just right for Devinon."

"I found a boot," Liandra added, "if anyone needs one of those."

"These rats weren't even a challenge," Pylara gloated. "Killing them was like chopping weeds in a garden."

"I suspect most weeds would be conquered easily with an axe like that," Liam laughed, pointing to one of the weapons on Pylara's back.

"I've certainly fought worse."

"Like what?" Liandra inquired. "Orcs? Trolls? Bugbears?"

"Three-headed goats that breathe fire, lightning, and hot potato soup?" Throg asked.

For a moment, everyone stared at the orc, unable to find the words for any kind of a response. The room was silent as Throg grinned uneasily, his green tusks looking particularly dirty.

"Mostly things like spiders—"

"Giant spiders?" Liam was riveted.

"Normal-size spiders," Pylara continued. "Squirrels, a groundhog or two, a particularly nasty carp, and, oh, turtles."

"Wait." Liandra stopped Pylara, obviously confused. "Turtles?"

"Aye, turtles. Those bastards can gnaw off your finger if you let them. And their armor is tough to beat."

"So," Liam said, "you're an exterminator?"

"Found it!" Devinon yelled from another room.

When the rest of the party arrived, Brutus was scraping away dead rats and their nests to reveal a trap door.

"Found what?" Throg asked.

"A trap door," Devinon answered, pointing to what was indeed a door in the floor. "Didn't you hear what the narrator *just* said?"

"We must search that door for traps!" Liam sang, writing down something on paper. "Wait, what's a good word that rhymes with 'traps'?"

"You ninny," Brutus, said, chiding Liam. "It's not called a 'trap door' because it's trapped. That would be silly!"

"Well, actually," Devinon retorted, "It is indeed trapped."

"Huh," Brutus chuckled. "A trapped trapdoor? What are the odds?"

"How you know, kid?" Throg asked.

"Because it's my job, and I have keen observational skills!"

"What you mean?"

"Because," Devinon sighed, "some nitwit wrote *that*."

Devinon pointed to one of the walls, on which was written in very clear lettering: "Deactivate trap with code 1234."

"Huh," Pylara said. "I never would've guessed. You have a keen talent for finding danger, kid."

Liam scrutinized the writing, moving his fingers over the letters and numbers etched into the wood. "Do you think it's case-sensitive?"

"Don't be foolish," Liandra sneered. "Nobody speaks in uppercase or lowercase." She moved closer to Devinon. "Besides, numbers aren't case-sensitive. Go ahead, kid, speak the password."

"What? Me?"

"Yes, you," Liandra urged. "You're the expert—you said it yourself."

"Fine." Devinon cleared his throat. "You may all want to step back. You know, just in case it blows up or something."

"Aw, that's cute!" Liandra said as she moved back to the doorway. "You care for your companions!"

"Um, yeah, that's ... definitely the reason!"

The rest of the group moved back as well, hoping the doorway was a safe distance should something go terribly wrong. It was foolish, of course, to group together merely a few feet away, but surely those in the back would be safe—you know, behind a meat shield the others provided.

"Besides, I need someone to drag my body back and resurrect me if this goes poorly," Devinon mumbled.

"Sorry, didn't hear you. What did you say?" Pylara asked.

"Nothing. Just, uh, disarming the trap and talking to myself."

"Well, get on with it already."

Devinon set to work, inspecting the trap door. He brushed away the dirt and debris until the trap door's surface was as clean as it would get. Set into the sturdy wood was a crude combination lock consisting of four dials, each set to zero. He turned each dial to its corresponding number, starting with the number one.

Everything went smoothly until he got to the last dial.

"Hey, guys? Uh ... the last dial has no number four."

"What do you mean?" Pylara asked.

"I mean it has no number four! It goes from three to five."

"You're the rouge," Brutus said. "You figure it out."

"The what?"

"The rouge."

"It's *rogue*, you loser. And it's not like it's a profession that you can simply walk up to someone and say 'I'm a rogue for hire'."

Brutus dismissed Devinon with a wave of his hand. "Whatever, just use three."

"Or use five," Liandra added.

"Five is right out," Brutus countered. "Use three."

Devinon wanted to punch something. Liandra and Brutus were combing over the finer points of combination locks and which number Devinon should use and here he was, possibly moments away from his own demise. He was about to yell at all of them when a green, meaty hand shoved him out of the way.

"Move, kid," Throg grunted. "This how I open locks."

"No, wait!"

Throg lifted his massive, dual-bladed battle axe high over his head and brought it down hard on the door, sending splinters and chunks of wood into the air.

"Huh," Devinon mused. "No trap after all. Good to know."

"Yes, no trap." Liandra appeared behind them. "No trap indeed, but now everyone in the entire city knows we're coming. Could you have been any louder?"

"Throg's axe fail stealth roll." Throg shrugged and stepped aside, quite pleased with the fact that he soundly defeated the trap door.

Liandra sighed, peering into the hole. A crude ladder led down to a basement but, past that, she could see nothing more. "I could simply lob some fire down the hole and clean out whatever might be down there."

For a moment, everyone looked at one another and considered the possibility. It was a sound plan and would expedite matters nicely. They'd been hired to kill rats, and that would most certainly kill rats.

"No, wait," Devinon said, holding out his arm to stop Liandra. "If there's loot down there, fire would surely destroy it. "It's best we deal with whatever's down there so the treasure remains unscathed."

"Fine," she pouted.

One by one, the party climbed down the ladder, finding themselves in a small, dimly lit room. Aside from a door on the opposite wall, there was nothing remarkable about the chamber.

"It's like a dining room," Liandra said.

"What you mean?" Throg asked, his axe held firmly in his grip.

"I mean, it's a worthless room. Sure, it sounds like a great idea, but nobody actually eats in a dining room. I mean, what's the point? Why is this room even here if it serves no purpose? Dining rooms usually just serve as storage. This room is completely empty."

"You've obviously put a lot of thought into this," Brutus replied.

"Poor house design," Liam added. "What a shame. This room has so much potential, yet it's wasted. It would only require minimal effort to spruce it up."

Devinon turned to Liam. "Did you really just say all that shit you just said? Who cares? Let's bust down that door and kill whatever's on the other side so we can go home."

Without hesitation, Throg brought his axe to bear on the simple, wooden door, shattering it in the same fashion as its trap door brother.

The room beyond was surprisingly large and contained several cages, each holding a prisoner, all of whom now yelled for help. In the center of the room sat a plump man on a dirty but opulent throne. Surrounding him were several dog-sized rats.

Admittedly, rat-sized dogs would've been adorable.

"Well, hello!" he said, his voice deep and raspy. "I've been expecting you." His tunic was covered in stains—whether food or rat poop, nobody knew—and his breeches appeared at least two sizes too small.

"Really? How did you know we were coming?" Devinon

smirked.

"Because you're the noisiest bunch of—oh, wait, that's sarcasm, isn't it? You're joking. Yeah, I get it now. Really funny." The man stroked his mangy stubble and scratched his bald head. "Anyway, I assume you have killed all my babies upstairs. Shame on you! Bursting into a man's home and killing everything in sight! That's deplorable! Who does that? A bunch of murder hobos, that's who!"

"Says the guy who's keeping people in cages, but lives with rats," Brutus retorted, pointing to the various ramshackle cells about the room.

"Help us!" one man shouted.

"I mean," the buxom man continued, "rats gotta eat. And, as you can see, these are rats of uncommon stature."

"I would've gone with rodents of unusual size, myself," Devinon quipped.

"I would have, but that moniker was taken."

"So, what is this?" Devinon inquired. "You just hang out downstairs all day, sitting on your throne and petting your rats? Don't you ever get outside and do stuff? This is, like, the absolute *worst* dungeon ever!"

"I don't sit down here *all* the time," the man retorted. "I go outside sometimes. It's not like I *only* hang around my mom's basement in the dark with people in cages. I've got a complex social life. I get out and do things!"

"Yeah?" Devinon quipped, "like what?"

"I get coffee sometimes."

"But you bring it back here, right?"

"You know what? Enough talk!" the man shouted, pointing at the party. "Attack!"

"Well that went sideways real fast," Liandra muttered.

The group watched as the rats advanced, snarling with drool dripping from their maws.

"I really thought boss villains always talked longer and

explained their plans," Devinon mused. "This is disappointing."

"I don't think he has any actual plans," Liandra replied. "We already established he has no life."

"Hey, Pylara," Brutus shouted. "This is your area of expertise. Go for it!"

"I only deal in small pests, priest," she replied, wielding her tree branch in front of her. "I'm not certified for this type of work."

"What does that even mean?" Brutus asked. His view of the fight was obscured on account of the fact that he was cowering behind his shield.

"Oh, fine!" Liandra shouted, her arms outstretched and her fingers splayed. She muttered some unintelligible words and, soon, gouts of flame spewed forth from her fingertips, creating a wave of fiery destruction that instantly consumed several of the rats.

"Ye gods!" Devinon shouted, retching. "The smell! It's like ... burnt toast and the bowels of an orc!"

"It's like rotten garbage, except the garbage is on fire!" Brutus added. "And burnt hair!"

Pylara pinched her nose. "Burnt rat smells way worse than raw rat!"

"Raw?" Devinon asked. "You mean live rat?"

"Whatever!"

"Sound about right," Throg agreed, cowering behind the rest of the party, also pinching his nose shut.

The three remaining super-sized rodents looked slightly singed but otherwise unscathed. If anything, they seemed angrier than before. One lunged at Devinon who deftly dodged out of the way, causing the rat to hit Pylara instead. She fell onto her back with the rat on top of her, gnashing its teeth wildly, but unable to find soft flesh to sink them into.

Everyone stood around, dumbfounded, watching as the

rat failed to hurt her in any way.

"I mean," Devinon started, scratching his head. "Maybe I should wear a bikini if its armor value is *that* good."

"I truly don't believe that anyone wishes to see that, kid."

"Shut up, Brutus! I'm not a kid!"

"Guys," Liam interrupted, pointing at the remaining two rats.

"Oh, right." Brutus turned back to the other two attackers. The rest of the party did the same, leaving Pylara on the ground to wrestle with a large, angry rat.

"It's too bad nobody brought a bow," Liandra joked, only half-sarcastically.

"Fine!" Throg yelled, pushing everyone aside. He charged both rats and, in one swing of his wicked axe, cleft them both in twain. Bloody rat bits soared high into the air, painting the area in a bright crimson hue. "That for Brog!"

The party stood in awe, mouths agape, at the instant carnage the orc had created. Pylara, having finally dispatched her rat, stood and whistled at the sight.

"My babies!" the man on the throne cried. He now wore the blood of his fallen pets. "You killed my babies! What did they ever do to you?"

"Uh," Devinon replied. "They tried to kill us? Remember?"

"Well, that's no reason to—you know what? Fine. I'll kill you myself and avenge their furry little souls!"

"Hey, Brutus," Devinon whispered. "Boss fight. Watch this."

The man stood and grabbed a sword. Holding it outstretched, he glared at the party, grinding his teeth. "You now face the undying wrath of ... the Rat Prince!"

"The rat what now?" Liam asked.

"The Rat Prince!"

"You're only a prince?" Devinon laughed. "I mean, you

could've named yourself the Rat King!"

"I didn't want a lawsuit. That name is already taken. Everyone took the good names before me."

"Okay, whatever," Devinon continued. "But how much wrath can a rat *prince* have, seriously?"

"Help us!" a man from one of the cages yelled.

"Shut up!" the Rat Prince shouted back. "Anyway, you're about to find out!"

"Yeah?" Throg taunted. "Well, you about to face wrath of … The Company of Eight!"

Everyone stopped at once, confounded.

"What kind of a name is that?" Brutus asked. "It's terrible."

"I have to agree," Devinon added.

"Yeah," Rat Prince said. "It's pretty bad."

"Hey, *you* don't get an opinion!" Liandra scolded.

"Throg not good at names."

"Besides," Liam countered. "There are only six of us."

"Throg also not good at math."

Devinon leaned over to Brutus. "Besides, the bard doesn't really count," he whispered.

"The Company of Five?" Brutus giggled.

"Anyway," Rat Prince interrupted. "Let's fight!" He lunged at the party who scattered. In most cases, this would be seen as a strategic move to attack a foe from all directions. However, in this situation, it was merely a way for every one of them to avoid combat.

Pylara attempted to gain a combat advantage against the man, wielding her mighty tree branch while Liam hung back in the corner, practicing vocal exercises. Liandra pelted their enemy with tiny fire darts that appeared to do minimal harm to the man. Brutus swung his sword blindly while hiding behind his shield, Throg cowered behind Pylara, and Devinon was nowhere to be found.

The Rat Prince lashed out at Brutus. Though his sword clattered off the priest's shield, he hit with enough force to cause Brutus to hit himself in the face. He staggered backward, now with a bloody nose.

"That's right! You will all die by my hand, and I will raise *another* rat army off your corpses!"

"I hope they get food poisoning from us!" Brutus yelled, wiping blood on his tabard.

Pylara jumped into the fray, swinging her branch and connecting with the man's shoulder. He grunted and stabbed at her with his longsword which, like everything, clattered harmlessly off her scantily-clad body.

Brutus stepped next to her, bringing his longsword down on the Rat Prince. The blade dug into the man's arm, and he yelled in pain.

"Sweet!" Pylara shouted triumphantly. "He is defeated!"

"You think you've won?" the Rat Prince growled through clenched teeth. He dropped his sword and clutched his arm. "This is only the beginning! You have angered the Rat Prince and now, you shall witness my *true* form!"

"Aw crap," Brutus muttered, "boss fight, phase two, I guess. I bet he's going to turn into a rat!"

The party watched as their enemy grunted and screamed, every muscle in his body clenching at once. After a few seconds, they squared off against their new foe.

"Uh," Brutus started, inspecting the Rat Prince. "You changed your hair color?"

"Throg see no difference. Look same."

"You don't see it?" the Rat Prince asked. "I mean, I'm more muscular and dangerous. Beware my new powers!"

"I'm not seeing anything," Liandra replied. "Are you sure you did it right?"

"I mean," Brutus mused, "the boss battle music got more intense but that's really all I noticed."

"Crap. I was supposed to level up and be more menacing. Are you *sure* nothing changed? I mean, I think I feel different but I'm not—"

Two daggers erupted from the man's chest, and he slid to the ground, choking on his own blood. Devinon now stood where the Rat Prince had been.

"Boring!"

"I wondered where you had run off to," Liam said, putting away his flute. "Good show, Devinon!"

"I find it slightly disturbing that a kid is doing all this killing." Liandra inspected the body on the ground. "Oh, he *does* look different! I see it now! He has bloody daggers sticking out of his chest now!"

"Are we done here?" Devinon asked, pulling his blades from the now ex-Rat Prince.

"What about us?" one of the prisoners shouted. "Please rescue us!"

"Oh, right," Pylara replied.

"Sorry, guys, but we can't!" Devinon started making his way toward the exit. "Our quest is over. We did what we came to do! Nobody said anything about rescuing prisoners."

"Please!" another prisoner pleaded. "We've been locked up in here for a long time! Let us out!"

"Devinon's right," Brutus agreed. "Our quest is done. We return triumphant! No time for side quests. Let us be off!"

"You guys suck!"

The room shook violently as the party made their way to the ladder. The walls began to buckle and the ceiling crumbled while the floor cracked.

They scrambled through the trap door, waded through the rat corpses upstairs, and darted out the front of the house just in time to see the house completely collapse, sending dust and debris into the air.

6

nce they were back at the inn, everyone reveled in
their glorious victory with a bountiful feast. I
watched as they tore into their food and knocked
back several tankards of ale each. I was pleased with their
performance and was hopeful that they might be ready to take
the next step. Though, I did wonder why it took them an
entire day and night just to clean out some rats. And, if I was
being honest, they looked as if they'd nearly lost.

It was a gamble, but what choice did I have? There was
trouble brewing on the horizon, and the world badly needed
heroes. Who was I to deny a whole world the privilege of its
existence?

"Did you see how Pylara hit him in the shoulder?" For
someone whose mouth was utterly full of food, Brutus
articulated quite well. "I could almost *hear* his bones cracking!
It was glorious!"

"You are a disturbing priest," Liandra said. She kept her
head low and stayed mostly quiet, apparently not interested in
the celebration.

"And then," he continued, "I got him in the arm!"

"And did anyone see me completely murderate him from behind?" Devinon asked. There was an alarming amount of glee in the boy's voice.

"Er, well, no," Pylara replied. "I mean, you were behind the Rat Prince, so we didn't actually *see* it."

"Oh, well it was pretty awesome. I mean, at least *I* got to see it."

"You are a very disturbing child," Liandra mumbled.

"You all did a wonderful job," I said, approaching the table. "I commend you on your success."

"So, do we get paid or anything?" Devinon asked.

"I do suppose some form of payment is in order," I replied. "Five gold coins for each of you." I laid down 30 gold on the table.

"So that's it?" Devinon turned his nose up. "That's a paltry sum for all we just accomplished."

"Is it really, though?" I asked, sitting down at the table. "You earned valuable experience and, more importantly, you rid the town of a vile menace. Is not the pride from your accomplishments payment enough?"

The group fell into silence.

"You did a wonderful deed. You should be proud. You helped people."

"Meh. I'll help myself to the gold." Devinon plucked his five coins and deposited them in his money pouch.

"Well, I think it was a fine adventure!" Liam said.

Or, well, that's what Liam *would* have said, had he been there, which I had just noticed.

"Guys?" I asked, "Where's the bard?"

Everyone looked around the table, as if he would be sitting among them but, alas, he was not.

"Oh," Devinon said shyly. "Funny thing. Well, maybe not so funny, I mean, if you're Liam. But, yeah, Liam's dead."

"Dead?" I asked. "But, how?"

"I'm sure it's a great story," Devinon continued. "You know, if I knew the story, but I don't." The kid rummaged around in his backpack for a second and produced a mangled, bloody leg which he plopped down on the table. "After the house went to shit, I found his leg!"

"Poor Liam," Liandra mumbled.

"Poor me," Devinon countered. "I didn't get to loot his body."

"Wait," she continued, "are you sure this is Liam's leg?"

"Who else's would it be?"

"Throg!" Pylara shouted, slapping the orc who was now chewing on the leg."

"This not part of breakfast?" Throg muttered, his mouth full of ... well, Liam. He swallowed, then dropped the leg which now had a bite out of it. "Throg sorry. Minstrel tasty."

It was at that very moment that I wondered if these guys might be a greater threat to the world than the real danger. But I still had to risk it. They were, in fact, our only hope.

Devinon chuckled, staring at Liam's half-eaten leg. "I mean, being breakfast is probably the most useful thing he's done for us so far."

"That's a terrible thing to say!" Liandra scowled.

"Oh, whatever, Liandra. You laughed too!"

"Did not."

"Did too."

"Okay, fine. It *was* funny. But now he's dead."

"Again," Devinon pointed out.

"Yes," Liandra sighed, "again."

"Look," I said. "I know a guy who can probably bring him back to life again for pretty cheap. I'll see what I can do."

"Throg!" Liandra shouted, smacking the orc's hand. He dropped Liam's leg and swallowed what he'd bitten off.

"Sorry ... again."

"Stop eating the bard!"

"Wait, wait, hold on." Devinon visually inspected the leg. It had been almost completely eaten. While Devinon didn't particularly care for orcish cuisine, he had to admit, they could devour their meals quicker than anyone or anything he'd ever seen. "How much of the bard do we need to raise him from the dead? Can't be much, right?"

"Hopefully not," Brutus chuckled, "since we haven't much of him left. And I'm not asking the orc to reproduce what he's eaten."

"Why don't I just take that?" Fearing the worst, I wrapped the severed, mostly eaten limb in a towel and placed it on the bar. I noticed Throg's eyes following every movement, like a dog would watch each bite its owner takes. It was then that I wondered if I should look elsewhere for the possible saviors of the world.

The truth was, however, the world was running out of time *and* heroes. No, there was no alternative. It *had* to be these guys. My stomach roiled and I wanted to throw up, but I composed myself as best I could and addressed the party.

"Okay, listen up guys," I said, trying not to sound as desperate as I really was. Though it took a couple of minutes, everyone finally calmed down and gave me their attention. It was, at that moment, when I realized that I had absolutely no idea what I was going to say.

"You've done very well on the two quests with which I have tasked you."

"Yeah, we did!" Devinon cheered proudly. "We totally stole that book and destroyed a house!"

"We kill book and retrieve rats!"

"Other way around, Throg," Pylara said.

"Yes, yes," I continued. "You all survived a bookstore and the foul rodents."

"Most of us, anyway," Brutus laughed.

"These were but mere chores, and I have a much more dangerous proposition for you."

"Not another errand, I hope," Devinon complained. "I require you to travel to the far-off land of Doofenheim and retrieve the golden toilet!"

"There," Brutus continued, "you must also acquire the golden toilet plunger of Stinkitor and use it to unclog the mighty throne of Turdstrom!"

"And retrieve the Sacred Kidney Stone of Infinite Anguish!" Pylara joked, barely able to speak through her laughter.

A part of me wanted to let them finish their shenanigans, because what they were about to embark upon might be the last quest they would ever partake. Laughter would be scarce.

But the other, much larger part of me wanted to smack the living crap out of them.

"Are you guys finished yet?"

"Wait," Devinon said, fighting through tears of laughter. "Not yet. We—"

"Okay, yes, you are." I could feel my own frustration rising. There was little time left. I felt like there was a giant rock about to crash into the world, and our only hope lay in the hands of some misfits who could somehow bore a hole in it and blow it up.

While that was a completely ridiculous—if somewhat humorous—premise, our situation was not at all amusing.

"Okay, it's time to get serious. Legend has it, when our world was created, it was created with a specific purpose. You see, there was an evil so powerful, so terrible, that it could never be killed. It could only be imprisoned. It's said to be older than time itself, and more evil than—"

"Brutus' mom, am I right?"

Liandra shot Devinon a disapproving glare, though Brutus giggled.

"I am sure Brutus' mom is a very nice lady," Pylara added. "And not that old."

"This evil spent eternity roaming existence and devouring everything it discovered."

"Well, it didn't get the bard's leg!" Devinon joked. "Throg saw to that!"

"When every alternative was exhausted, the creature was imprisoned for eternity. That prison … is our world."

"Wait wait wait. Whoa." Liandra stood, leaning on the table. Little black bits of singed hair floated to the floor as she ran a hand through it. "This world—*our* world—is a prison for an eternal evil? Like, there's some badass creature thing buried deep within our world and we've all just been going about our business every day, not knowing this?"

"Well, actually, yes. That's accurate. But it's been asleep all this time."

"Okay, good. It's asleep." Liandra sat back down.

"Well, actually, it's *not* asleep."

"Sonofabitch!" she shouted, jumping back up from the table. "But it's still imprisoned, right?"

"Um … so, the thing about that is, no. It's trying to escape."

"Damn it!"

"And it's hungry."

"But don't worry," Devinon said. His voice was calm, seemingly unfazed by this news. "It'll be fine. We killed a whole bunch of rats earlier and retrieved a book, so we did our part. It's cool."

"Which is why I have assembled you here. You are the world's last hope for survival. You five—"

"Six," Pylara interrupted, pointing to the leg wrapped in a towel sitting on the bar.

"Right. You *six* are going to defeat this evil and save the world."

"Does this evil have a name?" Liandra asked.

"Gobthorak. Eater of Worlds. Devourer of Souls. Bane of All Existence. And, sometimes, it's known as Brad."

Brutus shivered. "Yuck, Brad. So vile."

"Let us never speak that name again," Pylara agreed.

"Okay." Devinon stood which, being as short as he was, didn't change his height. In fact, he may have been shorter standing than when sitting. The least he could've done was buy some shoes with heels in them or something. But I digress.

"You finished?" he asked. "Good. Anyway, let's go get some shovels, dig a giant hole down to this Gobthorak guy, and kick his eternal ass."

"Were it so easy," I replied.

I found Devinon's eagerness to be extremely uplifting. Maybe these individuals *would* be able to handle this. Maybe the world could be salvaged after all.

"How hard can it be?" Devinon asked. "We should consult Brutus' mom!"

And there it was—the reassurance that these imbeciles would doom our very existence.

They all laughed, especially Brutus. There was a part of me that wanted to share in their jovial revelry, but there was too much at stake.

I sighed, shaking my head in dismay. The quests I had given them thus far were child's play compared to what lay before them. They were eager, but they had no idea what they were getting into. This was far more dangerous than a bunch of rats ... and we know how the rats turned out.

But they hadn't died yet. Well, except for the bard, of course. Twice, even. No, maybe this laughter was necessary. Let them have their moment, for it may very well be their last.

"So, when do we embark upon this noble quest?" Liandra asked. I couldn't tell if she was being serious or if the jokes were continuing.

"On the morrow, you will travel to Duskenheim to consult with—"

"Duskenheim?" Liandra enquired. "I am unfamiliar with that town."

"It's north of here."

"Still never heard of it. Are you sure it's a real town?"

"Why wouldn't it be a real town?"

"I believe I've heard of it," Brutus interjected. "I think it's a suburb of Dawnheim."

"Yes," I said. "You're correct. Anyway, you must find a man named Briskel. He is a sage and should have a map to lead you to Gobthorak's lair. He is the utmost expert on the matter."

"We destroy this Gobthorak," Throg growled, slamming his hand down on the table. "Will tear out his heart and eat for dinner!"

"That's the spirit, Throg ol' buddy!" Brutus laughed.

"Great," I said. "Then it's settled. You leave tomorrow. Be sure to gear up before you leave, and I'll see about bringing Liam back to life ... again."

Throg licked his lips.

Brutus leaned back in his chair, propping his feet on the table, and sighed contentedly. "Sounds pretty simple to me. We find this Gobthorak guy, eviscerate him, then we're done. We get his treasure and Throg gets a snack."

"I don't think you understand," I said, pulling a chair up to the table and sitting. "This is the most serious threat the Realm has ever faced or may yet ever face."

"Your face is face!" Throg laughed, pointing at me.

Silence overtook the table for a moment, and we all looked at one another, unsure of what to make of an orc telling a joke. Or was it an insult? It was simply baffling. If we laughed when we weren't supposed to, it might insult him.

Pylara patted Throg's hand. "It's okay, honey. You tried, and that's the important thing."

"As I was saying," I interjected. I could feel growing anger within me. It seemed impossible to impress upon these people just how dire our situation was. "This is no fool's errand. There is no fetching of books or dispatching of vermin to be done."

"Gobthorak extermination crew at your service, am I right?" Devinon held his hand up for a high five. Brutus promptly obliged. "We got this."

"You're basically going to take down a demon of the highest order. Gobthorak is a force even gods fear."

"Look, good sir," Pylara said, standing. She clutched her tree branch in her right hand. I could see it in her brown eyes —determination. There was no fear or hesitation. She would have probably challenged Gobthorak to a duel right then and there. "You sought us out. You gathered us here. And you have bestowed this epic quest upon us. You would not have done this had you not believed we were the best fit for the job."

"What she said!" Devinon cheered.

The rest of the party raucously agreed. Throg pounded his fists on the table, Liandra's hair blazed in red-hot fire, and Liam's leg ... still lay there, half-consumed.

"So ... yeah," I stammered, scratching the back of my head. "About that."

"About what?" Brutus asked, still seeming unconcerned.

"Well, uh ... you guys aren't the first to take on this challenge."

"What exactly do you mean, Gerald?" Liandra glared at me, her hair calming down to a smolder.

"Well, you see, everyone else who has set out to destroy Gobthorak in the past has failed."

"Failed?" Pylara asked. "How?"

"Miserably."

Liandra truly looked worried. She was obviously trying to calm herself by setting her fingers on fire. "Have we made it further than any of our predecessors?"

"Not yet."

"But you have come to us," Liandra continued, "because you trust us. You are confident we can get this job done. That means a lot."

I scratched my head again, trying hard not to make eye contact. I briefly feared for my life, wondering how the group would react to the information I was about to give them. But then I remembered that they barely escaped a bookstore with their lives.

"I have chosen you," I gestured to them all, "because you are the last available."

The room fell silent as they all looked at one another. I could see the concern in their eyes. I could almost smell the tension as they all worked it out in their heads.

"So," Brutus finally replied, his voice low and without feeling. "What you're saying is ... you saved the best for last!"

"No, that's not—"

"This is awesome!" Brutus shouted. "I am shoving my foot so far up this Gobblethorak's ass that he'll taste my boot! And I'm pretty sure my boot tastes awful."

"He will taste every weapon in my arsenal," Pylara growled.

"Throg eat his heart!"

Liam's leg remained silent.

It was obvious they had no idea what was happening or why. Instead of destroying their morale, I decided to let them revel in their ignorance in the hopes it would bolster their confidence. They needed every advantage they could get.

"Well," Devinon sighed, eyes closed and shaking his head with an obvious understanding the rest didn't share, "when do we start?"

"Tomorrow. Gear up and head to Duskenheim, which is north of here."

"We can handle that," Liandra said, extinguishing one of her fingers and lighting another.

"Yes," I replied, trying to stay positive. "You most certainly can—after you pass through the Haunted Forest."

Devinon looked at me. "Shit," was all he said.

7

orning came early. The sun hovered just above the horizon, making bountiful promises and bestowing hope of a new day. The birds chirped in the trees as the town of Ralph's Keep slowly came to life. From the looks of it, the weather was going to be perfect—perfect for an adventure. Because, really, who has time and resources to keep track of the weather every day? And, really, who actually cares about the weather? Weather is like rations: it's a necessary thing, but it tastes like crap.

Wait, I may have messed that up. Whatever. Anyway, the weather was great and nobody cared. Let's get on with it.

One by one, they all showed up in the market. Devinon was first, having already robbed several shops during the night, and stashing his loot in the inn. He was an annoying kid—

"Oh, you too? You know I'm a halfling, right?"

Sure, you're a halfling. A disgusting, filthy, smelly halfling with big, hairy feet riddled with lice and fleas like all the other halflings.

"Okay, you got me. I'm a kid. Now get on with it."

He was a disgusting, filthy, smelly kid with big hairy feet

riddled with lice and fleas, and he was now armed to the teeth and equipped for any emergency. But with his newfound possessions came danger, for he was now what normal townsfolk liked to call "overpowered." Fate had a way of coming back and biting munchkins in the ass.

But I digress. I seem to do that a lot. Deal with it.

The party members all trickled in and, once they were together, they set out on their noble quest ... to buy stuff! Said stuff was badly needed for their *real* quest—to save the world from the maw of the evil Gobthorak, the Eater of Worlds, the Prince of Eternal Torment, Landscaper of the fifteen-or-so-Hells!

"Ah, good," Liam exclaimed, his voice full of fervor and enthusiasm. "We're all here, I see! Let us wander forth in search of equipment!"

"Well look who's whole again!" Brutus snickered.

"Why, yes! Quite unfortunate it was but, thanks to a bit of magic, I'm feeling *much* better! Leg's a little sore, though. Also, can anyone tell me why the orc is staring at me all weird?"

They headed towards a blacksmith's shop in search of weapons and armor and whatever various other bits of equipment they would require.

"I think he's just hungry," Brutus remarked. "You know how orcs are. They'll eat anything—even garbage."

Devinon had a difficult time holding back his laughter. Brutus appeared ready to burst from the effort.

"Oh, well ... yes. Orcs do have voracious appetites, I hear. At least, it's the subject of several songs I know. I should sing one for you sometime!"

"Oh look," Pylara pointed out, "no time for singing. We've arrived."

"Welcome to Cillaron's Swords and Armor Emporium, LLC! What can I do for you?" a deep voice said as a man emerged from behind a pile of weapons.

"Well, met, Cinnamon!" Brutus exclaimed, clasping hands with the haughty, stout blacksmith. The man was short, stocky, and well-muscled. His fiery red beard made up for the absence of hair on his head.

"Uh, name's Cillaron. What can I do for you guys?"

"Right. Cigarlon," Brutus replied.

"Cillaron."

"Simmer on?"

"Are you deaf, boy? My name is Cillaron, fool!"

"Okay, okay, I get it." Brutus backed off a couple of steps. "So, Cillaron fool, we—"

"What my esteemed colleague is trying to say," Devinon interrupted, "is that we are in dire need of equipment."

"Big adventure," Throg added. "Much kill." He made a hacking motion with his arm and smiled. If you've ever seen an orc smile, then you know just how similar it looks to a snarl. Complex creatures, orcs are.

"Well, uh," Cillaron stammered. He looked puzzled as he scratched his head, averting his gaze. "Have a look around at the various weapon and armor racks and find what suits you."

"Thank you, sir," Liandra said softly. Everyone explored different racks that held assorted armor, weapons, and tools and began sifting through them in search of whatever it was they would require.

Cillaron kept a close eye on them, for he was suspicious they were up to no good. "So why do you need new equipment?" he asked. "Looks like you've got some decent weapons already."

"We are adventurers," Liam replied with a flourish of his cloak. "And we are on an important mission to banish an unspeakable evil from this world. And this is how all great adventures start—with capitalism!"

"Huh. That sounds familiar." Cillaron chuckled.

Everyone riffled through the various objects, looking for that perfect weapon. Devinon pocketed several items easily, slipping them into his backpack or a pocket. Pylara loaded her arms full of swords, axes, and spears, grinning wildly while Liandra sat patiently on a stool, observing.

"Adventurers, eh?" Cillaron continued. "Do you have, like, a name for your little group?"

"The Last Available!" Throg shouted over his shoulder, still inspecting a very large hammer.

"That is *not* our name!" Devinon yelled angrily.

"Gerald said it was. He said we last available."

"No, he didn't. He said—"

"Well," Cillaron interrupted, "it's certainly not the name I would've chosen, but it's heroic ... enough, I suppose?"

Devinon growled, obviously upset the name had stuck.

"So, members of The Last Available, I take it you have some epic heroic quest ahead of you? You need some fine weapons and armor, yes?"

"Yes!" they all shouted in unison—some of them excited, others perturbed.

"Well, you'll find no finer wares than mine. And you were fortunate to choose today to shop here. I just got in some nice, newly crafted items from the dwarves up in the mountain. Cost me an extra gold coin or two, but the purchase was worth it."

Throg was first to dump his items onto the counter, but the others soon followed suit, littering every bit of the flat surface with weapons, armor, bobbles, and tools. Cillaron diligently took inventory and scribbled notes on a piece of parchment while they watched.

Finally, quill in hand, he looked up from his work, smiling. "Right," he said, unable to contain his excitement. "The total comes to five-hundred and twenty-six gold coins."

"Yes," Brutus replied. "I guess it does, doesn't it?" He chuckled nervously as the party looked at one another.

"Right," Devinon said. "How much for us?" He gestured to himself and everyone around him.

"Five-hundred and twenty-six gold coins."

"But ... we're heroes."

"Sort of," Cillaron countered.

"What do you mean *sort of*?"

"Well, I mean, *real* heroes would have coin to spend on equipment. At the very least, they'd start off with a few coins or *something*, wouldn't they? I mean, even first level—"

"Listen, Cirgeron," Brutus growled.

"Name's still Cillaron."

"Whatever!"

"If I may," Devinon cut in, standing on his tiptoes so he could see completely over the counter. "What my esteemed colleague was going to say is that we are on a quest to bring the world out of darkness and into the light. Should we fail, we will all die. Me, you, that dude over there, definitely the bard —*everyone*!"

"That's not a dude, that's a sculpture."

"Whatever!" Devinon took a second to calm his fiery demeanor. "What this means is that this is all pointless. You should be throwing this equipment at us and pleading with us to save your sorry ass!"

"Sorry, rules are rules. If you want my equipment, you'll need to pay me."

"But what if," Brutus interjected, "without these fine goods, we die, and the world is plunged into eternal darkness?"

"That's not my concern. Are you buying it or what?"

"So, no free stuff, then?" Devinon pouted, arms crossed in front of his chest. When there was no response, he stormed off.

"I guess that's that," Liandra muttered, following Devinon's lead. "Come on, Throg, put down the hammer."

Throg, who was literally hugging his potential new weapon, frowned. Pylara approached and met his sullen gaze, hand outstretched.

The orc shook his head, snuggling the hammer even tighter.

"I'm sorry, Throg," Pylara whispered, "but you must let it go. Maybe we'll kill someone later who has a better hammer than this one!"

"And I can have?"

"Yes, Throg. If we loot a body with a better hammer, you can have it."

"The body, too?"

"We'll talk."

"Throg agree." He threw the weapon on the ground and stormed off, shoulders slumped.

Dejected, the adventurers left, having bought nothing.

"At the very least," Brutus chuckled, "we could've sold the musician to Cillaron. I bet he's worth a few gold coins!"

Pylara glared at Brutus, arms folded across her chest. "That's a terrible thing to say! Especially in front of Liam who's standing right there!"

"Uh, actually, he's not." Devinon looked around, noticing Liam was, in fact, nowhere to be found. The rest of the party scrutinized the area, as if they didn't believe him. Imagine that! Not believing Devinon! I'm sure that was a huge surprise to him. But I digress.

"Crap! Liandra shouted. "Why does he always have to wander off? Let's go back to Cillaron's. Maybe he's seen the bard."

It was at that time that the merry band of adventurers trekked back to Cillaron's Swords & Armor Emporium, LLC and asked Cillaron if he had seen Liam. When he told them he hadn't, the group fanned out, searching the area, until Devinon finally announced his discovery.

"Thanks for the summary," Devinon said.

Anyway, I believe Devinon had an announcement—some kind of discovery, right?

"Oh, yeah. Hey guys! I found him!"

"Oh good! Liandra replied, sounding relieved. "Tell him to get his ass over here and let's get this quest underway!"

"Right, yeah. So, uh, there's just one problem."

"What problem?"

Yes, indeed, there *was* just one problem. Well, unless they considered each weapon impaling the bard to be a separate problem. If so, then there were precisely twenty-two problems.

"He's buried under a pile of sharp weapons." "Devinon lifted two swords out of the jumble, both covered in bard blood.

"When did that happen?" Pylara looked over the weapon pile with Liam's foot sticking out. "He was just *right here!*"

Everyone stood around, awkwardly, unsure of what to do. For a few moments, nobody said a word. Brutus wasn't sure if he should laugh or be appalled. Devinon knew he should laugh but kept it to himself and *pretended* to be appalled.

Throg licked his lips.

"Well," Liandra finally said. "Let's not just stand around, gawking. We have to get him out of there."

A few more moments passed as everyone waited for someone to be the first to try and extricate Liam from his pointy demise.

"Fine," Pylara grunted. She approached the weapon pile and scratched her head. Then she grabbed Liam's boot and yanked. Her muscles flexed and tightened, and she grunted again, pulling even harder until, finally, the bard was free of his prison.

"Ew!" Liandra shrieked.

Throg vomited.

Cillaron vomited.

The statue vomited ... probably.

Liam's body was tattered and torn to shreds, having been ripped apart by the weapons on the way out of the pile.

"Maybe that wasn't such a great idea after all." Pylara dropped his leg, stifling her own urge to vomit.

"So now what?" Brutus asked.

"Well," Devinon said, inspecting what was left of the corpse. "He can't really take up much space now, on account of him being ... well, goo. Who's got the biggest backpack?"

And so it was, that the members of The Last Available set out on their quest to face terrible dangers, conquer impossible obstacles, and rid the world of an unspeakable evil ... without adequate equipment, and with a dead bard in Pylara's backpack.

"You guys all owe me one," Pylara growled.

"I'll let you have a weapon or two that I swiped from Cillaron," Devinon laughed. "They may still have a bit of Liam's blood on them though."

"Guys, Throg have idea" Throg muttered.

Liandra glared at the orc. "No, Throg, you are not nibbling on the bard."

8

"Run!" Pylara shrieked, desperately gasping for breath as she commanded her legs to carry her swiftly away. Everyone followed suit and soon, they were all sprinting across an open field.

"We *are* running!" Devinon yelled as he quickly fell behind. "I can't help it if my legs are shorter than everyone else's!"

"You're a kid! You should probably be in better shape than the rest of us!"

"Actually, I was always the last to be picked in combat class! And thank you for dredging up my painful childhood memories!

"Memories of what? Yesterday?" Liandra asked

"Can we just concentrate on the running away part?"

"I'd like to point out," Brutus interrupted, "That it's *your* fault we're running for our lives in the first place, Devinon."

"Hey! How was I to know I wasn't supposed to touch the rock monster?"

"Because," several of them shouted at once, "there was a

sign that said DO NOT TOUCH THE ROCK MONSTER!"

"And I would point out," Liandra added, "you weren't just *touching* the rock monster, you were trying to pry its eyes out."

"They were rubies! How was I supposed to know the thing had rubies for eyeballs?"

"Because it screamed 'ouch, those are my eyes, stop prying them out!' and you didn't stop trying to pry them out!"

"Okay, fair point, I guess. But it didn't have to be so rude to me!"

"Oh?" Pylara laughed. "And why is that? Is it because you called its mother porous?"

"She may have been made of volcanic rock! Jeez, nobody can take a joke! Besides, my diplomacy sucks, okay? It was my dump skill! You should never allow me to speak for the party!"

"If we'd been patient," Pylara panted, "Liandra could've hit it with some fire."

"Fire has no effect on rock," Liandra argued. "I believe only paper can defeat rock."

"That makes no sense!"

"Wait, guys," Brutus said, stopping at the top of a hill. "I think we're safe now."

The rest of the party followed suit. As they looked down the hill, they saw the rock monster, still in pursuit.

"Oh, this is just sad," Pylara snickered. "Poor little guy hasn't even made it 20 feet outside its cave."

"Not very speedy, is it?" Brutus continued. "I fear we'll all die of boredom before it ever gets to us."

"How about giving me another crack at those rubies, then?"

"No!" everyone else shouted.

"Fine." Devinon pouted, still watching the sluggish monster make its way in their general direction, painstakingly lumbering across the vast field. "But I feel we're missing out on an opportunity here."

"What opportunity would that be?" Liandra asked.

"The opportunity to be stinking rich, of course. We get the rubies, sell them, then go home and live lavish lives."

"I think you're forgetting one important detail."

"Oh, right," Devinon laughed, "I totally wouldn't share any of it with you stiffs."

"Not that." Lianda smacked Devinon in the back of the head. "The end of the world, remember? What good is wealth if you're dead?"

"Ow!"

"We're sorry!" Liandra shouted in the rock monster's direction. "Your mother is probably a wonderful lady! We're just going to go about our business now, okay? Let's get out of here before Devinon pisses off something else like a grass monster or a water monster."

"Or beef monster?" Throg joked.

"That's called a cow, Throg. And, yes, I'm not really in the mood to battle a pissed off cow right now either—they're jerks even when they're *not* angry. Let's just get to Duskenheim and find Briskel so we can get on with saving the world."

"Now Throg hungry. Want eat beef monster."

And so it was that The Last Available resumed traveling in their original direction, making sure to walk around the dangerous, but seriously slow, rock monster. As they passed the creature, it turned and pursued them. Though its pace was painstakingly slow, it was really super mad, for its mother was metamorphic, and not in the least bit porous.

To say the adventurers slowed down once the monster was out of sight would have been an exaggeration. However, at some point, they eventually stopped looking behind them to see if it was following.

"So how far is Duskenheim anyway?" Devinon inquired, with a familiar "are we there yet?" vibe.

"If we had horses, it would be faster." Liandra sounded as bored as Devinon. She was perusing a book while walking and appeared interested only in the words on the pages. "But we don't so, you know, it'll take a while."

"Ugh," Devinon whined. "Why couldn't we have gotten horses?"

"Because we're broke."

"And Throg would probably eat them," Brutus snickered.

"Neigh monsters tasty!" Throg licked his lips.

"I could've just swiped some horses when nobody was looking."

Lianda turned a page. "And get us kicked out of Ralph's Keep? No thank you."

"But we're saving the world from evil! We shouldn't have to pay for something like horses, or food, or fines when we steal things and get caught! And murder should be legal for us!"

The rest of the party stopped and glared at Devinon who simply shrugged.

Pylara darted through the grass ahead of them. "Squirrel!" she shouted, wildly swinging her tree branch. Several moments later, a rodent of unknown origin flew out of the grass and high into the air, landing in the distance where it exploded.

"What was that about?" Brutus asked when the party caught up with her.

"It's good experience," she replied. "And, apparently, not a squirrel after all."

Devinon nodded approvingly. "We wouldn't want an army of exploding squirrels to attack Throg."

"Not funny!" Throg shouted, arms folded across his chest. "Squirrels attack Throg once."

"How ever did you survive, my good man?" Brutus was

having a difficult time containing his laughter. "It must have been terrible."

"Squirrels delicious. Throg survive by eating."

"I'm sure they are," Brutus agreed, his mocking tone obvious to everyone except, apparently, Throg. "Liandra, don't you know some kind of teleportation spell or something so we can skip the boring travel stuff?"

"Teleportation spells are tricky, and above my current level of knowledge. The last time I attempted one—"

"Let me guess," Devinon interrupted. "You set something on fire?"

"No, mister smarty pants. As a matter of fact, I didn't."

"Oh. That's disappointing, actually."

"I set *multiple* somethings on fire."

"Ha! I knew it!"

The banter continued through day and night as they got to know one another. Well, except for Liam, of course. He wasn't in a talking mood on account of him still being very dead, and not particularly loquacious. It was a situation the party would have to come to terms with at some point and possibly try to return him to life again. But bringing someone back from the dead was costly, though Devinon was constantly thinking of ways to steal that ability and open a resurrection business, which was completely absurd, but absurd was Devinon's specialty, after all.

Day turned to night, then night to day, then again and again and—well, you probably get the idea. It was midday when our valiant adventurers finally arrived in Duskenheim. Also known as The Sleepy City. This was a misnomer, however. While, yes, it did indeed appear as if every citizen was tired or drowsy, the truth of it was they were all just lazy asses. During a typical day, it was a miracle if much of anything was accomplished. Often, entire fields of crops would rot due to the fact that the people who were supposed to tend them simply forgot or found a really neat-looking rock or, yes, maybe they overslept.

I exaggerate. Duskenheim wasn't *truly* that lazy. The real problem was that the entire town was shrouded in perpetual dusk. No sun shone upon the people, yet night never arrived. Needless to say, there was no active nightlife in Duskenheim.

"It appears," Brutus exclaimed, pointing ahead of them, "we have arrived at Duskenheim!"

"Hey, what happened to the Haunted Forest?" Devinon asked.

"What haunted forest?" Pylara asked.

"THE haunted forest. You know, the haunted forest Gerald said we'd have to go through?"

Ah, the Haunted Forest. That was a story for another time.

"Seriously?"

I had fully intended to detail the party's adventures in the Haunted Forest but, honestly, it wasn't in the budget, so they had to skip it. They expressed much disappointment about this fact but ultimately understood and were thankful for being able to skip the danger.

"I guess that's okay," Devinon continued. "I wasn't looking forward to that anyway."

"As I said," Brutus continued, "it appears we have arrived at Duskenheim."

"Great job pointing that out," Devinon laughed. "Which god are you praying to today? Captain Obvious, the god of ... obviousness?"

Brutus gave Devinon a sour look. "Gee," he sneered, "good one."

"Anyway, do you think we'll be able to find someone to bring the minstrel back to life?" Pylara shifted her backpack on her shoulders, grunting a fair bit as she did so. "He's gotten pretty heavy. I'm certain I'm going to have one super beefy shoulder from lugging him around."

Throg drooled.

"Must be bloating," Devinon chuckled.

"Hopefully," Brutus replied. "We could use a little music to stay awake. And if we can't have music, then we'll settle for whatever Liam usually calls music."

They continued toward the town, finally passing the first farms and homes as the duskiness enveloped them seemingly all at once. It was as if they had passed through a wall of utter boredom.

"Hey, who turned on the dark?" Devinon lit a torch which, while providing some modicum of light, didn't seem to pierce the gloom as much as everyone had hoped. Maybe *this* is actually the haunted forest!"

"It's not the haunted forest," Liandra replied.

"How do you know, miss smarty pants?"

"Do you see a forest around here, Devinon? Any trees? Hm?"

"As a matter of fact, I do." He pointed off to their right and into the gloomy duskiness."

"That's a bush."

"A bush is just a tree that hasn't realized its full potential."

"I think that would actually be a baby tree," Pylara interjected.

"There's no such thing as a baby tree!" Liandra growled. Her smoldering hair caught fire briefly before she regained her composure. "A baby tree would still be a tree. That is clearly a bush. And even if it *were* a tree, one tree does not make a haunted forest."

"Guys, this is kind of spooky, though. It's not night yet, is it?" Brutus yawned.

"No," Liandra replied, setting her hand on fire which, to everyone's   surprise,   provided   more   illumination   than

Devinon's torch. She seemed pleased with herself and, if she was in any pain, it didn't show.

"Then what's with all the darkness?" Brutus asked.

"It's because Duskenheim is cursed," Liandra replied.

"What do you mean, cursed?" Devinon asked, still scrutinizing the bush off in the gloomy distance.

"Seriously, Devinon. Didn't you read the sign?"

"No."

"Do you *ever* read signs?"

"Sometimes—when they're pointing me in the direction of treasure or when they say 'free treasure' and point to a mountain of free treasure nearby. Ooh, or when they're planted in a pile of treasure."

"When has that ever happened?"

"Never." Devinon bowed his head and frowned, kicking at the dusty road. "But I'm hopeful."

Liandra walked 20 feet down the road, from whence they came, and stood in front of a large, wooden sign that looked as if it had been assembled in, where else, the dark.

"Welcome to Duskenheim," she read. "The town is shrouded in eternal dusk because it is cursed by an evil wizard who lives atop the highest hill. Please help us by kicking his ass and making him reverse this horrible curse so that we can see the sun again. We're all so very tired. Also, please bring coffee." She walked back to the party.

"Huh." Devinon scratched his chin. "Who knew?"

"Apparently, everyone but you," Liandra growled as she headed into town. "Now let's go find this Briskel guy and get directions so that we can lay a smackdown on this Gobthorak guy."

Everyone else shrugged and followed her into the town which, while lit with lamps, appeared to be largely deserted. As with Devinon's torch, the lamps shed less light than they should have.

Brutus looked hard but couldn't see any movement. "How will we find Briskel if there aren't even any people about? Surely, they're not all inside."

"Maybe they are," Pylara argued. "Or asleep. Usually, in these towns, there's some urchin or random person about who will give directions, but I see no one."

"Throg sleepy, too." He let out a yawn that sounded like a dozen horses running through a pottery shop, followed by a belch with equivalent gusto. "Find bed soon."

"Throg, it's barely past noon! Besides, if anyone needs rest, it's me. Minstrel corpse-hauling is hard work! I think my shoulder's cramping up.

"What's wrong, Pylara?" Devinon asked, about to burst into laughter, "got minstrel cramps?"

The lady warrior rolled her eyes and groaned.

"Would you like to carry him?"

"I know you found that funny," Devinon smirked. "Anyway, maybe we could use Liam as monster bait and trap detection."

Pylara and Liandra glared in disbelief while Brutus and Devinon nodded their approval. Throg looked hungry. Liam didn't get an opinion ... for obvious reasons.

"What? I'm just saying ... he's already dead. If a monster chews on him or he gets hit by a trap, he's not going to care."

Pylara growled, obviously exasperated. Liandra followed her as they both stomped further into town. Devinon shrugged and Brutus chuckled. Throg said nothing, still looking hungry.

"Fine." Devinon pouted, but eventually headed into town. Brutus and Throg followed, having nothing better to do. "Let's find this Brisket dude and get on with it already."

Throg's stomach growled.

"Just listening to the orc's digestive tract is making me hungry. Being a priest is hard work. I hope the people of this town aren't too tired to cook us something tasty. I will certainly make sure they receive a god's favor."

"I could use a few pints of grog, myself," Devinon agreed.

"So, we find this Bristle guy and get directions to Gobthorak's home, then kill the fifteen-or-so Hells out of him, go back to Ralph's Keep and get some kind of reward, right?"

Devinon sighed but remained silent.

"Wait, what was that? You know something, don't you? Spit it out." Brutus poked Devinon's shoulder.

"It's probably nothing. Forget it."

"Oh no. No, you can't just sigh knowingly and then not tell me. What is it? Do you think we're headed into some kind of danger? Are we all going to die? That's it, isn't it? We're all going to die hideously! I knew it! I should consult the gods about this!"

"Oh, no, it's nothing like that. I fear there is something far worse on the horizon."

"Worse than death? What could that possibly be?"

"Another errand quest."

"Son of a bitch," Brutus groaned.

9

And so it was that The Last Available entered the town of Duskenheim. They walked the deserted streets, hearing only their footfalls, their breaths, and Throg who was loud and gassy. Whether on purpose or accidental, it mattered not, for each transgression smelled like rotting bard and cheese.

The shops were closed, the taverns were empty, and the brothel was dark, but that was most likely normal for that particular establishment. Everyone kept quiet, both watching for danger and also simply feeling the lack of motivation to utter a sound. Brutus toyed with the idea of finding an inn and taking a nap but even that seemed like too much work. The street looked comfortable enough, and he could use his shield as a pillow, since he never really seemed to use it for much else.

"This place sucks," Liandra said. "It's boring—like watching two goblins—"

Brutus and Devinon both gasped with shocked looks on their faces.

"What?"

"Nothing," Devinon replied.

"No, what?"

"I just didn't expect you to … you know."

"To what? Not know what goblin intercourse is?"

"To swear. Or to have a sense of humor. Also, yeah."

"Well, if you must know, I once had the unfortunate opportunity to witness two goblins go at it and, let me tell you, it was unpleasant, smelly, and messy."

"Let us never speak of this or even think about it ever again," Pylara replied, a sour look on her face.

Liandra shrugged it off. Her hair was smoldering, and tiny tendrils of smoke rose from her head. In the dim light, however, nobody noticed.

"What are we even doing here?" Pylara asked. "How are we supposed to find this Brisket guy? We've yet to see anyone at all! Isn't there usually some dude standing outside these places, welcoming adventurers to their humble village and giving them directions?"

"At the very least," Devinon responded, "there's usually some kind of quest marker on our compass."

Everyone stopped and looked at Devinon, too confused to know what questions to even ask about the nonsense he'd just spewed.

"I'm sorry!" a voice from above shouted. "Did you say you were looking for Brisket?"

"Who's that?" Pylara yelled. "Show yourself!"

"Up here! In the house to your right."

Everyone looked above them, searching for the source of the mysterious voice. Leaning out a window two stories up was a not-so-mysterious boy, waving at the party. It was too dark to see his actual features, and Throg suspected this boy may have really been several rats in a tunic. He stood behind everyone else, watching from safety.

"Yes!" Devinon shouted. "Do you know him?"

"No! I have no idea who that is!"

"Then why in the fifteen-or-so Hells are you bothering us?"

"Because I'm hungry, and some brisket sounds really tasty! Can you bring me some?"

"Brisket sound tasty for sure," Throg mumbled.

Liandra pushed everyone aside and stood in front of them. "Briskel! We're looking for Briskel!" She paused and, when there was no response, continued. "We're supposed to find him here so that we can get a map!"

"Oh!" the boy replied, sounding excited. "Yeah, I bet he's significantly less tasty, so that's a shame. Oh but you need directions! Are you lost? Where are you trying to go?"

"We just need to find Briskel!"

"Oh right, Briskel! Yeah, that guy!"

"You know him?"

"No! I don't know him!"

Liandra sighed, obviously frustrated. The tips of her hair glowed red, and more smoke wafted upward. She balled her fists at her sides but remained composed, fighting the urge to lob fire at this weasel of a kid.

"Do you know of anyone who *does* know this ... Briskel?"

"Oh sure! I mean, I've met him before and all, but I just don't *know* him. I mean, when do you really *know* someone? Is it after a week? A month? Do you have to share a near-death experience, stranded without food, and wait for them to offer to let you eat them if they die first before you *know* them? Who can say?"

Throg's stomach growled.

"Okay, I think we get it! But can you tell us where he lives, at least?" Liandra continued.

"Sure, I totally could!"

"Great!"

"I probably won't, though. I mean, if there's something in it for me, then maybe ..."

"Excuse me?" Liandra clenched her fists tighter as her frustration grew. She felt her fingernails digging into her palms.

"I mean, what are you going to give me?"

"I like this kid," Devinon whispered, snickering.

"How about a high five and our thanks?" Liandra growled.

"Uh, sorry, but no dice. I can't buy anything with that. And, anyway, you mentioned food and you have none."

"This kid is reaching halfling-level annoyance," Brutus whispered. "Someone should kick his ass. Halflings are so filthy and irritating."

"Uh ..." Devinon stammered. "Yeah ... damned annoying halflings ... yeah. I ... really hate them, too. Good thing I'm a, uh, kid and not one of them." He slipped away and sneaked inside the house. Nobody noticed as they were all preoccupied.

"Okay, fine!" Liandra shook with rage.

Pylara put her hand on the mage's shoulder to calm her but pulled it away instantly from the intense heat.

"What is it you want from us?"

"I want to sleep!"

"I'm sorry ... did you say you want to sleep?"

"Yeah, sleep. You know—that thing everyone around here does pretty much constantly, nonstop? I want to sleep! It's so boring, being the only one here who doesn't sleep!"

"Wait," Brutus interrupted. "You don't sleep? Ever?"

"Nope. Why is that so hard to understand?"

"I mean, it's just ... everyone else apparently sleeps all the time!"

"Yeah, well, I don't do everything that everyone else does! If everyone else jumped off a cliff, would you?"

"Hells yes!" Brutus laughed. "I'd wait for them all to go, then I'd jump off and let their broken bodies cushion my fall! That would be so much fun!"

Liandra gasped. "You are one really messed-up priest, you know that?"

Brutus only laughed, sensing their jealousy.

"You're a priest?" the kid yelled. "Man, she's right—you *are* messed up! Anyway, yeah, I don't sleep. I try but I end up just lying in bed, staring at the ceiling. Ever since I drank that quad-shot super strong grog soy latte with extra whip, I've not been able to sleep."

"Ooh, that sounds tasty," Pylara remarked.

"I might have a spell that could help with your condition," Liandra replied.

"Does it involve fire?" Brutus asked under his breath.

"They *all* involve fire," Pylara chuckled.

"Why would you drink such a thing?" Liandra continued, ignoring her companion's subtle jabs at her spellcasting ability.

"Cramming for finals, of course! Well, I was *supposed* to be, but I was actually just playing games. Anyway—hold on a sec, I need to check on something."

The party stood in the quiet, abandoned street, waiting patiently for whatever was about to happen. This whole quest was going nowhere fast, and the general attitude soured with each passing minute. There was apparently no town more irritating than this one. In fact, a more proper name for Duskenheim might have been Jerksville or Buttholetown. No, Jerksville ... that sounds much better. Forget that other one.

Anyway, silence. Yes, the band of sort-of-brave adventurers stood in silent desolation, waiting for a response from the kid who had mysteriously fallen just as quiet as the rest of the village. In fact, they couldn't see his shady outlined form in the window any longer. Had he abandoned them? Maybe he had finally fallen asleep! That would be excellent for him, but terrible for the party—assuming he had any *real* information to give them in the first place. With their luck, he was just using them for his own amusement. He did indeed seem like the kind of annoying individual to do such a thing.

Eventually, Devinon emerged from the house and casually strutted back to join his companions. He seemed rather pleased with himself, but that was nothing unusual.

"Okay," he said. "We can go now."

"But we still don't know where this Briskel guy is," Brutus replied.

"We do now."

"Devinon," Liandra said sternly, glaring at him. "Tell me you didn't *kill* that kid."

"Okay. I didn't kill that kid."

"Why do I not believe you?"

"Why do you always think I killed someone?"

"Because you *always kill someone!*"

"I'm a man of action."

"You're a kid," Pylara interrupted.

"Anyway, I get things done. While you guys stood out here, useless as usual, I did what I normally do."

"What you normally do is kill people," Liandra argued.

"Well," Devinon sneered. "This time, I didn't! I mean, sure, I had to... coax the information out of him. I knocked him out so he's happily sleeping. He got what he wanted, and we got what we required. Sure, he's going to have quite the lump on his head when he wakes, but he deserved far worse."

"How so?"

"Only a monster drinks a *soy* grog latte. Kid's got worse problems than a simple lack of sleep. His taste in beverages is abhorrent. Also, completely unrelated, did you know the other end of the dagger can knock people unconscious without killing them? I just discovered this!"

Liandra shook her head and sighed—partially out of

frustration, partially out of relief. "Fine," she said. "So where is this guy?"

"Turns out, he's just a few blocks down the road."

"How do we know which house is his?" Pylara asked.

"The kid didn't say. He only said we'd 'know it when we saw it.' I'm not entirely sure what that means because my dagger's hilt sort of clocked him before he could finish. I couldn't stop it. I tried. You know I tried. But things just happened so quickly … and violently."

Liandra rolled her eyes and sighed again. Without a word, she headed down the street with the rest of the party following her lead.

"Come on! That kid was a dick! Besides, he's getting the rest he so badly needed. I provided a valuable service! If anything, he owes me twice."

"Twice?" Brutus inquired.

"Sure. Once for putting him to sleep and once for not killing his smarmy ass."

They, again, walked in silence amid fits of yawning and stretching. The oppressive nature of the town was getting to them—seeping into their very beings like a cancer—and they knew they were doomed to nap if they didn't leave in short order. So, they made haste, keeping their eyes open for Briskel's house but quite unsure of what they were looking for.

"So," Pylara said, "he didn't tell you anything about this guy's house *at all*? Nothing?"

"Nope. Nothing." Devinon scanned the area, looking for any house that would stand out among the others.

"From now on, you don't get to do the talking," she continued.

"And you'd rather stand out in the street, yelling up to some jerk kid? I got us the information while you all stood out here and argued."

"Information?" Liandra growled. "You call what you got information?"

"Well, yeah. I mean, he said we'd know it when we saw it and that it's a few blocks down the road."

"That could be any of these!" Liandra gestured around them. There was nothing about any one of the houses that stood out from the others. "I think we need to go back, apologize, and see if we can get him to tell us more."

"I ... wouldn't recommend that."

"And why is that?"

"Oh, no reason. It's just ... it's a long walk back and we don't want to waste time, do we? We might succumb to sleep before we get there. Besides, I think I see the house!"

"Where?" Throg perked up and he gazed about.

"Right there!" Devinon pointed ahead and to their right.

"Wait," Liandra said, squinting. "Which one? How do you know?"

"I'm guessing," Brutus interrupted, "it's the house with the giant yellow exclamation point hovering over the roof?"

"Bingo."

"I hope you're right," Liandra scowled. Let's get this over with."

Thus, the band of adventurers headed toward the suspected abode of the one called Briskel. Though the beacon was evident, they had to wind and twist their way through the deserted streets. The air was still and eerily silent, though, and the party's footfalls were obscenely loud against the stone beneath them.

Everyone kept largely to themselves, oppressed by the town's eternal dusk. Everything not only looked dark but *felt* dark as well. It was as if the town sapped the happiness out of their very beings, replacing it with scraps of discarded onion and fish bones. No, you know what? Scratch that last part. It was unnecessary.

"Dog!" Throg yelled, pointing ahead of them. That adequately got everyone's attention and they all looked in that direction.

Lying on a building's doorstep ahead of them was a large, flaxen-haired dog. It, like everyone else in this lazy town, appeared to be dozing, but it cocked one eye open when it heard the band of adventurers approaching.

"Don't anybody move," Pylara whispered as she clutched her trusty tree branch. "I will exterminate it. Stay here, for this is a dangerous situation."

"Pylara, no!" Liandra grabbed the branch and tried to push it down, but Pylara was apparently very strong. "It's just a dog. We don't need to kill it!"

"But it's good experience. Besides, it could be a horrible monster in disguise."

"Ooh, maybe it's Gobthorak himself, right here!" Brutus held his shield aloft. "We can get this whole thing over with right now!"

"Or," Liandra countered, "maybe it's just a dog."

"How are we to be sure?" Pylara asked. "I tell you what— let me kill it and, if it's not a brain-sucking, flesh-eating horror, then I owe you a grog."

While the party stood in the street, bickering, the dog slowly rose to its feet and sauntered toward them, stopping a good ten feet away. It sat, waiting patiently for them to finish and finally notice what a good dog it was.

"But what it if *is* a monster?" Devinon asked.

"We should slay it now, before it has a chance to murder us outright!" Pylara exclaimed.

"Dog tasty!" Throg added.

"Guys," Liandra insisted, holding her hands in front of her. "It's *just a dog*! It's not a monster, we don't need to kill it, and we are *certainly* not eating it! It's ... just a dog."

"Fine," Pylara groused, obviously disappointed. "It would've been easy experience points, though."

Throg, too, looked disappointed … and hungry.

For a brief moment, Liandra stopped and considered the situation, but quickly regained her resolve. "Anyway, the dog looks like it's waiting for us."

Devinon put away his daggers. "Maybe it's come to lead us to the right house!"

"Like some kind of guide dog?" Brutus asked. "That's evil sorcery, and I should smite this animal!" Brutus courageously held his longsword aloft, pointing it at the dog that, in response, scratched its chin with its hind leg.

"Brutus, dear," Liandra said in the sweetest voice she could muster. "What did I say already?"

"You said … you said that we're not going to slay the dog."

"Right." She carefully pushed his longsword down to point at the ground.

"But I was talking about *smiting* the dog."

"Brutus, now, that's the exact same thing, isn't it?"

"Not even a little smiting?"

"No smiting."

"Fine." Brutus sheathed his blade, pouting and making his displeasure known.

They approached the mysterious canine enigma and, just as they were within petting distance, the dog took off.

"Stop!" Brutus shouted, giving chase. "Come back here so I can smite you!"

The rest of his companions followed suit, armor clanking and jingling as they raced down the street.

"I really hate running!" Devinon growled.

"But you're so good at it!" Liandra laughed. "What with all the trouble you get into!"

"I don't get into trouble! Trouble finds me!"

"Sure. It's all fun and games until a rock monster's involved!"

"Are we going to keep bringing that up?"

"Absolutely!"

The dog stopped in a cul-de-sac and promptly sat, panting and tail wagging, near a well. When the band of adventurers arrived, the dog remained, waiting for them.

"Well," Pylara muttered, both hands gripping her deadly log, "here we are. Someone remind me why we followed this mutt again?"

"I think it's pure-bred," Liandra whispered.

"The well?"

"No, the dog. It's not a mutt."

"How can you tell?" Brutus asked.

"It just doesn't seem to have traits of—"

"Why does any of this matter?" Devinon impatiently inquired. "We ran after a dog that led us to a pit and now we're standing around a deserted street with a pit in the middle like a bunch of dinguses."

"Wouldn't the plural be 'dingi'?" Liandra asked.

"Also," Brutus added, "it's not a pit. It's a well, actually—"

"Help me!" came a voice from the well.

Liandra moved closer to the well. "Did you guys hear that?" she asked. "I think it came from this well. Someone may be trapped down there!"

"Are we sure it wasn't the dog?" Devinon asked sarcastically.

"Sweet," Brutus muttered, "more easy experience."

Liandra pointed her finger. "We are *not* killing whatever's down there, Brutus!"

"But what if it's, like, an evil dragon luring us into a trap? Sure, it *sounds* innocent and trapped but once you stick your head over the edge of the well, foom! Your head's a soufflé."

Nobody spoke. Liandra looked as if she wanted to argue

but, also, thinking what Brutus had said might, in fact, be a possibility. "Hey, Throg," she said. "Can you just peek over the edge of the well real fast and tell us what you see?"

Throg, not having paid attention to anything within the last few minutes, gladly poked his head deep into the well for a few seconds before pulling it back out, completely unharmed. "It delicious little boy."

"Ah, yes," Pylara affirmed. "I knew it. See, Brutus? Nothing to worry about."

"Well," Brutus mumbled, "maybe he breathes fire."

They all poked their heads into the well to get a look. Sitting at the bottom, on dry ground, was a boy dressed mostly in rags. Nobody could make out much more detail than that in the relative darkness.

"Oh good! Goldie found you! I knew she would! I fell down here and can't get out. Can you guys help me get out of here?"

"No thanks, we're good!" Devinon shouted.

"Wait, what?"

"Sorry, but we're on a mission and we can't be waylaid by such a pitiful side quest!"

Liandra pulled Devinon out of the well by his tunic. "What are you doing? He's a frightened little boy trapped in a well! We should save him!"

"Kid fell down the well. There are consequences, blah blah. Look, the point is, this is a side quest. There's nothing in it for us—no coin, no equipment ... no *experience*. Someone else will come along and help him, I'm sure."

"That's rude, Devinon. I can't believe—"

"Look. If anyone was going to pay us to retrieve him, we would've heard about it by now. His dog is probably the only thing worth anything. Look at him! He's barely wearing clothes! What if he's an evil villain and he's *supposed* to be down there? Maybe someone defeated him and banished him to the bottom of the well!"

Liandra scratched her head and frowned for a moment, obviously lost in thought. "None of that made any sense, Devinon. But we *are* on a pretty tight schedule."

"Exactly."

"Sorry, kid!" Liandra shouted down the well. "Maybe next time! We're on a *real* quest at the moment!"

After a moment of contemplation, one by one, they all stepped back from the well.

"Wait! Come back! I need your help! How can you just leave me down here?"

Devinon pointed to the exclamation point in the sky. "We're close," he said. "Let's go find this Brisket dude."

They filed away, making haste to the house where their *real* quest lay.

"I *am* a real quest!" the boy shouted. "Hello? Are you still there? Okay, screw you, jerks!"

10

fter they knocked for what seemed like forever, a short, plump man answered the door. "Who are you?" he asked, wiping a bit of food out of his bushy white mustache.

"Are you Briskel?" Liandra inquired, fidgeting. She wasn't so much nervous as she was afraid her companions would either accidentally kill the man or, worse, *purposely* kill him.

"Aye. What do you want?" He yawned and scratched his bald head.

"We were told you could help us—that you know where we can find Gobthorak, the Eater of Worlds or whatever his name is."

"We aim to slay him," Pylara added, striking her best heroic stance by holding aloft her mighty branch.

"Gobthorak?" Briskel laughed. "You ... you guys are on a quest to defeat Gobthorak?"

The party remained silent, obviously a little deflated by the man before them, laughing. He was almost shorter than Devinon and resembled more of a ball with arms and legs. For a moment, Liandra wondered, if he fell over, would he roll?

"Aye," she continued, speaking over his laughter. "We have been chosen for a noble quest to free the land from his corruption. We will find him where he lives and cut him down."

"Really?" the man continued, tears streaming down his face. "You ... you're just going to walk in and ... *kill* Gobthorak? Just like that?"

The party exchanged uneasy glances while Devinon looked past the man to see if there was anything worth stealing.

"Well, yes," Liandra replied. "But I'm not sure I see the humor in keeping the world from ending."

"Very well," Briskel giggled, partially containing his laughter. He dried his eyes with his fingers and giggled some more before continuing. "Okay, yes, I've conveniently got this map. It was given to me to decipher after it was found by looters among a pile of bloody bones and various other bits of disgusting carnage."

"Yay!" Throg cheered. "This easy. Follow map, kill Gobthorak!"

"Yes, yes, the map should lead you straight to Gobthorak's lair so you can ... kill him." Briskel snickered.

"Wait a minute," Brutus said, the hesitation on his face painfully evident. "Guys, this sounds a little suspect, don't you think?"

"What do you mean?" Devinon inquired. He didn't bother looking up as he used a dagger to clean under one of his fingernails. "It's perfectly simple. Some skeletons had the map, and they were destroyed. Dead skeletons. Free map. Seems simple to me."

"That's ridiculous, Devinon," Brutus laughed. "What would skeletons need with a map?"

"Hey, I'm sure skeletons get lost, too. It's not like they

have eerie skeleton powers of direction sensing. Why are you hating on skeletons, man?"

"You seem to know an awful lot about skeletons."

"Yeah, genius, because I have one inside me!"

"Hmm." Brutus scratched his chin, obviously lost in thought. "I guess that makes sense."

"Besides, it's all written down in the manual—you know what? Never mind. The point is, the ex-skeletons don't need the map anymore, so it's ours, right Briskel?"

They're not really ex-skeletons, though," Brutus replied. "I mean, they never stop being skeletons."

"Um, yeah, right." Briskel sighed, no longer laughing. In fact, his face showed sadness, as if he pitied the group, which made what he was about to say even sadder. "You see, the thing is, I need a favor."

After having conversed with the party for only a few minutes, Briskel wondered if he should even continue. It would be like asking a favor from a corpse—a severely incompetent corpse at that. But he sighed again and mustered all the courage he could.

"You see, Duskenheim is cursed."

"Oh, right." Liandra perked up. "We saw the sign on the way into town. Well, *most* of us saw the sign." She glared at Devinon who was oblivious due to the fact that he was casing the room, presumably for something to steal.

"Yes, well, you see ... Duskenheim's curse was bestowed upon us by a wizard."

"An *evil* wizard?" Brutus asked. "Wait, I know—a *skeleton* wizard, right?"

"He's not a skeleton, and I don't know about *evil*. I mean, I think he's just a dick. But he's cursed our town and, as I understand it, someone must defeat him to lift the hex and free us from this eternal sort-of-night."

For a moment, thoughts of possibly getting to incinerate someone without repercussions filled Liandra's mind. A smile so wry crossed her lips that several of her fellow adventurers stared at her with concern. "So, we defeat this wizard and lift the curse, then you'll give us the map to Gobthorak's lair?"

"Aye, that is correct. Once the curse is lifted, return here and I'll give you the map as payment."

"What if we get lost?" Devinon asked. "Can you put a waypoint on our HUD?"

Everyone looked confused, except Devinon who simply stared back, beaming. "Seriously, you guys should get out more."

"You won't get lost," Briskel continued. "It's the tall, spindly castle situated atop the seemingly impossible hill, accessible by the ridiculously illogical road. You could probably find it blindfolded."

Everyone paused for a moment before Brutus held aloft a finger and started to speak up.

"Which I do *not* recommend ... so I suggest you all go in with your eyes wide open."

"Then I shall pray to Lycernia, the blessed Goddess of Not Getting Super Lost. You know, just in case."

"You won't get lost! It's just right out there—on the hill! You can't miss it! Why are you so worried about getting lost?"

"We shall return victorious," Pylara exclaimed, hefting her tree branch above her head, nearly punching a hole in the ceiling. "Huzzah!"

The party, one by one, filed out of the house and onto the street. Briskel stood in the doorway, sizing up his new would-be saviors. "Oh, and there's one more thing, if you would be so kind."

"What now?" Devinon groused.

Briskel dry-washed his hands in front of him. "It seems my

son, Tommy, has gone missing," he said. "He left earlier today and hasn't returned. I was wondering, you know, if you saw him, could you make sure he's okay and maybe send him home?"

"What does your son look like?" Pylara asked.

"He's got short, blond hair, brown eyes, and isn't much taller than me. He went out in his dirty old play clothes and never came back."

"Yes, Briskel," Liandra said, clapping the man's shoulder. "If we see Tommy, we will make sure he is safe."

"Excellent! Thank you so much! Oh, his dog is with him —she's sort of a gold color. She never leaves his side!"

The party paused for a moment, soaking in the awkwardness of the moment that seeped into their bodies, down to their bones.

Throg licked his lips at the thought of the dog.

"Uh, that's good to know," Liandra stammered as they hurried away, making sure not to look behind them.

And so it was that the band of brave adventurers left a boy in a well and wandered through the dusky town, following Briskel's waypoint, until they found themselves standing at the edge of a deep gorge, over which a long, meandering road made its way towards a steep, shadowy hill atop which sat a dark, spindly castle.

"Obviously," Liandra said, "this guy is an evil wizard." The party nodded in unison. "Just look at the number of adjectives."

Brutus secured his shield and gripped his sword tightly. "I mean, if he's *not* evil, he's certainly giving off the wrong vibe."

"I bet he's got, like, twenty cats." Liandra's body shivered at the thought. "So evil."

"Yep," Brutus agreed, "super evil."

Throg fearlessly tromped down the winding road, axe in

hand, courageously leading the way. Devinon shrugged and followed with the rest of the party behind him.

"What's gotten into Throg?" Devinon whispered. "Why's he so bold, walking into danger like this?"

"It's probably the promise of cats," Brutus whispered back.

"Oh, right." Devinon made a disgusted face he was pretty sure nobody could see. "Gross." He also made a mental note under the category of "Ways to motivate the orc."

The road was a land bridge, narrow and twisted. Nobody could see the bottom of the gorge, a fact for which several of them were thankful. It was ridiculous, this bridge, but par for the course for such an evil wizard.

"So," Pylara mumbled. "What's the plan?"

Liandra wondered if it was even worth it to propose a plan. She hesitated before speaking up. "Maybe we can knock on the front door and—"

"And stab the jerk in the face!"

"No, Devinon, and *talk*. Maybe he's just lonely, living atop this hill in this dark, creepy-ass, isolated castle, without anyone to talk to."

"Except his cats."

"We don't even know *why* he cursed Duskenheim." Brutus added.

"Brutus is right. Therefore, I suggest we talk to him and get the whole story."

"And I say we stab him. He's obviously a seriously evil wizard and we should act before he casts a seriously evil spell. Seriously."

Liandra glowered at Devinon who didn't seem to care. He was used to those looks. He *expected* those looks. The truth was all he was thinking about was what kind of things he could steal from a wizard's castle.

"You know I can hear what you're saying, don't you?" Liandra scowled.

"Wait, what?" Devinon asked.

"You just said you were used to scowls and you were going to steal something from the wizard."

"No, I didn't."

"You totally did."

"No, the narrator said that. And, by the way, thanks for that, Narrator. And, while we're discussing it, doesn't the narrator sound a lot like Gerald? Weird, huh?"

"It's not like anyone's surprised by your motives," Pylara scoffed. "And, yes, the narrator does sound a bit like Gerald."

"Well," Brutus interrupted, clutching his sword and standing at the ready. "We should probably decide what we're going to do, because we're here, standing in front of the evil door of the evil castle of an evil wizard."

"Oh, wow." Pylara looked up, marveling at the mighty structure before them. The massive wooden door was black as night. It was difficult to even discern it from the black bricks comprising the wall. The door pull was black, the banners hanging from above were black. Even the flags flying from the tops of the spires were black. "So, is this a goth wizard or a necromancer or what?"

"I think those are the same thing," Brutus giggled.

"Keep it down!" Liandra put a finger to her lips. "We're supposed to defeat this guy to bring the light back to Duskenheim! Let's not piss him off before—"

"Before we smash some skulls?" Pylara asked.

"Preferably one skull—and none of ours but, yes."

As the party of heroes … deliberated, the door to the castle creaked open, causing them all to give pause as they waited to discover what lay behind it. They watched the door open until the moment it stopped, then they peered into the darkness beyond. To nobody's surprise, it looked no different than when the door was closed—black.

"I was really hoping for something more," Devinon grumbled, releasing a heavy sigh and pouting. "I mean, this is just more darkness. What's the point?"

Liandra ran a hand through her smoldering hair and scratched the back of her neck. She had to admit, she, too, had expected to see some heinous beast or spell-slinging mage ready to do battle with them. But, no, they were all left with an open door and inky blackness beyond. "Well," she said, "I guess that's an invitation for us to go on in. Who wants to go first?"

Nobody said a word or even made a motion to move. Along with the confusion they all felt, there was the obvious cowardice present within them.

"If only the minstrel were alive," Brutus snickered, trying to conceal his laughter but failing miserably.

"Well, he *could* be of use to us." Devinon turned to his companions, finger in the air to quell any counterargument that was inevitably about to arise.

"How, exactly?"

"Pylara, why don't you chuck one of his legs through the doorway and see what happens?"

Liandra gasped. Brutus laughed. Throg's stomach growled.

"We will do no such thing, Devinon!" Liandra scolded. "I told you, Liam is *not* monster bait!"

"Calm your fireballs, lady, his legs aren't doing him any good right now are they? Besides, this way we determine if there are any traps or monsters on the other side of the darkness—the darkness we totally *cannot* see through and have no idea what's on the other side of. How convenient."

Liandra gave pause, obviously mulling the idea over inside her head. She kept up the appearance of utter disgust, but

Devinon made a good case. Would it hurt just to borrow one of Liam's legs? *If we're eventually able to bring him back to life, would the leg heal up or what?* And, besides, he'd be that much lighter on Pylara's back.

"Besides," Devinon whispered, "maybe the orc would run into the darkness to fetch a snack."

As Liandra was lost in her deep medical conundrum, a voice boomed out from somewhere within the darkness.

"Would you just come in already?" it said—its tone low and slightly perturbed. "By leaving the front door open, you're letting in all the flies!"

The party members looked at one another, some of them shrugging, others more frightened now than they had been previously.

"Well," Devinon said, gazing at the dark portal ahead. "He *did* invite us in. He doesn't sound like a bad guy, right?"

"Are you kidding me?" Pylara gasped, "did you not hear his raspy voice? He sounds evil!"

Liandra nudged Pylara with her elbow, receiving an annoyed gaze in return. "Look who this is coming from," she whispered. "If Devinon thinks this wizard is friendly, then *of course* he's evil!" Pylara nodded but her face soon showed confusion. "We'll get Devinon to go first—willingly."

Pylara shrugged and nodded.

"Come on, guys," Devinon said, motioning to the party to join him. "I'm going in. How terrible can this be?"

"I wouldn't go in there," Liandra replied, only pretending to try and discourage him.

Devinon promptly disappeared into the darkness beyond the door before she could finish her sentence.

The rest of the group stood in awkward, impatient silence, waiting for something—anything—to show them if this had been a good idea.

Nothing. No screams, no explosions. Nothing.

Pylara shrugged, clutching her branch in both hands. "Well, that was easy. I guess we go in, then?"

She stood just outside the doorway for a few seconds then, holding her breath, she walked into the darkness. Everyone else cautiously followed until they were all through and found themselves within ... yep, a dark chamber. Surely you saw that coming. We had to lower production values and darkness is cheap.

A single, flickering candle provided enough illumination to avoid running into anything but any specific details about the room were difficult to discern. Devinon felt around the area, finally stumbling upon a chair.

"This guy really likes it dark," he muttered. "I bet he wears a tunic with at least one skull on it or something. He's probably got boots with more zippers than anyone's ever seen in one place. Or belts! Yeah, I bet he has leather straps and belts all over his clothes."

"You know what?" Liandra growled, "screw this. It's time for some light." She began a subtle incantation and moved her hands about in the air in front of her. Not that she or anyone else could really see that.

"Ooh!" Brutus exclaimed, rubbing his hands together. "Some kind of light-providing spell would be great! Is that what—"

A column of fire engulfed the chair, setting it ablaze and flooding the room with a red-tinged illumination. Devinon jumped back from the blaze, barely avoiding the flames.

"In a matter of speaking, yes." Liandra grinned.

The rest of the party stared awkwardly.

"You said you wanted light. I gave you light. Next time be more specific."

"More specific how?" Devinon asked. "Maybe more specific as in 'don't set anything on fire' specific? You almost got me with that spell."

"I'm confused about the 'don't set anything on fire' part," Liandra snickered.

"Let's just get on with it." Pylara impatiently fidgeted which, for her, meant she was about to smash something with the tree trunk she carried. Deadly, destructive fidgeting.

It was then that everything rumbled and shook.

11

"guess," a gravelly voice boomed, "since you've let yourself into my home, I should welcome you. But you also set fire to my favorite chair, and that makes me unhappy."

Everyone stopped in their tracks, as if standing still would make them invisible. Devinon looked around slowly, hunting for the voice's source but the room was empty still—well, except for the chair next to him, completely engulfed in flames and emitting a foul odor that resembled old feet.

"Uh," Liandra stammered, "who said that? Who's there?"

"What kind of a question is that?" the voice continued. "You're in my home, I presume you know who I am."

Liandra saw the voice's point. "Well, yes."

"So, then, why ask? Who waltzes into someone else's house and asks who they are?"

"I'm just making conversation. What would you have me ask? How many people can the average dragon fit in its stomach?"

"Oh, that's an easy one!" the voice laughed. "But it

depends on how big the people are, and if they're wearing armor or if they're naked."

"Well of course they're wearing armor!" Liandra said. "Why would naked people fight a dragon?"

"It's your question," the voice answered, "I was merely setting parameters."

"Whatever," Liandra scoffed. "It was a simple question."

"Throg bored."

"I agree with the orc." Brutus yawned. "Can we just get on with this?"

"Show yourself, Necromancer!" Pylara yelled, hefting her tree branch. "Show yourself so we can righteously kick your ass!"

Everything shook again and the air felt charged, as if lightning would strike them all in an instant. A column of smoke plumed from the floor and, when it dissipated, a black-robed figure stood in its place. Whoever it was, their robes obscured every feature, and they were motionless as the party readied their weapons, waiting for any sign of danger.

"We should probably just attack," Devinon whispered.

"Don't you want to hear his droning monologue about how he's going to destroy us?" Liandra asked.

"Not particularly."

"Suit yourself. Sometimes it's just nice to be in the know."

"Welcome to my home," the figure said. "I am Gargalog."

"Wait," Devinon snickered, "Garga what?"

"Gargalog."

"Fart log?"

"GARGALOG!"

"Don't piss off the bad guy," Liandra warned. "We did just break into his house and set his favorite chair on fire."

"Uh, *you* set his favorite chair on fire."

"We could argue for days about who set what on fire. The point is, he's probably already really mad."

A moment of silence passed until, finally, the figure spoke again.

"Are you always so mean? I can't help that my name is Gargalog. I didn't get to choose my name, you know. It's not my fault."

Everyone in the party exchanged confused, somewhat ashamed glances—even Throg who was apparently paying attention for once despite what everyone may have thought.

The figure sighed and removed its hood to reveal a bare skull. The party gasped in unison and clutched their weapons tighter.

"Ha!" Devinon shouted, pointing at Gargalog. "I *told* you he'd be wearing a skull! Though, honestly, this far exceeds my expectations."

"You're a necromancer!" Liandra shouted, pointing at him. "You're an abomination to the natural order of magic! You must be destroyed!"

"Vile creature of darkness!" Pylara shrieked, hefting her tree branch with both hands. She looked ready to tear Gargalog apart with her teeth.

"Whoa there, wait!" Gargalog stretched out his hands in front of him, slowly backing up until a wall stopped his progress. "Just hang on a second! I'm a wizard, but I'm no necromancer!"

"That sounds exactly like what a necromancer would say!" Pylara continued. "How are you *not* a necromancer?"

"Yeah," Devinon added, "you literally have a skull for a head which, by the way, is *super* cool, but also a little concerning because, like, how do you even see without eyes?"

"Having a skull for a head is unnatural and sinister," Liandra added.

"Everyone has a skull for a head, you ninny."

"Uh ... well, yeah, but only necromancers wear their skull on the *outside*!" Devinon shouted.

The party exchanged quizzical looks as if they understood what Devinon had said, but they absolutely wished they hadn't.

"That ... only barely makes sense," Gargalog replied. "Listen, let's all just calm down a moment. Killing me won't put an end to the perpetual dusk out there and—"

"Well," Devinon interrupted, "maybe not but you're probably worth, what, a couple thousand experience points right?" He looked at the wizard much like a hungry dog would eyeball a juicy steak.

"What does that even mean?" Gargalog sighed and dropped his hands to his sides. "Look, it's a chronic condition. I'm seeing a healer about it and using an ointment for it, okay?"

Everyone lowered their weapons and eased their stances, bowing their heads a bit in shame.

"Can we kill him anyway?" Devinon whispered.

"Absolutely not," Liandra replied, glaring at him. "At least not yet. If he attacks us, then yes."

A wave of sadness and shame washed across Gargalog's face. Or, well, it probably would have, if he'd actually had a face. Nobody's sure just how that really works when your head is just a skull. It's quite uncommon, really, and maybe Gargalog should've been proud to be so unique. But I digress.

"Anyway," Gargalog continued, "I would assume you're here in my lair to stop the endless dusk, am I right?"

They nodded.

"Well, I'm sure your intentions are pure and it's a valiant effort but there's nothing that can be done, I'm afraid. Follow me if you please, and I'll show you."

He motioned to them and walked out of the room. Liandra shrugged and went after him, soon followed by the rest of the party.

"You see, I am a very powerful wizard. *Very* powerful. I

partake in the types of magic nobody else has the talent, intellect, or courage to even whisper about in the darkest corners of the most forgotten city.

"So," Pylara interrupted, "you do more than just pull rabbits out of hats then?"

"I pull rabbits out of hats, incinerate the rabbits, then reanimate them and teach them to speak orcish."

"Why would you even do that?" Pylara asked.

"Because I can? Because why not? Because now I can have an undead army of rabbits that will do as I please?"

"No," Pylara continued, "why would you teach them to speak orcish? It just seems like a waste of time."

"Have you ever tried to order from an orcish food cart? You'll never know what you're getting unless you speak orcish.

"Also," Devinon added, "raising rabbits from the dead is what a necromancer would do. I knew it! And if you're such a great and powerful badass wizard then why can't you ... you know." He motioned to Gargalog's face.

"Okay, okay. So I *dabble* in necromancy. Even super powerful wizards get bored from time to time, and rabbits make great pets. Plus, when I light them on fire, they keep me warm. It's really just being environmentally conscious. I play with necromancy like anyone plays with their food when they're not hungry or like this kid here probably plays with a toy."

"I'm not a kid!" Devinon shouted.

"Disgusting, gross halfling, then."

"Fine, I'm a kid or something. But my toys are daggers and when I play with them people get stabbed."

"Whatever helps you sleep at night, little guy. Anyway, are you going to help me or what?"

"Why we here again?" Throg appeared to have just woken up, wiping drool from his chin.

Liandra sighed, shaking her head, and swearing under her

breath. "We're here to put an end to this endless dusk so it can end!"

Everyone looked confused for a moment as they puzzled out what the mage had just said. Throg's confusion never abated, but he stopped caring. There was a loud, very disturbing growl and it either came from Throg or his stomach.

"Yes," Gargalog replied, "what she said. I think. Though I don't know how you're going to stop it. I've tried everything and it won't respond."

"I don't understand." Liandra had a puzzled look on her face. "What won't respond?"

"Oh, yes. I guess I should explain about the darkness orb. Follow me."

"That what necromancer would say," Throg growled.

"Anyone could say that," Gargalog retorted. "I'm sure necromancers say lots of things that anyone else would say."

"Throg," Pylara whispered, "don't piss him off please."

"Better him than me," Brutus quipped. "Let him be distracted by the orc while we pound him into goo."

Liandra growled, the embers in her hair coming alive. "We're *not* killing him ... well, not yet."

"Okay, then when?" Brutus appeared impatient.

"After we find out where all his loot is of course," Devinon responded. "Duh."

Gargalog the NOT necromancer led them out of the room and into a hallway decorated with ornate rugs and tapestries. Torches sat in skull-shaped sconces that lined the walls and as the party passed each one, they got the feeling they were being watched.

Brutus kept his eyes on each skull as he passed, sneering at them, and making other faces to try to get a reaction.

They descended a dark staircase at the end of the hallway. Gargalog waved his hand, and a skull-shaped ball of light sprang from his fingertips, floating ahead and illuminating the area.

"Pfft," Devinon scoffed, "like that's supposed to be impressive."

"This ball of light used to be a living creature known as a boolag. I incinerated it and raised it from the dead. Not that I need to impress you or anything."

"Necromancer," Pylara whispered, gripping her branch tighter.

"So, this darkness orb," Liandra said, "what is it?"

"Well, I don't mean to get technical, as it's very complex, but it's … an orb that's really really dark."

"Is this something else you've incinerated and brought back to life?" Liandra asked.

"I'll bring your mom back to life," he muttered under his breath. "No, it's not. I was researching a way to make it darker than dark so I could get some quality sleep and things … sort of got away from me."

"Define 'got away from me.'"

"Let's just say it would be prudent for them to include the disclaimers and warnings *before* the spell text."

"Okay," Liandra agreed, "I feel you there."

"Liandra?" Brutus queried.

"Yes?"

"Is that why you constantly set things on fire?"

"Would you like to find out?"

"I'll pass, thank you. That doesn't sound like something I need a definitive answer to."

"Smart man."

They stepped off the stairs and into a large, open room containing all manners and sorts of strange items. As they looked around, they saw shelves of cannisters containing herbs, powders, and various body parts from a variety of creatures.

Several tall stacks of books lay in one corner while a pile of books filled another. Strewn about the room in more piles and stacks were devices that could have been torture implements, kitchen gadgets, or simple toys. Even Liandra with her vast wealth of magical knowledge had no idea what they were.

"Well," Brutus said, "this is sort of a ghastly place, isn't it?"

"Hey everyone's got a junk-filled storage room in their house. No judging. Now follow me, we're almost there."

"I feel like I'm in an overly-loquacious fantasy novel spanning far too many books that focus way too closely on traveling," Devinon quipped.

"Sometimes, Devinon," Liandra replied while tugging on her hair, "I have no idea what you're talking about."

"I think that goes for most of the time," Pylara joked. "At least for me."

Gargalog pushed open a door and motioned to the object within.

Inside the room was a twisted pedestal constructed from bones. Floating a good foot or two above the pedestal was an orb made from the darkest darkness. It was so dark it made something normally dark look like daytime.

Okay, look, that was a bad comparison that didn't make a lot of sense. Just know that it was super-duper dark, all right?

"There it is. The Orb of Eternal Dusk."

"I thought you said you wanted everything to be totally dark." Devinon scrutinized the floating ball of darkness. "So why stop at dusk?"

"The darkness wasn't even supposed to go past my castle but, as you can see, everything out *there* is dusky and nothing in here is."

"So, you screwed up," Pylara snickered.

"Yeah. I screwed up. I didn't even get the darkness right and half-assed it to dusk."

"So, how do we turn it off?" Devinon asked.

"I could set it on fire," Liandra suggested.

"Fire won't affect it," Gargalog replied. "Besides, the guy I spoke to when I contacted technical support said fire might make things worse."

"I think you underestimate my fire."

"It won't work."

"Seriously, my fire is special."

"How so?"

"It just is."

"Look, I've tried everything I know. I've thrown every spell in the book at it and it's still here, floating in the air and mocking me. Though, I will admit I've slept really well since I cast the land into eternal dusk."

"So has everyone in town," Brutus added.

"Anyway, I don't expect you guys to have a solution as my magical knowledge is vastly superior to—"

At this point, a bored Throg Axehammer muscled his way past the party and approached the orb where he proceeded to obliterate the pedestal with his wicked, double-bladed axe. Bits and pieces of bone flew in all directions as he swung one last time and destroyed it.

But the orb remained floating in mid-air, continuing its function of spreading duskiness across the land.

Determined to be an orc of action, Throg punched the orb, sending it flying into the wall where it smashed, releasing dark, wafting energy that soon dissipated.

"Throg fix."

"Now why didn't I think of that?" Gargalog asked, astonished by the solution.

"I guess," Devinon snickered, "you should always start by turning it off and turning it back on?"

"Well," Pylara added, "we at least turned it off. Turning it back on might be a little difficult."

"Throg powerful mage. Throg cast axe, then Throg cast fist."

"Well done, Throg!" Gargalog shouted, clapping the orc on the back but quickly withdrawing when he saw the orc's look of disapproval. "I really wish I'd thought of that. Of course, that setup was rather expensive and time-consuming to create, but I guess that's just part of being an all-powerful wizard of unlimited potential."

"Excellent!" Devinon exclaimed. "So, we get paid now, yes?"

"Paid?" Gargalog laughed. "You just destroyed a precious artifact I created, not to mention setting my priceless chair on fire upstairs."

"That chair was an old piece of crap," Liandra argued "It wasn't worth anything."

"It had sentimental value! You can't replace memories."

"Memories of what?" Brutus asked, only whispering to Pylara next to him. "Dingy and stale aromas?"

"Surely whoever gave you this quest agreed to pay you. Isn't that how it works? I'm not even sure, since I haven't left my castle in quite some time."

"Gargalog is correct," Liandra said. "Briskel agreed to give us the map to Gobthorak's lair. That will be payment enough, as per our agreement."

"What a scam." Devinon folded his arms across his chest and pouted. "I knew we should've asked for more."

"How much stuff did you steal from Briskel during the short time we were in his house?"

"Lady, I am *appalled* that you would accuse me of thievery! How dare you!" Devinon grinned. "I merely borrowed with the intent to keep. Also, I took a lot of stuff. A *whole lot* of stuff. Dude's gonna wonder where his toilet brush is!"

"Gross," Pylara muttered, disgust clear on her face.

"Yes, yes," Gargalog interrupted. "This is all well and good, but I'm a busy man and I have important things to attend to, so please get the fifteen-or-so Hells out of my house now."

"Oh, hey," Devinon said. "You're apparently good at raising things from the dead, right?"

"Yes."

"Any chance you can help us with a little bard problem?"

"Alright it's time to go." Liandra ushered everyone out of the room, literally pushing Devinon until he begrudgingly complied. "We'll be leaving now. We'll show ourselves out."

"Try not to set anything on fire on your way out."

Gargalog waved his hand and the door slammed behind them, leaving the party to find their own way out of the castle.

Which they did quickly, eager to get the map from Briskel and continue their quest to rid the world of the foulest, evil being ever known.

The sun shone brightly as they made their way back into town, pleased with the successful conclusion to their quest. The Last Available had fought darkness and won.

12

ook," Devinon whined, "all I'm saying is, the townsfolk sort of seemed like a bunch of ungrateful jerks."

"I tend to agree with that assessment," Brutus concurred.

"Well, yes," Liandra continued, "but I'm pretty sure that bright sunshine was uncomfortable after so much time in perpetual dusk. Even my eyes had trouble adjusting at first."

"Yeah, but they could've at least been happy about it. All I heard was 'ow my eyes' and 'I'm blind' and 'great, now I need to find sunscreen!'"

"Whiners," Pylara added, flicking a bug off her tree branch. "One man was crying about having to go back to work."

"And that kid in the well," Brutus added, "was not only whining about still being stuck down there but also about how bright it was. Seriously, what a bunch of asshats."

Liandra looked annoyed. "You know, we could have pulled him out of that well."

"Liandra," Brutus replied, "we're on a mission to save the

world! We can't be waylaid by situations that don't concern us. We have important business to conduct with Gobthorak."

"Business that involves kicking his ass, am I right?" Devinon held out his hand for a high-five. Brutus obliged. "If we stop for every single thing along the way, we'll never reach our destination, and the world goes boom."

"But obviously," Liandra continued, "wasting several hours killing squirrels in the forest is a fantastic use of our time."

Devinon pointed to Pylara. "That one's on her."

"I needed to kill something," Pylara retorted. "Devinon said I was super close to leveling, whatever that means."

"And what about the time we spent getting coffee?"

"How was I supposed to know the walk-thru line would be so long?" Devinon snorted. "If the people in front of me hadn't ordered the most complex drink in the realm, we would've been in and out with no problems."

"Throg like coffee." The orc appeared to be vibrating after the super mocha triple goat milk brulee latte he drank in ten seconds.

"Throg is right," Brutus agreed. "We can't possibly save the world if we're all super tired. Heroes need downtime."

"Fine, whatever. According to this, we should be getting close." Liandra scrutinized the various symbols and scrawlings on the poorly drawn map. "But I'm not entirely sure."

"What exactly does that mean?" Brutus leaned in to get a look at the map in case he could make better sense of it, but he quickly gave up.

"Yeah, what does that mean?" Pylara asked.

Liandra huffed, looking quizzically at the map from all angles. "It means this map sucks and was probably drawn in crayon by a five-year-old who wasn't paying attention. If I'm reading it right, there should be some sort of giant rock around this bend. After that, we should see the town of Littleton.

"Uh, Liandra?" Brutus interrupted, staring at the map again. "I don't think that's supposed to be a giant rock." He flicked his finger at the symbol and ejected it from the map. "That was a fly."

"Well," Liandra continued, "either way, we *should* be coming up on Littleton shortly."

The party walked a little further, passing a whole lot of boring terrain that isn't worth describing because, really, who wants to read a bunch of rambling text about people walking?

Anyway, the road led them a little further before it took them to some rocky cliffs that jutted up from the ground.

Devinon inspected a nearby sign. "Watch for falling rock," he read.

Throg immediately hefted his axe and scanned the area, squinting. "No falling rock get past Throg," he growled.

"Do not worry!" Brutus exclaimed. "We shall not befall a most unfortunate fate today, for my goddess Felistra shall keep us safe from the menacing stones!"

"Felistra?" Pylara asked. "I've never heard of her."

"She's the goddess of rocks."

"Goddess of rocks? She sounds very ... specialized."

"Well, she has a wide dominion, but she usually focuses on jagged, heavy rocks. She leaves the smooth pebbles and river rocks to other deities. Felistra is widely worshipped in the southern realms where boulders routinely kill people."

"Wait," Liandra said, "stop for a minute. Why do so many people get killed by boulders?"

"Oh, well, because boulders are jerks. Also boulders are really heavy."

"I don't even know why I'm discussing this." Liandra went back to studying the map.

"So, could she have aided us in our valiant fight against the rock monster Devinon angered?"

"Oh, heavens no. She has no sway over rock monsters. Just rocks."

A small stone broke off from the cliff and tumbled to the road, rolling in front of them. Throg motioned for the party to stop before crushing the rock with his axe.

"Safe now," he said triumphantly, looking quite proud.

"Seriously, fly, get off!" Liandra screamed, shaking the map vigorously. "I couldn't care less about rocks but if someone would kill this damned fly, I'd be eternally grateful!"

Brutus swatted the map, killing the fly but leaving a chunky smear of goo.

"Gross but thank you."

"Oh look!" Devinon pointed ahead of them where the road angled around the cliff to the right. "Looks like we're finally close!"

"What are we going to do in Littleton again?" Brutus asked.

"Hopefully restocking supplies," Pylara responded, "and maybe getting a good meal."

"With a name like Littleton I wouldn't expect much." Brutus adjusted his shield on his back briefly and wiped sweat from his forehead. "But at least it's not eternal night or anything."

Liandra yawned. "It may as well be. I'm bored just thinking about it."

They followed the road for a bit longer until, indeed, it curved around the cliff which slowly tapered off and gave way to flatter terrain.

"Well, that's unexpected," Liandra said, pointing off to their right.

Lying in a field was a giant fly-shaped smear.

"That doesn't even make any sense," Devinon replied. "Also, super gross."

It was only a few minutes more before the party gazed upon Littleton.

"This map sucks." Liandra rolled up the parchment and put it away, sighing in a way that effectively conveyed how tired of nonsense she was. "We definitely didn't get paid properly for putting an end to that eternal dusk."

The towering, ornate structures of Littleton reached high into the air as they stood outside the city gates, gazing at the unexpected grandeur of a city that absolutely belied its name in every way possible.

"Well, now," Brutus gasped, "this is a welcome surprise. Ascalan smiles upon us this day."

"Who Ascalan?" Throg asked.

"God of majestic cities, of course! He puts Crosti to shame."

The party remained silent, assuming Brutus would continue on his own.

"And Crosti is ... " Devinon eventually acquiesced, instantly wishing he hadn't asked.

"God of shithole towns, of course."

"I should have known."

"He's usually referred to as Crusty."

"Welcome to Littleton!" a voice boomed. A woman approached hastily, pushing through a small crowed that had formed as people traveled in and out of the city. "Oh, but you're late! This will not do!"

"Hello!" Pylara announced. "What can we—"

The woman scurried up to them, clearing her tousled, brown hair from her face. "You were supposed to arrive yesterday!"

"Wait," Devinon interrupted. "We're expected?"

"Well of course you are!"

To the party's surprise, the woman before them broke into song and dance.

"♫ *We've awaited your arrival for days and days. To help with our survival and lift the heavy haze. We—*"

"What in the fifteen-or-so Hells is going on here?" Devinon whispered.

The woman continued her song and dance which was bizarre enough, but when the crowd joined in, singing harmonies and coordinating their dances, he knew they had arrived at one of the deepest depths of the fifteen-or-so Hells.

"Throg scared."

The party gazed on in terror as the musical number continued, now incorporating magical pyrotechnics and illusions which piqued Liandra's curiosity.

"When does this torture end?" Devinon asked.

" ♫ *Please shut up!*" Brutus sang in a surprisingly melodious tone.

Everyone came to a halt and the crowd went back to what they were doing as if nothing weird, bizarre, or even ridiculously annoying had ever happened.

"That was ... odd," Pylara said. "I wish the map had warned us."

"That's putting it lightly," Brutus replied. "So, anyway, I wasn't listening. Tell us again why we're expected?"

"♫ *You've come to—*"

"No no," Devinon interrupted. "Just *tell* us what's going on please."

"♫ *We—*"

"No!" Liandra shouted. "*Tell* us! No singing!"

"But we have to sing," the woman whispered, shifting uneasily and fidgeting. "It's what we do!"

"Well, it's not what *we* do," Liandra replied.

"What *do* we do?" Pylara asked.

"Blow shit up," Devinon laughed.

"Very well," the woman continued, "we need your help to free the city from an evil—"

"Please let it be an evil burrito," Brutus suggested, his eyes filled with hungry hope.

"An evil curse," the woman continued.

"Aw, damn it," Brutus growled. "Just once—JUST ONCE—I would like it to be something awesome and delicious. But nooo! It's always an evil curse or an evil necromancer or whatever!"

"He wasn't a necromancer," Liandra replied.

"He was totally a necromancer," Devinon mumbled. "And a liar. But he had fantastic taste in home décor."

Liandra sighed. "Anyway, I'm not sure we're the people you were expecting. You see, we're just passing through on our way to save the world from Gobthorak."

"Gobthorak!" the woman shouted. "Oh, if you plan to face him, then you will need Surok's help!"

"Surok?" Devinon asked. "Who's that?"

"Oh crap," Pylara grumbled, "here we go."

"You see, ♫ deep down dark where the water flows red lives a ..."

It was at this time the party all suffered through the next musical number, largely ignoring everything, and just waiting for it to be over.

"Someone kill me," Devinon growled. "Literally. Just kill me."

"Anything to end this," Brutus agreed.

Throg danced and joined in, more grunting than singing, but he also appeared to know the words and the choreography perfectly.

"And Liandra accuses *us* of wasting time," Pylara said.

"Look at him go, though." Liandra marveled at the orc's surprising talent. "I mean, he's not going to win any awards, but I was unaware Throg had it in him."

"I wish he would've kept it in him," Devinon joked. I mean, he was serious, but it seemed like a decent dialog tag to include. You get the point. I'm sorry, I did the whole meta thing there.

Anyway, where was I?

Liandra looked nervous, as if she was concentrating on something with great effort. Her pursed lips trembled, and her hands shook.

"Uh oh," Brutus said, pointing at Liandra's slowly increasing undulations. "Don't do it! Fight it!"

"Crap!" she shouted just before she, too, burst into a song and dance, looking pained and under great duress as she tried to resist but failed.

"Her dancing," Brutus whispered, "it looks like a dying pelican."

"That's ... oddly specific," Pylara responded. "But clearly, you've never actually seen one. I've killed pelicans and they die more gracefully than that. They sound more pleasant, too. Liandra's got nothing on a dying bird."

"Wait." Brutus scratched his head as he scrunched his face. "A pelican's a bird? I thought it was one of those things—you know, with the eight legs, wings, and three faces."

"Yes, a pelican's a bird. I have no idea what you're thinking about but, whatever it is, pelicans aren't it."

"Apparently I, too, have no idea what I'm thinking about."

"Whatever they are, are they worth a lot of experience?"

"Listening to you two prattle endlessly is only slightly more enjoyable than listening to this song," Devinon grumbled. " ♫ I believe it's high time we left this terrible place," he sang.

"Not you too!" Brutus shrieked.

"Oh, no I'm fine. I'm just bored. I wondered, if I sang

something, if it would get everyone else to shut up. Sadly, it didn't work."

Eventually, the song wound down and while Liandra appeared thankful, Throg was disappointed. They rejoined their friends, both out of breath.

"Okay, now that that's over, what are we supposed to do?" Devinon asked.

Liandra was still trying to catch her breath. "We locate Surok, apparently. And, hopefully, without that singing garbage happening again."

"Who's Surok?" Devinon asked.

"Were you not paying attention to that horrible song Throg and I just helped sing?"

"Duh, no. As you just pointed out, it was garbage, so I was busy thinking of something else. Just skip to the part where you tell me who or what a Surok is and how we can profit. Or if we, you know, have to kill him."

Liandra rolled her eyes and groaned. She clenched her jaw and grimaced, obviously wanting to wrap her hands around Devinon's neck. Her hair was a lovely, bright shade of crimson and the smoke rose in thick black plumes.

"Surok is the mayor of Littleton. This kind lady said he could help us reach Gobthorak."

"We have a map," Devinon scoffed. "We don't need anyone's help."

"She disagrees and, honestly, I'm willing to believe her. We could use all the aid we can get because, apparently, Gobthorak is really nasty."

"How do you know?"

"If you had listened to the song, you would—"

"Song shmong. Let's just get our supplies and move on."

"Oh!" Gianna shouted. "You need supplies? ♫ The best place to go without spending lots of dough ..."

"Wait a minute!" Devinon waved his hands in the air trying to get Gianna to cease her song, but she continued crooning without so much as a pause. "The woman has a name now?"

Of course, she has a name. If you'd listened—

"Yeah yeah, if I'd listened to the song, blah blah. You keep saying that as if I was actually going to listen to that garbage. I really hate this place."

Gianna continued singing.

Throg danced.

Pylara nearly vomited.

Devinon pushed past Gianna who appeared unfazed as her song continued. "Come on," he said, motioning toward town. "Let's get whatever we need and get out of here."

They were certain they could still hear Gianna singing in the distance as they shuffled through town, many of them keeping their heads down and trying not to attract attention. Being noticed most likely meant another song, and nobody wanted that except maybe Throg.

"Too bad Liam's not alive," Brutus snickered, "he'd absolutely *love* this town."

"Which is why I'm glad he's not," Devinon added, his voice low so only Brutus could hear. "The orc singing and dancing is bad enough. In fact, I think he's better than Liam ever was."

"Wait," Brutus said. "Liam knows music. If he were alive, then maybe he could help the town with this musical curse thingy and they'd—"

"Shower us with riches and treasure?"

"Well, I was going to suggest they'd be free of the curse, actually."

Devinon said nothing, but merely stared at Brutus, disappointed.

"I'm just kidding!" Brutus laughed. "Obviously riches and treasure are more important. Man, the look on your face! I thought you were going to stab me for having the wrong priorities!"

"Yeah," Devinon laughed nervously, "wrong priorities ... I knew you were joking." He removed his hand from one of the daggers hidden behind his back. "Though, honestly, I would prefer to be free of this curse myself."

And, so, the group continued through the crowded streets, of which there were many, keeping their heads low but watching out for any establishments that might suit their needs. Several groups of people hindered their travel as they broke out into songs with four-part harmonies and well-designed choreography. It might have been a nice spectacle if it hadn't been such an inconvenience.

Also, Throg tried to join in at every opportunity, somehow knowing all the words and dance moves. Half the time they spent making their way through the crowds was trying to drag the orc out of some elaborate musical number about boots or the price of a banana.

Finally, Devinon pointed to a simple, unassuming shop that just said "STUFF" in big letters on the sign. "You know what? Let's just go in there and see if they have what we need."

"Good idea," Liandra agreed. "Ear plugs would be nice. And then maybe we can talk to Surok and enlist his aid against Gobthorak?"

"One thing at a time."

13

really thought that shop would have everything we needed," Brutus said as they exited the store. "I mean, with a name like 'Stuff' how could they possibly not?"

"Seems like false advertising to me," Liandra added, obviously disappointed. "I really could have used some materials for my magic research. They didn't even have dried sochra root! Can you imagine?"

"The nerve," Devinon said, rolling his eyes where Liandra couldn't see. "There wasn't even anything good to steal."

Pylara shot Devinon a disapproving glare.

"Did I say steal? I meant buy. They had nothing good to buy. But I think Throg had a good snack."

"But there wasn't anything edible in there." Liandra paused and looked at the orc who finished chewing and swallowed. "Wait. Throg, what did you find to eat?"

"Just ... stuff, like sign said."

"Just stuff, huh? Stuff like, say, the things that were in the little bins and bottles?"

"Things."

"Throg, those were spell materials! You're not supposed to

eat those! Some of them are poisonous and others can cause strange effects!"

Throg burped and a plume of smoke erupted from his mouth.

"See? Yes, just like that!"

"Give it time," Devinon laughed, "and we'll have spell effects from the other end! I hope I'm around to see some of that … just not up close or, you know, in the blast radius."

"Some of those materials were for destructive spells."

"You're not doing a good job of changing my mind," Devinon laughed.

"And others were for gaseous clouds of noxious fumes that eat organic matter."

"On second thought," Devinon mused, "maybe I don't want to be around for that after all. The orc sleeps outside tonight. Though, if I'm being honest, I'm not certain that would differ from Throg's usual emanations."

"Well," Brutus shouted, "I truly hope nobody starts a song and dance about destructive flatulence!"

He waited for the crowd to break into a musical number but was quickly disappointed when nobody paid him any mind. "Seriously? I left the door *wide* open for you people."

"Are you *trying* to annoy us?" Liandra asked.

"Pretty much, yeah," Brutus laughed.

Throg burped butterflies, then proceeded to try and catch them. Usually, when orcs swat at the air, they're trying to murder something, so it was mildly amusing to watch him try to catch illusory butterflies, especially since nobody but him could see them.

Which meant most people assumed Throg was attempting to kill them.

"So now what?" Pylara asked. "I'd prefer not to run around this city looking for supplies and dodging low-budget musical productions."

"I guess," Liandra suggested, "we find this Surok fellow and see what aid he can give us against Gobthorak. Nobody seems to be able to shut up about him."

"And then we get the fifteen-or-so Hells out of here?" Devinon asked.

"Absolutely. I'm a good ten seconds away from just lobbing fire in all directions."

"I would very much like to see that."

"Why am I not surprised?"

"So then," Brutus interrupted, "does anyone know where this Surok lives?"

The party exchanged dubious, confused glances but remained quiet. Nobody dared suggest what they were all thinking until Throg finally broke the silence.

"Hey!" he yelled, sending several people scurrying away. "Where Surok at?"

They all braced themselves for the musical onslaught that was about to befall them. Throg, of course, was ready to dance ... or whatever he called his undulating, noisy mess.

"Where is Surok?" someone whispered.

"Where is Surok?" someone else whispered.

"Seriously, Throg?" Liandra smacked the orc on the back of the head. "Thanks a lot."

"Where is Surok?" another person whispered as music from somewhere began to build.

"Where where where is ..."

"Surok!" Throg yelled.

Everyone on the street erupted into song, complete with colorful costumes, an orchestra, and even confetti. People danced on balconies and even atop roofs, though why they were up there in the first place remained a mystery. Nothing in this city appeared to make any sense.

"How do they not fall off the roof?" Pylara asked,

pointing to several jovial dancers high above. "It seems an impractical location for revelry."

"And in those shoes, too," Devinon added. "Precarious footwear for such heights."

"This entire city is an impractical location," Liandra grumbled. Her growing irritation was no mystery to anyone observant enough to notice the tiny yet radiant flames flickering within her hair. The plumes of smoke they sent into the air were darker than the normal, smoldering fumes her head produced.

"Your mom's an impractical location," Devinon joked, careful to only mouth the words to avoid Liandra hearing them. Passing up a joke was painful, but death as a result of a joke was a tragedy. Today was not the day to get incinerated. "Your mom" jokes weren't good enough for that.

"♫ Surok is the man, the man with two hands…"

Several revelers danced a ring around the party, choreographed perfectly to the upbeat music that seemed to come from everywhere. Yes, there were musicians about, playing their instruments, but no way could they have produced such a robust, complex melody.

"♫ He also has two feet and many sweat glands."

"This is truly a song worse than any other," Liandra griped.

"But it's educational," argued Brutus. "We're learning the man's anatomy! This is important stuff!"

"♫ His arms, like ropes, are big and thick and deep down below is his massive—"

"You know what?" Brutus continued. "I think we've all had enough education for one day."

"Or a lifetime," Pylara added.

Throg sang the lyrics nobody wanted to hear but everyone knew were coming, and they winced.

"I assume," Brutus said, "we'll be forced to listen to this

disaster to figure out where Surok lives."

"Oh, screw this," Devinon shrieked. "He lives up there, on that hill in that house. Let's just go already."

Liandra looked perplexed as the song and dance number started in on the second verse about Surok's hobbies and favorite color.

"How do you know this?" she asked.

"While you guys were busy listening to this monstrosity, I took the liberty of interrogating one of them. People change their tune when presented with bodily harm."

"I don't condone your methods, Devinon, but thank the gods. Let's get out of here before they tell us about Surok's favorite food!" Liandra grabbed Throg's arm and with much effort, finally convinced him to follow. And he *did* follow, but was obviously unhappy about it, so he hummed the tune as they hurried through the crowded streets, headed for a simple, unassuming abode perched atop a grassy hill.

They kept to themselves, taking the utmost care not to speak to anyone. Everyone but Throg attempted to avert their gazes lest they trigger another songasm. The orc, however, appeared to be purposely trying to set off another performance piece, so their quick pace was crucial. Frankly, I'm glad they made it without any major musical altercations, because even I have my limits.

And so, it was that the steadfast adventuring party braved the throng of townsfolk, keeping to themselves, remaining silent, and gently lifting every bit of coin from each person they could.

Well, Devinon was solely responsible for that last bit but, as it turns out, most townsfolk didn't carry much beyond a few coppers and maybe a silver. Not as if that fact discouraged him or caused him any hesitation, of course. Each new purse or pocket was another opportunity.

The crowd thinned as they left the bustling merchant

areas behind and found themselves in a more residential area. Everyone breathed a sigh of relief when they realized they would encounter very few people here and the chances of a full-blown musical disaster were slim.

Throg, of course, looked disappointed. Or maybe he was hungry. Sometimes, orcs could be difficult to read which has surprised many scholars throughout the ages and resulted in no small number of untimely deaths.

"Why does this guy have to live atop a hill?" Liandra asked, slightly out of breath.

"Important NPCs always live atop hills, apparently," Devinon griped. "Necromancers, mayors ... whatever."

"He wasn't a necromancer," Liandra replied.

Pylara laughed, apparently enjoying the workout. "A little exercise never killed anybody."

"I'm pretty sure it has, actually," Liandra growled. But do you know what's more common and kills people?"

"No idea. What?"

"Snide remarks from tree branch-wielding smart asses."

Liandra's hair lit up with many hues of red, orange, and yellow before it resumed its normal smolder. She was not having it. Even Devinon decided it best to remain quiet. He and Brutus exchanged an uneasy glance, and both came to the same conclusion. Don't piss off the mage.

"You can obviously guess what *her* dump stat is," Devinon whispered anyway. He was no fool but, as we established a few paragraphs ago, he also couldn't pass up a joke. Well, he *could*, but he would never.

The street leading to Surok's abode wound its way through town, passing houses of all kinds, two large, overly elaborate fountains, and a dog licking itself.

Brutus eyed the dog as they passed by. It paid him no mind, seemingly unconcerned with anything but its hygiene.

"Uh oh." Brutus pointed at another dog emerging from

behind a house. "Another dog."

"Big deal," Pylara scoffed. "What are you afraid of?"

"That." He pointed to two more dogs emerging from behind a statue.

"They're dogs, Brutus. They're cute! Look at them! They're fluffy and cute! Here poochy pooch!"

Pylara made kissy faces at the dogs, but they didn't approach. "I bet they're worth at least two experience points each, too."

Devinon laughed but also did the math in his head in case she wasn't joking. Several more dogs appeared.

Throg looked terrified. Even more dogs came in from all around them, eventually surrounding the party. Liandra readied a fire spell while Pylara gripped her branch. A lighthearted moment suddenly turned dark as the pack of dogs closed in, growling and snarling and sometimes even nipping at one another. Drool dripped from the mouths of several of them that bared their teeth.

"It looks like things are going to get ugly," Brutus warned, his shield held in front of him as he clutched his sword.

"They're just dogs," Pylara said, reassuring everyone. "What are they going to do, lick us to death?"

"Hopefully not," Devinon replied. "I've seen where their tongues have been."

"I can probably take out most of them with some fire," Liandra added.

Throg trembled and remained quiet, his mighty battle axe in both hands.

The pack of animals closed in, slowly inching forward until they were a mere few feet from the group.

"Why aren't we attacking?" Pylara asked.

"I mean, they're dogs," Liandra replied. "They're cute! And, besides, you're supposed to never kill the dogs. It's, like, an unwritten rule or something."

The dogs moved in closer.

"Even if they're going to kill you?" Brutus asked.

Liandra's hands erupted in red and orange flames. "I mean, it's a gray area," she growled, grinning.

All at once the canines lunged at the party, growling, drooling, and snarling in a fit of fur, teeth, and rage.

Throg yelped in terror while Liandra prepared to release the fire from her hands. Just as she was about to give the puppies what for, they stopped and sat like the good dogs they apparently were. Everyone breathed a sigh of relief except Throg who didn't notice and had possibly peed himself.

"What," Pylara began, "what's going on?"

"I've got a bad feeling about this," Brutus warned.

"They're not attacking," Pylara continued. "Why aren't they attacking?'

"Crap," Devinon growled. "It's even worse than a dog attack."

"Worse than a dog attack?" Liandra appeared confused, the flames from her hands still licking the air.

"Way worse."

"You don't mean—"

"Yep. That."

As if on cue, the dogs broke into a spontaneous song and dance number complete with harmonies and full choreography. Nobody in the party spoke dog but Devinon thought the song was about the tragedy of an empty food dish.

Throg still lay on the ground, sobbing even harder now. The rest of the party sympathized with him.

"Okay," Liandra said, her voice calm and steady. She was so serene; it was surprisingly frightening. "I've had it."

Without warning, she launched searing flames from her fingertips, engulfing the circle of dogs in a ring of fire. The animals didn't seem to notice, however, dancing and howling until they were nothing more than piles of ash. Dancing piles of ash. Don't ask.

"What in the fifteen-or-so Hells?" Devinon asked, completely astonished. "I was going to say you cursed us by killing the dogs, but this is a whole new level of disturbing—even for me."

"To be fair, though," Pylara added, "they're better at dancing now that they're ash piles."

"I think I would've preferred a dog attack to this," Brutus said, hiding behind his shield. "At least everything would've smelled better. Or maybe that's Throg."

The orc, still cowering, burped sparks.

"I can't argue with that," Pylara agreed. "Can we go now?"

"I think that's best," Liandra said. "Someone get Throg off the ground."

The piles of soot and ash continued dancing which looked like little more than bouncing mounds of dust hopping around. If the party weren't convinced before, they now knew the magnitude of the evil curse that loomed over the city and everyone in it.

Their pace quickened as they left the surreal and terrifying dancing dog ash piles behind them, none of them ever looking back at the scene. Several of them wondered if Gobthorak could possibly be any more disturbing than the horrors they just witnessed.

When they reached the front door of Surok's house, they all breathed a deep sigh of relief. With the horrors of the city behind them, they could finally get the help they required to continue their quest.

If you want the party to knock on the door, turn to page 150.

If you want the party to kick in the door, turn to page 200.

Just kidding. This isn't that kind of book. Just read the next chapter. Or not. I'm not the boss of you.

14

So, as I was saying before the chapter break so rudely interrupted me, the group of adventurers stood outside Surok's front door, still reeling from ... well, pretty much everything that happened to them up to this point.

This might have included that one time Devinon picked someone's pocket only to discover the pocket had a huge hole in it and the person wasn't wearing undergarments.

But that was years ago, and we try not to mention that.

They knocked on the door and when I say, "they knocked on the door," I mean all of them knocked on the door. All at once. They were desperate to get inside somewhere safe lest another sickening song start up somewhere.

"Let us in!" Brutus shrieked.

"Please open the door!" Pylara screamed. She looked as if she might bust it down at any time. Doors weren't worth any experience points, but she didn't know that.

The door opened. On the other side stood a relatively plain, unassuming portly man in a sleeping gown and slippers. He yawned and scratched his balding head while he stared at the strange, terrified people who had just appeared outside his house.

"They sang," he said, "didn't they?"

"Holy crap, yes," Brutus replied. "Everything and everyone sang. They danced. There was music everywhere."

"It was horrible," Devinon added.

The man sighed and motioned for them to enter. "You may as well come in," he said. "You know, before the trees burst into song."

Brutus laughed, but the man didn't. At that point, everyone thought it best to get inside and they quickly and quietly slipped through the door.

"Well, I'm Surok. So, what in the fifteen-or-so Hells do you want?" He shut the door and bolted it, then peeked out the window. "You're obviously not from Littleton or you'd be crooning up a storm and knocking stuff over with your dance number and I would probably have to kick you out of my home. This is a no-singing zone. I crafted the spell myself."

"Believe me," Liandra said, "we have no desire to stay in Littleton, but we do need your help. We've been tasked with a quest of the utmost of importance."

"You're here to lift this terrible curse?" Surok looked excited.

"What? No. Definitely not."

"Oh. It's just as well. It's a powerful enchantment. I also crafted it."

"Wait a minute." Devinon stepped forward with a puzzled look upon his face. "*You* unleashed this musical horror on Littleton?"

"Well, no."

"Okay good. For a minute there—"

"Wait, actually, yes. Yes, I did."

"What were you thinking?" Pylara growled.

Surok sighed and bowed his head in shame. "Can you keep a secret?" he asked.

"Yes," everyone responded.

"No," Devinon said to no one's surprise. "I mean, unless it's *my* secret. Otherwise, definitely not."

Surok pulled up a chair and sat, staring out at the party. Nobody moved, unsure of what was going to happen, but they were all ready to strike should trouble, or song, arise.

Except Throg. He was scrutinizing the décor choices, debating whether the wall color clashed with the floor. He would address the drapes later.

The man before them remained still. He appeared frozen in place. Just when everybody thought Surok might have died, they saw something emerge from the back of his neck and scurry up to the top of balding his head.

"Is everyone seeing this?" Brutus whispered, keeping his eyes affixed to the creature that now perched atop the man's noggin. "It's not just me, right?"

"What is that?" Devinon asked.

"I can hear you perfectly well," the creature said, licking its eyeball.

It was a blue lizard—possibly about a foot long—with six legs, tiny wings, and a thin tail.

"Your next question is going to be what am I," the lizard continued.

"You can read minds?" Brutus gasped.

"No, you're just predictable. Besides, it's the first question I would ask. Also, the thief already asked it. The answer is unimportant. You said you weren't here to lift the curse so why exactly *are* you here?"

"I'm not a thief," Devinon mumbled. "I just like stuff."

"Just wait a minute," Liandra said, holding her palms out in front of her. "You cursed Littleton and now you need help lifting your own evil curse? Why would you do such a thing?"

"I had to do it to survive. You see, my kind live off music. Whereas your kind eats things like meat and vegetables—you do eat your vegetables, right?"

"Meh," Devinon responded. "They're overrated."

"Anyway, whereas you consume food, my kind live off the power of music. Without it, we wither and go into a forced hibernation. Eventually, we will die."

"This unacceptable," Throg said.

"Correct. I had to boost the town's musical output in order to survive."

"Color of puny lizard not match décor. It clash with everything."

"Let me make sure I understand," Liandra said, ignoring the orc completely. "You were starving so you forced everyone to sing and dance for you?"

"Aye, that's the sad truth of it."

"That's ... diabolical and genius." Liandra looked eerily happy. Even Devinon found himself a little taken aback by the sheer devious nature. "But you look well-fed to me."

"I'm usually much larger."

"That makes sense I suppose. So why, if you consume song and dance as your sustenance, would you plead with us to help you lift your own curse?"

"Ah, yes. It's tricky. You see ... well, there's just no other way to put it, this town is absolutely terrible. They can't sing at all. They're awful. Their singing sounds like a herd of dying squaremahn."

"What's a squaremahn?" Pylara asked.

"It's like a circle, but with four sides, mahn" Surok laughed. "That joke never gets old."

Nobody made a sound.

"Really? Nothing?" Surok continued. "That joke kills at open mic nights."

Everyone remained silent, unsure of what had just happened.

"Fine. Just know the people of Littleton might be the worst singers in existence."

"So, wait," Devinon interrupted, "I mean, don't get me wrong, yeah, they suck. I mean, they *really* suck, but their singing isn't good enough for you? Are their songs somehow not nourishing enough? I can't believe I just asked such a question. What even is going on?"

"Their songs sustain me just fine, but they taste abysmal. It's like eating ... have you ever eaten a garbage and dirt sandwich?"

"Can't say that I have," Pylara chuckled.

"Well, I can't say that I have either, but I assume they taste like the inside of someone's butt."

Devinon raised a finger and was about to speak.

"Which I *also* have never tasted," Surok responded quickly, "but I would guess it's not pleasant. Hopefully you get the idea. Trash. Their horrible songs taste like hot garbage, okay?"

"It's better than cold garbage," Brutus muttered quietly.

"I can't handle it anymore. If you're not here to help lift the curse, then I need to find better accommodations. I've heard excellent things about Yellowbridge. It's a much smaller town but they have a choir there! Less music is certainly better than eating sweaty feet dipped in garbage juice."

"Why do you need us?" Brutus asked. "You've got this ... uh ... meat body ... thing. You can certainly travel on your own."

"He's not exactly a marathon runner, is he? I imagine his body would collapse after a mile or two of just brisk walking. Plus, I'm the mayor. I doubt I can just flit off in the middle of the night and get away with it. The lousy townsfolk will probably sing about my journey and follow me there. That's unacceptable."

"So, what, you want us to take you with us?"

"Yes. Given my distinct lack of options, I believe you can help me. In return, I will help you. You said you had a quest of the utmost importance, yes?"

"Indeed," Liandra replied, perking up a bit. "Gobthorak has awoken. We're going to kill him."

"Oh, are you now?" Surok laughed. "That's an easy job, no problem."

"Why does everyone laugh when we tell them?" Brutus asked.

"Really? It's easy?" Liandra added.

"Absolutely not! What fool gave such a monumental task to ... well, you guys?"

"It doesn't matter who gave us the mission. What matters is stopping Gobthorak before he consumes our world."

"So that's it, then? Just find Gobthorak, march in, and kill him?"

"Pretty much," Pylara said "I mean, we've got a map."

"Oh, well then you should be set! You don't even need my help!"

The party was silent, with nobody sure what to say next. Was Surok joking?

Yes, Surok was joking.

"Okay, listen," he finally said, "you get me out of this fifteen-or-so Hellshole and I'll tell you what I know about defeating Gobthorak."

"How do we know we can trust you?" Devinon eyed the lizard suspiciously. "What makes you such an expert on Gobthorak?"

"Because ... you see, he's my brother."

The party gasped in unison—even Throg, but that might have been because he'd just noticed the antique coffee table.

"Really?" Devinon was nearly speechless.

"Of course not!" Surok laughed. "But you totally should've seen the looks on all your faces," he stammered through tears streaming down his little lizard face. "Priceless." He took a few moments to regain his composure. "But seriously it's because I'm super smart and really old and I'm a mystical lizard and just go with it okay? I don't really have the time or energy to go into my entire backstory. Maybe someday, in a short story or micro fiction. Ooh, a feature-length movie would be great! Anyway, not today."

"Okay, fine," Devinon scoffed. "Whatever. You're super cool, we get it. So, what's the best way to get out of here without an entire three-act musical between us and the edge of the city?"

"We could escape during intermission!" Brutus suggested.

"We'd probably best wait until after nightfall. There will still be people about, however, so the musical risk is still great."

"Too dangerous," Pylara argued. "I don't think we can handle that. What other options do we have?"

Surok scratched his chin with one of his legs, obviously weighing their options.

"Well," he finally said, "there are the catacombs that run under the city that spill out near the river east of here."

"That sounds perfect!"

"But they're crawling with dangerous monsters and unstable ground."

"Still better than singing," Devinon added.

"No," Surok replied, "it's not. These are the foulest creatures you will ever meet. They're deadly, bored, hungry, and bloodthirsty."

"Yep, better than singing."

"They will descend upon us, tear us to ribbons, and eat us. We won't last more than a few minutes, I assure you."

"Look," Devinon argued "I don't relish the thought of

wading through monsters just to get out of the city. But there are two things you must know. First, I don't think I can handle any more of what's out there. I swear a group was *this* close to bursting out into a full-blown opera." Devinon presented his thumb and index finger barely spaced apart. "Second," he continued, "I've leveled up several times and I have some really cool shit I can do, and I'm really itching to try it all out."

"There's one other thing," Surok said.

"Fine, what?"

"Everything down there ... in the catacombs ... is probably also going to sing."

"Son of a bitch!" Devinon yelled, kicking a desk. "You really are the worst! And now my foot hurts!" He kicked the desk again. "And now it hurts worse!"

"Well," Liandra sighed, "The choice is clear. We leave town in the dead of night and try to avoid detection."

"What if we're seen?" Brutus asked. "What if they ... sing?"

"We'll do what we must to survive."

15

veryone waited anxiously for darkness to befall them.

They desperately tried to keep themselves occupied, attempting to shake off the dread of having to go back outside and face the possible disaster of the Littleton amateur musical troupe.

Throg slept.

Brutus shined his shield. Also, that's not a euphemism, so don't start.

Pylara stared out the window, expecting danger.

Liandra buried her nose in a musty book.

Devinon stole anything that wasn't nailed down. Anything that *was* nailed down, he still stole, but he stole the nails first, covertly cramming various items into his backpack.

Liam remained dead.

"Oh, which reminds me!" Liandra perked up and looked around the room. "Surok, you command great magic, right?"

"You could say that." The lizard was trying to snooze atop the desk. His previous body still lay slumped in the chair. "Not great enough to get the townsfolk to sing in tune, apparently, but sure."

"Can you help us with a friend of ours?"

"What kind of help?"

"The kind dead people need."

"That's a tall order."

"Yeah, well, remember who's sneaking you out of the mess you created." Pylara gave Surok a stern look.

"That's fair—a little harsh, but fair. And I suppose I should repay your kindness once we're out of the city."

Pylara pulled Liam out of her backpack and plopped his body on a table. Even though everyone knew the bard's corpse had resided in there this whole time, there was still no lack of amazement and wonder that Pylara managed to stuff the man into a tiny backpack.

And why wasn't he a bubbling pool of rotting goo by now?

"A bard, huh? Surok hopped onto the table and scrutinized the body, sniffing the air and poking different spots. "Are you really sure you want to bring him back to life? They sing, you know."

"This one didn't actually do *anything*," Brutus chuckled.

"That's a good point," Devinon noted, "he *was* pretty annoying. And what was with that flute of his?"

"How could you say that?" Liandra gasped. She looked truly shocked which, in turn, surprised Devinon who'd always assumed nobody liked the man.

"Liandra's right," Brutus agreed. "How could you say that? He was never alive long enough for anyone to get annoyed with him!"

Both Brutus and Devinon erupted in raucous laughter while Liandra and Pylara scowled, though Devinon was quite sure they wanted to laugh. Even Surok appeared to chuckle ... or maybe it was gas. Nobody really knew what humor looked like on a lizard—this was new territory for everyone.

"Very well," Surok said, once he was done scrutinizing

Liam's body, "when we're safe, I'll see what I can do. You'd best tuck him away until then."

Pylara effortlessly returned Liam to her backpack which, just as miraculous as before, remained the same size either way.

"It'll be getting dark soon. We must be ready to move quickly and quietly. Littleton is a vast city crowded with people who can't sing worth a damn, and a good number of them are night owls."

And so it was that everyone valiantly awaited the darkness, bravely cowering inside Surok's house, preparing for their opportunity to courageously flee the city.

"Wait," Liandra said, turning from the window as the sun sunk below the horizon. "What would it take to lift Littleton's curse? I mean, you cast the spell, Surok, can't you undo it?"

"Not this curse, unfortunately." Surok walked across the table and hopped to the window to look out over the darkening city. "There is only one way I know of to lift this curse, and it's a terrible, frightening prospect."

"I'm almost afraid to ask."

"The only way to lift a curse this sinister is ... a dance off."

Throg immediately jumped to his feet, quite eager to participate in such a competition. He began to limber up by stretching.

"What?" Devinon shrieked. "No way! I say we take our chances escaping the city."

"I'm with Devinon," Pylara agreed.

Throg appeared disappointed, but he continued stretching just in case.

"There's not a chance we'd win any kind of a dance off," she continued. "We're adventurers, not entertainers!"

"Unless ..." Liandra interrupted.

"Unless what?" Brutus asked, seemingly intrigued, and hoping her suggestion involved fire of some sort.

"Unless Liam were here."

"Could he even dance?" Devinon asked. "Not that any new information would change my mind from disagreeing with that option, but he never really did anything except occasionally try to sing or play the flute."

"And die," Brutus added.

"And tasty," Throg also added.

"Listen," Devinon said, holding his hand up to silence everyone. "We're sticking with the original plan."

"Running away, then?" Brutus laughed.

"Yes, running away. We're getting the fifteen-or-so Hells out of here. This city sucks."

"Besides," Surok interrupted, "if we lift the curse, they're bound to discover who cast it in the first place and I'd prefer not to be around for that. Have you any idea how difficult it would be to explain who I really am? No, it's better I start fresh somewhere else ... somewhere with people who can sing much better than anyone here. I don't think I'll ever get the taste out of my mouth."

"Right," Devinon confirmed. "So, we're running away."

Throg looked disappointed but continued stretching. He wanted to be prepared ... and flexible.

"So," Devinon continued, "is it dark enough out? Can we finally escape this city where happiness goes to die?"

Surok peered out the window with a pensive look on his face ... probably. "There's no better time like the present. Hopefully most of the citizens are in their homes and we'll encounter no problems." He hopped onto Liandra's shoulder and motioned to the front door.

"Aren't you going to ..." Devinon began.

"Do what?" Surok asked.

"You know," he continued, nodding toward the inert body slumped in a nearby chair. "Get back in your, uh, body or something?"

"Most certainly not. He was going to die of heart

problems pretty soon anyway. Besides ... it smells like old cheese in there." Surok turned his nose up and made gagging motions. "Nobody will recognize me in my true body."

Throg sniffed the motionless meat sack.

"That's fair," Liandra agreed. "I'm not sure he could keep up with us if we needed to run."

"Oh, heck no," Surok laughed. "He was definitely not an athlete but, oh man, could he put away a plate of chicken wings."

Surok licked his lips.

"So, what are we supposed to do with the body?" Liandra continued. "I mean, it's not alive right?"

"With me outside the body, it will eventually expire."

"I ..." Brutus stammered, pointing to the body. "I think we've found our answer."

Throg had already eaten the man's arm.

"Why am I not even surprised?" Liandra sighed. "You know what? I don't even care. Let's just leave. I hate it here."

Pylara carefully pushed open the front door and peeked out, inspecting the sprawling city beyond. From the hill atop which Surok's house was situated, she had a great view, and it was easily apparent the city was largely empty except for small pockets of movement. In the dim light of the city's lamps and at this distance it was impossible to make out just how many people there actually were, but she felt any encounters should be easily avoidable.

The city at night was a stark contrast from earlier. Instead of a bustling, active organism, it was serene and picturesque. As much as she hated it during the day, she found it almost charming as she gazed out at it now. It might almost be a good place to live if it weren't for Surok's curse.

"All clear," she whispered and stepped out onto the patio.

The rest of the party filed in behind her with Devinon

bringing up the rear. He pulled the door behind him, and it shut with a click.

It was a click that echoed across the city. As if it were somehow amplified, it rang in their ears for several seconds until it finally dissipated, leaving the group once again in serene silence where they stood, motionless, afraid to move and looking around in fear.

"That," Liandra whispered, "was a really loud door." The irritation in her voice was unmistakable and the choking black smoke wafted from her hair.

"Sorry," Devinon replied sarcastically. "I wasn't aware doors in this city were so rambunctious!"

"You're a thief, you fool! If anyone should be able to close a door quietly, it should be *you*!"

"I'm not a thief! I'm just unemployed and super good at taking things! Besides, *opening* a door quietly is always far more important than closing it. If you're going to break into a place, you need to—"

"Uh, I don't mean to be rude," Surok interrupted, "but now would be a good time to shut the fifteen-or-so Hells up and run!"

Moving up the hill, in full song and dance, was a crowd of people clad in colorful costumes with a full contingent of minstrels in tow.

"Well, crap," Pylara growled. "I wonder what they want."

"Who cares?" Brutus looked ready to fight them all. "Let's just get out of here."

"♪ We're going to kill the mayor because he cursed the town. We'll find him, we'll stew him, and then we'll drink him down!"

"Oh," Pylara said, "so *that's* what they want. I wonder how they found out."

"Who cares," Surok hissed, "let's just get out of here now

before we find out the answer in a performance piece! Also, I'm not a fan of being killed, so if we could hurry up ..."

"Nor am I," Liandra agreed. "Let's move."

"What shocks me the most," Devinon added, "is that they want to eat you. That's rude."

Throg licked his lips.

"That is a rather unexpected development," Surok agreed. "Apparently you can learn a lot about someone through the miracle of music."

They hurried off the patio and down a sidewalk that led to a side street that led to another side street that led to ... well, you get the idea. They stayed off the main streets and kept to the shadows, avoiding any people and dogs they spotted. The squirrels were unavoidable, but everyone knows they hold a healthy disdain for the musical arts and therefore would be unaffected by the curse. They were not, however, happy at all about the state of things and they threw nuts at the party to express their disapproval.

"♫ We'll string him up and set him ablaze for what he's done, he'll burn for days!"

It appeared the song was the same throughout the city as if the townsfolk were all connected somehow. The tune was catchy, though, and if it hadn't been for the frightening lyrics, the song would have been quite appealing.

"♫ When we find him, we'll give him a smack and sacrifice him to Gobthorak!"

"Okay, now, that's just uncalled for," Surok said.

"I'm not sure I really feel sorry for these townsfolk anymore," Devinon added.

"Did you ever?" Liandra asked.

"Not really. But now I definitely don't. I also don't feel bad about all the stuff I stole from them along the way and, because they're jerks, I'm keeping it all!"

Liandra rolled her eyes. "Whatever helps you sleep at night, I guess."

"So, what's the easiest way out of the city?" Pylara asked. "Surely we don't have to go through the front gates."

"Absolutely not!" Surok replied. "There are the back gates, the side gates, the under gates, over gates, the *other* front gates, and even the forgotten gates!"

"Good." Pylara motioned for everyone to move as they skittered across an empty street and into an alley. "So where are the forgotten gates?"

"Uh," Surok stammered, "I forgot."

"Lovely."

"Let's just keep going this way and we're bound to run into some gates at some point."

"You're not filling me with confidence, lizard dude."

And so it was that the party, with lizard dude in tow, escaped into the night, fleeing the city through a set of nondescript gates that hadn't existed before just now. And, by that, I mean Liandra blew a damned hole in the city walls with fire and they passed through, disappearing into the darkness beyond Littleton and leaving the musical mess behind them.

"I hope," Liandra said, "that you're not going to treat the next town the same way. I don't want to have to save them from another one of your curses."

"Technically," Surok retorted, "you didn't actually save the last town, now did you?"

"He's right," Devinon laughed.

"I hate you all."

16

ll I'm saying is, as far as accommodations go, this isn't so bad."

"Shut it, Devinon." Liandra was, as always seemed to be the case, disgruntled, and she probably had every right to be.

She liked to think of herself as intense but everyone else saw her as cranky and mean. It wouldn't have been out of the question to say that both were accurate descriptions. In this particular case, however, she was absolutely justified.

Well, as far as she was concerned, anyway.

"Hey," Devinon continued, "at least we dumped that Surok guy off and no longer have to deal with the song and dance numbers."

"We need to find a way out of this dungeon," Pylara growled from the cell next door. "Though I do tend to agree with Devinon. As far as dungeons go, I'd rate this one pretty highly."

"Right?"

"What did I just say, Devinon?" Liandra growled, glaring

at him. Though she *did* agree the dungeons were tidy and clean, she would much rather have been stuck in a cell with anyone but him.

"Why are you mad at me? It's not like this was my fault!"

"It's *exactly* like it was your fault!"

"How so?"

"You killed that merchant!"

"Okay, that's a fair point, but *aside* from that."

"There is no aside from that. You killed the man in plain sight!"

"Okay, first of all, my knife killed him, not me. That's two totally different things. Second of all, he wasn't a merchant. He stole my stuff!"

"He stole *his* stuff that you took from him in the first place!" Liandra fumed.

"We can argue over who stole whose stuff—"

"No, we can't, because I'm through arguing about it. Let's just find a way out of here."

"I agree with Liandra," Pylara said. "While these are truly immaculate dungeon cells, I feel this would all be more pleasant if my cellmate wasn't trying to eat me."

"Oh man," Brutus laughed. "You got stuck with Liam?"

"Yes, I got stuck with the minstrel, and apparently, he's got an appetite for ... flesh now. It's not only most inconvenient but also really disturbing, and kind of stinky."

"You know," Liandra said, "I really wish we would've known Surok was a necromancer lizard before we asked him to help with the bard.'

"This definitely could've turned out better," Pylara growled, pushing Liam away. "I'm used to men coming on strong but not like *this*."

"I bet still tasty," Throg added, at which point the party collectively grimaced and made disapproving noises.

Liam drooled and groped for Pylara. Fortunately, thanks

to her ridiculously highly rated, skimpy armor, she was literally untouchable. She still kept him at bay with her tree branch, though, pinning him against the wall as he struggled to reach her. The guards allowed her to keep her weapon because she convinced them it was a mere walking stick. Also, they were captivated by her dress code.

Also, Liam only had one arm because Throg reluctantly admitted to eating the other one at some point. In any case, the minstrel had certainly looked better.

The problem was, yes, he was trying to eat Pylara. Of course, it was a problem! Nobody wanted to be eaten. To make matters worse, he kept singing and trying to tell jokes and everyone knows zombies don't sing well to begin with. And almost nobody thinks their jokes are funny because their vocabulary is limited to mostly grunts and groans and sometimes fart noises which, if we're all being honest *are* actually funny.

At least Devinon got a chuckle out of them, which was no surprise to anyone.

"The zombard notwithstanding," Brutus began, "what is our plan to get out of here anyway? I should like to be away from here as quickly as possible. Though Lenfilia would be suitably impressed with our accommodations."

"Lenfilia?" Liandra inquired, suddenly wishing she hadn't.

"The goddess of dungeons, of course. She'd probably give this a four-star review."

"That's really great to know," Devinon replied, "if I cared."

"The kid's cranky today," Pylara laughed.

"I'm not—you know what? Never mind. Pylara, do you see anyone coming?"

Pylara struggled to both keep the zombard away from her while also peering down the dungeon's hallway. "Nobody. There's nobody down here except us, apparently."

"Hey!" a gravelly voice shouted, "I'm down here too!"

"Who are you?"

"Name's Don. Don Gen."

"Who cares?" Devinon snorted.

"Well, you asked. One of you asked, anyway. So, I told you. It's only polite to respond to questions when asked, you know."

"Okay, okay, just shut up already. We weren't specifically looking for some old dude when I said nobody was around."

"How do you know I'm old?"

"You sound old." Devinon was trying to ignore this annoyance, but the man wouldn't stop talking.

"So just because I *sound* old, you assume I'm old? I could be a spry man of twenty-five, but you judge me based on my voice?"

"We're sorry, sir!" Liandra shouted. She was trying to be diplomatic but had to admit this man was particularly annoying. "It's just, we're stuck in a dungeon and would like to get out of here and we're all a little on edge."

"Oh, well, that's understandable. I've been in this dungeon cell for thirty-five years."

"Holy crap!" Devinon exclaimed. "You *are* old!"

"I'm thirty-seven!"

"Wait a minute." Liandra waved her hand in the air as if anyone could actually see the gesture. "Hold on. How have you been in your cell for thirty-five years but you're only thirty-seven years old? How is that possible?"

"Well, I haven't been in this cell for thirty-five years."

"Oh, well, I thought—"

"I was two cells down for most of the time. I only moved to this cell a few years ago. Well, I think. I don't even know what day it is anymore."

"How could you have been in a dungeon cell since you

were two years old?" Brutus asked. "What did you do at two years of age that was so terrible?"

Liam grunted. Throg grunted back.

"I've made some terrible life choices. But there's no rent and the food's delivered. Still, I think I would like to see the world."

"Meh," Devinon shrugged, "the world's overrated. It's like everything wants to kill me."

"That's because you steal everything," Liandra replied.

"Anyhoo. Hey Pylara, can you snag me one of Liam-zombie's fingers, please?"

"Devinon!" Liandra shrieked.

"What's the problem? I said please, didn't I?"

"That's disgusting! Not to mention insensitive. Liam's already got significant problems without you taking his body parts for fun. And that's a sentence I never thought I'd say." Liandra leaned against the wall and rolled her eyes at Devinon, trying not to acknowledge what was about to happen.

"Did I hear you right, kid?" Pylara asked. "You want one of his ... fingers?"

"You heard me right. If you could get his pinky finger, that'd be the best option."

"Dare I ask why the pinky finger?"

"Because," Devinon sighed, "he rarely ever uses it while playing an instrument. Duh."

"You're such an altruist."

"I have the utmost of altruisticism."

"That's ... not a word," Brutus stated.

"You're not a word."

"You don't actually know what an altruist is, do you?" Pylara asked.

"Whatever. It sounds lame. Now, can I get the finger or not?"

Devinon waited patiently along with everyone else as they listened to the sounds coming from Pylara's cell—zombie sounds mixed with her trying to remove a zombie finger. The expression on Liandra's face was one of disapproval, frustration, and disgust.

Eventually, the sounds of probably the most awkward fight scene known to anyone subsided and a finger bounced and rolled in front of Devinon's cell. He promptly scooped it up, grinning, and inspected the digit.

The bard had long, slender fingers—even more so now that they were decaying and falling apart.

"This'll do just fine," he mumbled, ignoring Liandra's scolding gaze. It took some work and finesse to get the finger to fit properly in the cell's lock but, eventually, it slid in. It was then that the *real* work began.

Liandra's expression went from disapproval to surprise when she finally understood Devinon's intent. The disgust remained, however.

"Finally," he muttered, "the minstrel will serve a useful purpose." Squinting, he scrutinized the lock and his makeshift lockpick. Then he pressed his ear against the mechanism and moved the finger around slowly, diligently paying attention to each motion.

"I hope that was worth it," Pylara yelled. "He smells even worse now. It's really quite disgusting."

"What in Lenfilia's name is going on?" Brutus asked.

"Oh, nothing," Devinon replied. "Just picking my nose with Liam's finger because I can.

"Throg want extra finger!"

"If you're quiet and you behave," Brutus continued, "You can eat the old dude in the cell down the way."

"I heard that!" Don yelled. "And I'm not old, damn it!"

Throg drooled.

After several minutes of maneuvering, the locking mechanism popped, and the squeaky cell door swung open.

"That is both the coolest and the grossest thing I think I've ever seen," Liandra said, exiting the dungeon cell. "Get to work on Pylara's and Brutus's doors and I'll go fetch our equipment."

"Good work, Devinon," he mumbled to himself. "What would we do without you, Devinon? Oh, I know, we'd probably be dead without you, Devinon."

He got to work on Brutus's cell next. The finger was shedding flesh quickly which, thankfully, made it easier to pick the lock.

Liandra scoured the dungeon and finally found their belongings locked up in the cell across from Don's. She peered into his prison and saw a gaunt man dressed in rags. His facial hair had overtaken his head and somehow melded with wispy hair on top.

"Ah," he wheezed, "there you are. I see you're escaping, which is quite excellent for you. I'm proud!"

"Uh, thanks," Liandra muttered, inspecting the cell containing their equipment.

"I think one of the jailors keeps the keys to the cells," the man continued. "But since you found your way out, you should have no problem getting your stuff back, I suppose."

Liandra wasn't paying much attention to the rambling man in the cell. Instead, she focused on channeling magical energy into her hands as she gripped the bars.

"Which, of course, means you can open *any* cell you want, I suspect. Yep ... you should have no problems whatsoever."

Liandra felt what began as a pleasant warmth flow into her hands, but it quickly intensified into a deep, burning sensation that spread to the bars she gripped in her palms. It wasn't long before they themselves radiated heat and glowed—first red, then white.

"Ah, you're obviously a powerful sorceress I see. I bet you

could melt the bars of, say, my own cell with ease, couldn't you?"

The bars soon melted completely, puddling on the ground and immediately cooling as steam wafted off the floor.

"Oh good!" Pylara exclaimed. "You found our stuff!"

The rest of the party filed in behind her, taking turns entering the cell and reclaiming their belongings. Except Liam, who was now a motionless heap in Pylara's arms.

"A pet zombie," Don muttered from behind them. "You guys are full of surprises. You seem quite powerful."

"The bard's dead again," she muttered. "I accidentally caused his current condition while prying off his finger." She shoved the bard's corpse into her backpack once again and sighed.

"Oh," answered Devinon, "we are absolutely powerful. We're on our way to defeat Gobthorak and save the world."

"It sounds like a truly noble quest. I could maybe help—"

"So," Brutus interrupted, "where are we off to now?"

Liandra pulled out the map and stared at it for a moment. "Well," she said, "we have two options. We can either go through the Sandwich Mountains or around them, which takes us through Murderville. The journey around them is longer by several days if I'm reading it right."

"Sandwich Mountains?" Devinon shouted? "That sounds delicious!"

"While I share some of Devinon's enthusiasm," Brutus agreed, "I'm sure the mountains aren't made of sandwiches."

Devinon immediately looked disappointed.

"However," he continued, "Sandwiches of any sort sound far more benign than ... what, a town full of murder?"

"I don't even understand what kind of a thing that is." Pylara scratched her head, appearing quite confused. "Is there ... is there just murder lying around on the streets?"

"I'll admit," Liandra added, "I'm a bit curious myself."

"Are you joking?" Devinon shrieked. "Why would we intentionally go to some place called Murderville? That's just asking for trouble ... and murder, obviously. Though, I guess if we were doing the murdering, that wouldn't be so bad, would it? Hey, Liandra, does the map say anything else? Like, can we be doing all the murder?"

The party got quiet for a moment.

"You really worry me sometimes, kid." Pylara said, shaking her head.

Devinon resisted the urge to, once again, argue against his stature as a child but thought better of it. Better to be thought of as a child than a filthy halfling.

"I commend your choice," Don said. He was now pressed against the bars, gripping one in each hand. "So now that you have a plan, I was wondering if you could ... you know, get me the fifteen-or-so Hells out of here?"

The party all looked him over, exchanging glances with one another in the process. They shifted uneasily and fidgeted, coming to the same conclusion.

"So that's a hard 'no' there, Don," Devinon replied.

"Seriously?" the man shouted.

"Yeah, no. I mean, unless you can fight or kill or steal or destroy stuff with magic."

"I'm a baker! Of course I don't do any of those things!"

"Wait," Liandra interrupted. "How can you be a baker if you've been imprisoned since you were two years old?"

"I've led a full life."

"I'm willing to leave you in your cell simply to avoid the confusion."

"Plus," Devinon added, "we'll get, like, only five XP a piece if we let you out."

With that, the party turned and exited the dungeon, leaving Don in his cell cursing their names and shouting obscenities, some of which Devinon enjoyed and filed away for later use.

They had once again heroically overcome adversity and defeated a dungeon that ... you know what? They did some stuff. I can't really pretend this was a heroic endeavor. Don certainly wouldn't, and he was usually slow to anger.

Of course, he was now super pissed, but what can you do?

17

hunder boomed overhead as lightning rippled down through the sky and impacted on the ground in front of Devinon, sending grass, dirt, and stone high into the air.

"Dandy!" Devinon shouted. "This is just dandy!" He dodged some incoming debris and hunched down behind a tree. The rest of the party was doing much the same, trying to figure out their next move. "Whose idea was this again?"

Nobody answered.

"And who was the person who would've rather gone to Murderville?" he shouted. "We could've been causing corruption and mayhem but noooo. Instead, we're stuck here getting blasted. Oh, this is certainly *much* better."

"Are you finished?" Liandra shouted.

"Am I ever finished?"

"I'm going with no!" Brutus shouted, cowering behind his shield behind a tree that was behind a boulder that was behind another, larger boulder.

Liam was still dead.

Throg cowered behind cover, unsure of what to do.

Several chunks of rock sailed over their heads, impacting mere feet behind them.

"How was I supposed to know the mountains were this dangerous?" Liandra shouted.

"You were reading the map!" Devinon countered. "This isn't what I signed up for! You said sandwich mountains and I expected sandwiches! At the very least, I didn't expect *this*! And now I'm hungry! AND WHERE ARE THE DAMNED SANDWICHES?"

"It really hurts me to say this," Pylara replied, "but I agree with Devinon for once."

"It's not my fault it was misspelled!"

"So, yay!" Devinon cheered, the mocking tone in his voice quite apparent. "We get to fight these ... are they really made of sand? Is this actually happening? Witches made of sand?"

"Looks that way."

A herd of strange animals trampled the area, trying to maul the party who remained behind what little cover they could find.

"And they're throwing ... what are these things?" Devinon peeked out from behind the tree, then pulled himself back to avoid the herd.

"They're just energy in the shape of animals!" Liandra yelled. She had to admire the witches' skills but decided fire animals would have been far more effective.

"I really hate that map! And I hate these sand bitches—"

"Witches!" Pylara shouted, correcting Devinon.

"I said what I said!"

"So, what's our plan?" Brutus shouted, blocking several energy projectiles with his shield. "They seem really pissed off!"

"You think?" Liandra asked, sarcastically.

"And this time," Devinon added, "I'd like to point out I didn't do anything to them!"

"I'm sure you did *something* to piss them off," Liandra replied.

"Does anyone have a sandcastle mold?" Pylara asked, squeezing out a small bit of laughter as an explosive magic effect shredded the grass next to her.

The three witches laughed and cackled, hovering in the air and lobbing whatever spells they felt like. Though nobody was sure how sand could do any of the things these three creatures were doing, their awe was suppressed by their survival instinct.

"How in the fifteen-or-so Hells are we supposed to fight ... what, sentient sand?" Brutus asked. "How do you defeat sentient sand?"

"How about with a sentient ocean?" Devinon suggested. He wasn't sure if he was joking or not, but he knew it had to be said.

"Your mom ocean," Throg said through raucous laughter. Nobody else seemed to appreciate his orcish attempt at humor but Devinon at least had to give him credit for the valiant attempt.

"Throg's attempt at humor may have failed," Brutus shouted, "but Devinon did have a decent idea."

"Which one?" Devinon replied. "I have lots of decent ideas!"

"Maybe water would take care of the sand witches!"

"That's a terrible idea!" Devinon shouted as thunder boomed.

"Wait, what?" Brutus was genuinely confused. "Why is that a terrible idea?" Something whizzed past his face, but he didn't get a good look at it.

"Have you ever eaten a soggy sandwich? They're disgusting!" Devinon replied.

"I ..." Pylara stammered as the ground near her erupted in flame, "I can't tell if you're being serious. I mean, you're right

—soggy sandwiches are terrible. Fresh sandwiches are fantastic, but I'm not sure that's really pertinent to—"

She was cut off abruptly as a sheep collided with the boulder she hid behind and exploded.

"They're throwing lambchops at us!" she shouted.

"Is there mint jelly, too?" Brutus joked. "That sounds delicious!"

Pylara eyed the slurry of now partially liquified sheep parts strewn about the area. "I don't know. You're welcome to come take a look!"

Brutus eyeballed the scene. "No thank you! My goddess wouldn't want me to eat it anyway!"

"Wait ... which goddess is that?"

"The goddess who also hates witches made of sand! I don't know specifics, but I'm sure there's one somewhere."

The three witches cackled some more, moving about in the air and controlling combat with relative ease. They had never given any warning when the party first stumbled upon them. They'd simply unleashed their foul magic and shrieked with glee. I mean, who does that? It's so rude.

A fresh barrage of magical effects flew from the sand witches as they drew upon their powers to cast whatever spells they desired, causing the party to continue bravely cowering behind cover.

"So, anyway," Brutus continued, "about that water idea— Why can't we just douse these witches in water? Sand hates water, right?"

"It would be a lot like rock-paper-scissors except with sand and water! It's a fine idea!" Devinon agreed.

"It can't be rock-paper-scissors," Liandra said.

"Why not?"

"I mean, sure, water beats sand but sand doesn't beat scissors, does it? And then what beats water? It's a terrible analogy."

A small sapling nearby exploded into splinters.

"Sand might actually *sharpen* scissors!" Pylara added.

"Yeah," Liandra agreed, "see? It doesn't work! Wait, this is silly. Why are we even discussing this?"

"Do you know any water spells you can hit these witches with?" Devinon asked.

"Devinon," Liandra replied, "have you ever .. EVER seen me cast anything but fire?"

"Well, no but—"

"So, there's your answer."

"Okay, fine," he pouted. "I guess I'll just have to do this myself!"

"Wait, you have a plan?" Liandra felt hope. Devinon was largely an imbecile, but he was crafty and if he had a plan, it would probably be a good one.

And deadly.

Devinon hopped up from behind his rocky cover and slung three daggers—one at each sandy witch blob thing. Each blade connected solidly and then passed through the creatures harmlessly, falling to the ground nearby. He ducked back behind his cover.

"Wait," Liandra said, "that was it? THAT was your brilliant plan?"

"Well, yeah. I mean, it seemed like it would work. To be honest, I'm pretty surprised it didn't."

"Well, it didn't work, and I'm not surprised at all. It was a terrible plan!"

"Leave me alone! At least I tried something, and now I'm out three daggers!"

"Oh no!" Pylara said, the mockery in her voice quite evident, "now you'll only have, like, ten or so!"

"Twenty-one, actually! I'm always prepared for anything! But I'd much rather have twenty-four."

"Wait," Brutus said. It was obvious he was doing some

kind of mental math work. "How does having an excessive number of daggers help you remain prepared for everything?"

"Brutus is right," Liandra agreed as the ground nearby exploded. "I mean, you can't *eat* daggers."

"Of course you can't eat daggers, genius. If I get hungry and I have no food, I can stab someone and take their food. Problem solved."

"Or eat them," Throg added.

Liandra wondered if Devinon had possibly tried to eat a dagger in the past. He sounded very sure of himself. "I don't even know how to respond to that."

"Probably with fire," Brutus added.

Everyone laughed except Liandra. Also, Liam didn't laugh, but that's no surprise.

"Well *now* what do we do?" Pylara asked as fire erupted all around them, setting their surroundings ablaze. "They appear to be stepping up their attacks."

"I think," Liandra said, "it's time to fight fire with fire."

"Wait, what?" Brutus asked, seemingly worried.

Liandra calmly stepped out from behind her tree almost in slow motion like one of those plays you see in big cities with the cool effects and the birds taking flight. She began moving her hands in front of her and speaking sacred incantations.

"Uh, Liandra?" Brutus continued. "Fighting fire with fire is bad! It's the last thing you should do!"

The flames began at her fingertips and crawled down to her hands, then up to her elbows and further past until both arms were entirely engulfed in fire.

"Fighting fire with fire is a *terrible* idea! It just results in more fire! That particular saying shouldn't even be a saying! Whoever came up with it probably died in a fire."

"This is going to be so cool," Devinon laughed, making sure he was firmly planted behind his rocks, hoping they would protect him from whatever was about to happen.

Liandra couldn't hear them. She was too full of rage and fire. Rising slowly into the air, she completed her spell at the same moment the witches cast theirs. Fire collided with fire in mid-air, mixing and creating something so hot, everyone had to shield themselves from the blast and look away. Everyone but Liandra, of course. She cackled and grinned as her hands belched forth searing flames, casting smoke high into the air and producing a new smell Devinon would never forget.

Fire fought fire above the party as flaming bits of ... well, fire rained down upon them. No one had ever seen Liandra so happy as she covered the area in her wicked flames, cackling maniacally.

"I think the fire is on fire!" Brutus shouted. "This is *not* normal!"

"I think my spleen is on fire!" Devinon added.

"Can anyone see anything?" Pylara asked. "Is it working? There's too much fire!"

"There's *never* too much fire!" Liandra cackled, still spewing flames from her hands. Her hair had also erupted in a full blaze. She was beginning to look like the embodiment of fire itself.

"Is anyone else a little worried about Liandra?" Brutus asked, his voice shaky. "She seems a bit ... unstable."

"You're *all* unstable!" Pylara shrieked. "In fact, I'm surprised we haven't all died or killed one another by now!"

"Not for lack of trying," Devinon mumbled under his breath, grinning.

"Not helpful!" Brutus replied.

As quickly as it began, the torrent of fire ceased, and Liandra floated gently to the ground. Still laughing and apparently quite pleased with herself. The fire atop her head petered out and her hair returned to the smoldering embers it normally exhibited.

When the smoke cleared and everyone had finished

snuffing out the tiny blazes all around them, they witnessed the result.

"So," Brutus gasped, "they're no longer sand witches then?"

"I'd say not," Devinon replied. "They look like ... glass witches. I guess nobody will ever fall into *that* trap again."

Indeed, Liandra's fire had been so intense—so hot, that it had melted them and turned them to glass. It was truly a sight to behold and, if they hadn't been so ugly to begin with, the glass sculptures might have been majestic.

"Well done, Liandra," Pylara said. She nearly clapped the mage on the shoulder but thought better of it both out of fear of burning her hand.

"I guess fighting fire with fire really *does* work," Devinon chuckled.

Pylara subtly shook her head at him.

"You have defeated us!" a deep voice boomed overhead. "Congratulations! Now that you have emerged triumphant, we need your help."

The party looked around but saw nobody—no source of this mystical voice. Nevertheless, they all drew their weapons just in case.

"There is no need for weapons," the voice continued, "you may put them away. We mean you no harm."

"Well," Devinon shouted, "maybe you don't *now*, but you certainly did a few minutes ago! And now you want our help? After trying to obliterate us?"

"That takes some nerve!" Liandra shouted, the glow in her hair intensifying.

"You have defeated our champions and now we are defenseless."

"You tried to kill us!" Liandra growled.

"We must be careful when intruders wander into our hills.

Without our champions, we are vulnerable. We knew not your intentions."

"You could've just asked us."

"Are you kidding? Have you been paying attention to your actions so far? You guys are the worst sort."

The party was dumbfounded. It became obvious the source of the voice had read the book up to this point. Hopefully, when it was all over, they would leave a review— LIKE ALL RESPONSIBLE READERS! But I'm getting ahead of myself.

"We will consider helping you," Liandra said.

"But only if you have treasure!" Devinon interrupted. "After all, you attacked us first and ... uh ... you should learn your lesson from this incident."

"Okay, whatever," the voice mumbled. "Are you going to help or not?"

"Yes," Liandra replied. "We'll help you. Just tell us what you need us to do. And if you double-cross us, you'll end up like those witches." She pointed to the three glass statues, just in case the mysterious voice could see her.

"Yes, yes, bravado and all that stuff. There's a cave entrance on the other side of a hill nearby. Enter and follow the tunnel. Shortly thereafter, you should reach us. We'll discuss more then."

"This is a trap, isn't it?" Brutus whispered.

"Probably," Pylara said, clutching her tree branch tightly. "But I doubt it's a dangerous trap. We just glassed their champions. What else could they have to throw at us?"

"I hate it when people ask that," Devinon groaned. "And it's usually me asking it."

"Come on." Liandra motioned forward as she walked toward the next hill. "Let's just get this over with already."

"More walking?" Brutus whined. "Why can't they just kill

me now instead of making me walk to my doom? My feet are killing me!"

The cave wasn't far—a development for which they were all thankful if only because that was less time for Brutus to gripe about walking. They cautiously entered the cave mouth and traversed its dark depths using Liandra's smoldering scalp as a light source. Devinon wondered if he could write an entire cookbook based around dishes made on Liandra's noggin stove.

The tunnel wormed its way down and in all other directions, but it wasn't long before it opened into a room of sorts. It appeared to be a natural formation but in the center was a small pedestal upon which sat three ... sandwiches? Wait, am I seeing this right? Seriously? That's the gag?

Okay, fine, we'll go with it. Three sandwiches. In order from left to right: ham on rye, grilled cheese, and a hotdog.

"Why am I not surprised?" Liandra sneered. "So, the map *was* right! You jerks all owe me an apology."

"I don't understand," Devinon said.

"An apology. You should apologize for blaming me for the fiasco up there."

"No, I mean, I don't understand the word. What's an apology?"

"Never mind." Liandra haughtily stepped forward, annoyed and ready to burn down the whole cavern. "Well, we're here. So start talking. Or whatever sandwiches do."

"No no, wait," Devinon interrupted.

"What, Devinon?"

"Aren't we going to address the elephant in the room?"

"Throg see no elephant."

"I mean the hotdog."

"What about it?" Liandra asked.

"A hotdog is clearly not a sandwich."

"This ... this is what we're going to argue about?"

"I'm with Devinon," Pylara agreed. "Hotdogs aren't sandwiches."

"I am indeed a sandwich," the hotdog replied.

"No, you're not," Devinon argued.

"I'm an open-faced sandwich. Look it up and do your research, kid."

"You're not a sandwich and I'm not a kid." He drew a dagger in each hand. Not that there was any danger; it was simply a reflex. But if that hotdog made a wrong move ...

"I am too a sandwich."

"Are not."

"Does it really matter?" Liandra finally asked. "We're wasting time bickering."

"Agreed," the grilled cheese said. "As we said, we need your help."

"With what?"

"You killed our sand witches," The ham on rye added.

"Yeah, we did. And nice pun, that."

"Thank you. Anyway, we are now in need of three new champions."

"If you're asking us to be your champions," Pylara said, pushing her way to the front of the party, "the answer is no."

The two sandwiches and the hotdog—

"Oh, now the NARRATOR'S against me too?" the hotdog asked.

Anyway, the two-and-a-half, possibly three sandwiches burst out in mocking laughter. It was oddly disturbing, being looked down upon by food items, but such things sometimes happen.

"Most certainly not!" the ham on rye continued. "You'd be the worst champions! No, we need you to gather supplies for our three new champions to defend us!"

"You defeated our previous three," the hotdog interjected, "so now you owe us."

"We will reward you with riches beyond your wildest dreams," the grilled cheese added. "We need only more sand to create three more champions. You can find bountiful dunes about twelve miles to the east of here."

"So, yeah," Devinon interrupted, "about that. I don't see any riches."

"Sand heavy," Throg added.

"And it's coarse and it gets everywhere," Pylara also added.

"That is our proposition," the ham on rye retorted. "We promise we have treasure to pay you, but we need the sand first."

"Please return promptly," the hotdog continued, "for we need time to craft the spell."

"We wish you safe travels," the grilled cheese added.

18

id we do the right thing?" Pylara asked. "I mean, they were complete jerks and they did attack us, after all. It just seems weird, after all that, them needing our help."

The party relaxed under the night sky, listening to the crickets sing their nightly songs. It had been a truly surreal day and apparently Pylara was thinking too much about it.

"Are you having second thoughts?" Liandra asked.

"I'm definitely not." Devinon replied, burping shortly thereafter. "That grilled cheese was super tasty!"

"You should've tried the ham on rye," Brutus laughed. "It really is a bit sad, though."

"What's sad? That we ate our adversaries who tried to kill us?"

"Oh, no, that's not sad at all!" Brutus flicked a piece of grass at Devinon. "It's sad the hotdog got away. It smelled delicious."

"That it did," Liandra agreed. "Still not sure it was actually a sandwich."

"It's dubious," Pylara said. "Almost like it just wanted to

be part of the 'in' crowd or something. But what's confusing is how did it get away? Not only was it possibly not a sandwich, but it had no legs!"

"That's the one thing you're confused about?" Liandra's hair sizzled for a brief moment. "Anyway, I don't condone eating our enemies, but it's been a while since we had a truly good meal."

"I guess," Devinon chuckled, "that's why they needed champions to defend them. So, what does the map say is next?"

Liandra produced the map from a pocket and unfurled it. She scrutinized it for a second with a perplexed look on her face, using her hair as a light source to read it.

"Well," she said, "we *are* getting nearer to Gobthorak's lair —albeit slowly. It looks like the next important point on the map is a city called Obvious Distraction."

Wait, crap. Ha, that's uh … that's my bad. I wrote that down a while ago and forgot to change it. Let me just scratch that out and make a correction … there, that should do it. Carry on.

"I mean, it looks like next important point on the map is a city called Candyville."

"Sweet!" Devinon exclaimed.

"That sounds pleasant," Brutus agreed.

"Yeah, it does sound pleasant," Liandra agreed, "but we all know how the sandwiches thing turned out. This map is not to be trusted."

"Liandra has a point." Pylara stretched and yawned contently. "Maybe, the better the city sounds, the worse it is? Perhaps we should just skip Candyville and see what's next."

"Hopefully it's Painful Death Town or Colonoscopyville," Devinon laughed.

"Well," Brutus added, "we *did* pass on Murderville."

"I don't think we can skip Candyville, guys." Liandra

scrutinized the map in the dim light, squinting and moving the parchment around in front of her. She even turned it upside-down, frowning.

"Sure we can," Brutus argued, leaning against a tree with his eyes closed. "We just pass it right on by and continue to the next disaster."

"No, I'm serious. I don't think we can."

"Well why not?"

"Because there *is* nothing beyond Candyville on the map."

"That sounds like lies to me," Devinon scoffed.

"You're free to take a look for yourselves but the map clearly shows Candyville as our next waypoint, and it shows nothing after."

Devinon grabbed the map and scrutinized it. "That's clearly lazy," he said, dropping it on the ground next to Liandra. "It's like the map is making everything up as we go along. It's a godsdamned pantser map."

"Well, that's just lovely," Brutus groaned, still keeping his eyes shut and looking quite comfortable. "So. we're basically *forced* to follow this map then? It's like we thought we had free will but, guess what? We don't!"

"It looks that way," Pylara replied. She was busy sharpening her tree branch. Don't ask me how one does that because I really have no idea how or why. Lots of things don't make sense. For example, why do bastard swords have no parents? Why do monsters just hang around dungeons waiting for adventurers? And cats. What's up with cats? These are all far more confusing issues than a tree branch, so get off my back, okay?

"Well, that's garbage," Devinon grunted. "No map's going to tell *me* where to go! I go where I want, when I want. If I want to go that way, I will!" Devinon pointed to the sky, which was a little confusing. "No map is my master!"

"Okay well," Liandra interrupted, "where would *you* like to go then?"

Devinon stopped his rant and appeared confused. He thought about it for a moment but had no answer.

"Fine," he finally relented, "we'll go to Candyville. Whatever."

Liandra chuckled quietly. "We went through the trouble to get a map that told us how to reach Gobthorak," she said, "and we have it. So, while it does seem odd for it to lead us along like this, we did kind of ask for it. It seems silly to not follow the map's advice."

"Okay, fine," Devinon consented, "but Candyville had damn well be a sugar-filled paradise. And if it's all that garbage peanut butter taffy stuff, I'll rage."

After a bit of traveling and a mishap with some quicksand and a donkey, the party finally laid eyes upon the city known as Candyville.

"Well, this is just fantastic," Devinon moaned as they traveled through one of the city's main streets. "What a fetid trash heap of a city."

Candyville, indeed, was not a sugar-filled paradise but, rather, it was a crumbling, dirty city where the streets were filled with garbage and some of the buildings were filled with more garbage. Some of that garbage was people. Yes, I called some of the people garbage. I said what I said.

Anyway, you get the idea—the city was dirty, falling apart, and filled with some of the sketchiest garba ... er, people, you could possibly imagine. And five of them just arrived. I say five because I'm not sure if a corpse counts. Liam, in fact, may have actually raised the prestige level just by sort of existing.

"Well," Brutus said, trying hard not to touch anything, "We've arrived. So can we now get the fifteen-or-so-Hells out of here?"

"I am an ardent proponent of Brutus's suggestion," Devinon added.

"Same," Pylara agreed.

"Throg agree."

"For once, I believe we're all in agreement," Liandra said, constantly scanning the area for any sign of danger. "I, too, would like to leave this place."

"And why Candyville?" Devinon asked. "It obviously doesn't live up to that name."

"Probably because naming it 'Festering Crapbag' would adversely affect tourism," Brutus laughed.

"You're not wrong," Devinon agreed. "I just feel we're being played or tricked here. Is it possible to be catfished by an entire town?"

"It would seem so, yes."

"Let's just pass through and get out of here as quickly as we can so we can leave." Liandra lithely glided between people, obstacles, and garbage as she avoided contact with all of it, simply looking for the shortest route out of the city.

"Leave?" a pile of garbage shouted. "You can't leave Candyville! It's too perilous! Nobody leaves Candyville and lives to tell the tale!"

"Or you mean nobody leaves Candyville and returns to tell the tale," Brutus laughed.

"Wait," Liandra said, stopping and scrutinizing the trash pile from afar. "Magical pile of garbage, what is the danger?"

"Are you daft? I'm not a pile of garbage you fools!"

The pile shifted and a man emerged, wearing the garbage as clothing.

"See? Not garbage," he continued.

"The jury's out on that one," Brutus whispered.

"Nice one," Devinon laughed, fist-bumping the priest.

"Nobody leaves because those who do are slaughtered by the wild boar that lurks just outside of town. I hear he's mean and I hear you can see his sinister green eyes from afar, but it's already too late. To see them means certain death."

"Dude," Devinon laughed, "we just vanquished three sand witches. Surely we can handle a little irate bacon."

"Sandwiches?"

"Yeah, sand witches."

"You defeated three lunches? Were there chips?" The man looked genuinely perplexed as he tried to make sense of Devinon's words. "I mean, how deadly can a couple of pieces of bread and—"

"You know what?" Liandra interjected. "It doesn't matter. We've fought deadlier enemies than pork products. We can handle this."

"Technically, we've run away from deadlier enemies," Pylara added.

Liandra held up a finger in Pylara's face. "Shut it, Pylara. Good … sir, we can handle ourselves in a fight. If an angry ham steak wishes to confront us, we shall show it swift justice."

"Excuse me."

A man approached. Clad in a full suit of immaculately shiny armor, making enough noise to alert probably the whole city to his presence, and possibly several neighboring towns.

"So sorry," he continued, "but I couldn't help but overhear your conversation."

Devinon and Brutus exchanged glances. They both knew the joke needed to be told.

"I'm surprised you could hear anything at all," they both muttered at the same time, giving each other a subtle fist bump.

"And I couldn't help but wonder if you could be of some assistance to me. You see, I have come to Candyville to rid it of the wild boar menace!" The man struck a heroic pose and almost fell over.

"You've come here," Liandra said, "clad in a full suit of armor to kill a simple animal?"

"Aye, that is correct. But it's not just any simple animal. It's a ferocious killer!"

"It's slaughtered so many of our people," the trash man added. "The moment you step foot outside the city it begins hunting you. Supposedly, some people have made it maybe a mile or two before they are finally slain. I hear it's horrible."

"Which is why I am here!" the armored man proudly exclaimed, striking another pose, and causing a cacophony. "I will free this troubled town from the shadow that lurks in the other shadows."

"Hey guys," Liandra announced, "let's huddle up for a moment."

The armored man moved to join them.

"Uh, not you ... what's your name?"

"Darwin Goodblood, good lady."

"Just give us a sec, okay?"

The group huddled up to discuss.

"So, what do you think?" she whispered.

"I think his name is atrocious," Devinon replied. "Goodblood? Who comes up with these names? What do they do, just combine two random words and slap them together? I'm surprised his name isn't Sir Reginald Beneficialriver."

"That's not what I'm talking about. Should we let him travel with us?"

"I mean, it doesn't sound like a bad idea." Fylara wasn't as sure as her words sounded. "If there *is* some evil creature lurking out there, it would be beneficial to have another sword to fight it."

"And if things don't work out," Devinon added, "at least he's monster bait. No way is a monster going to ignore the noise he makes."

"That's horrible," Liandra scolded.

"Plus, if we need to retreat," Brutus said, "We'll all be faster than him!"

Pylara nodded in agreement.

"Come on." Liandra motioned to Darwin. "We'd best be off before it gets dark. There's no need to provide any tactical advantages to this beast."

"Excellent!" Darwin exclaimed. "We shall vanquish this foe once and for all and allow Candyville to live in peace!"

And so it was that the brave party of five found a companion with whom they could travel. They ventured to the edge of the city where few people lived, so it was eerily quiet. They would've been able to hear their own breaths if it hadn't been for Darwin's armor.

"Looks like the road leads through a forest," Darwin said, pointing ahead of them. "Let us travel onward, find the beast, and vanquish it once and for all."

19

re we sure we're even going in the right direction?"
Pylara asked. "Do we even know if there *is* a right
direction?"

"I think we've been walking in circles," Liandra agreed.
"Why can't this road just go straight? It's like it wants us to see
every inch of this forest. Maybe the reason people keep dying
in here isn't because of some creature, but because they get
lost and never make it out. Or they starve to death."

"Or they never return to Candyville," Devinon added. "I
mean, who would go back there anyway? I smell lies and a
conspiracy."

"Are you saying they don't want to hurt the town's
feelings by never coming back so they spread rumors of their
demise?"

"Why not? We've certainly seen stranger things.
Remember the rock monster thing?"

"Oh, the one you pissed off?"

"It was an honest mistake! When I steal something, I don't
ask if it's their eyeball!"

"You stole someone's eyeball?" Darwin asked.

"Well, no, not technically."

"He *tried* to steal someone's eyeball," Brutus laughed.

"That sounds terrible. Why would you want someone's eye?"

"You know what? I should stop bringing that up. Let's just forget I mentioned it."

They walked in silence for a spell, keeping their eyes open for any sign of danger. The fact that none presented itself was both a relief but also an annoyance. Worse yet, Liandra's map showed nothing new, so they were left in the dark, bored.

"Why does Gobthorak have to live so far away?" Brutus whined. "You'd think, if he were going to eat the world, he'd want to do so from a more central location."

"I suspect he probably doesn't want to be bothered," Liandra sighed. Small talk wasn't something she often enjoyed but there was literally nothing else to do while they traveled. "I guess we can ask him when we arrive."

"And then hand him his own ass," Devinon added. "Here, Gobthorak, here's your ass we just beat!"

"Hold up there," Darwin interrupted, "who is this Gobthorak fellow of whom you speak, and why do you wish to ... beat his ass?"

"Gobthorak is an evil, powerful being that wishes nothing more than the destruction of our world," Liandra said. "It is a scourge and must be completely removed from living so that *we* may continue living."

"He sounds like quite the unsavory chap." Darwin clapped a fist against his breastplate, sending a loud echo through the forest and scaring a flock of birds in the trees. They quickly took flight.

"He's foul," Devinon said. "I hear he's got tentacles and teeth and lots of eyes and I bet his breath smells like farts."

"Wait," Brutus interrupted. "If his breath smells like farts, then what do his farts smell like?"

"I guess we'll find out."

"Stop it, you two," Liandra scolded. "We don't know if any of that is true."

"It's just what I heard is all," Brutus said sheepishly.

"From whom?"

"Devinon."

The tips of Liandra's hair got brighter, and thick plumes of smoke wafted into the air. "We don't actually know what to expect," she said. "Nobody who's seen Gobthorak has lived to report their findings."

"This is a truly noble quest. I have decided I shall help you vanquish this horrible evil." Darwin clapped his chest again. The resulting sound once again shattered the forest's relative calm. "We will emerge victorious! We will be epic heroes for the ages!"

Darwin grabbed Brutus by the shoulder and then clapped him on the back, sharing his excitement.

"Well," Liandra said, once again finding herself as the voice of reason. "One thing at a time. Let's focus on eliminating this wild boar first. After that, we'll see where the map takes us."

"I hate that map," Pylara grunted. "It doesn't feel right."

"It's obviously a magical artifact, and they always function in weird ways. Don't worry though, I'm certain it will lead us to Gobthorak's lair, and I feel we're getting close."

"Well, maybe. I can't say I understand magic, so I defer to you." The look of uncertainty remained on Pylara's face as she tried to shake it. "So how close do you think we are?"

"If I had to guess," Liandra replied, "I'd say possibly five or seven chapters."

Everyone exchanged puzzled glances—everyone but Liandra who continued pushing through the forest without hesitation.

It was only several minutes later when the party stumbled upon a clearing, in the middle of which sat a ramshackle house built from various logs, sticks, and apparently scrounged bits of wood and metal. Scattered around the clearing were people sitting with their backs to the party. At the center of them all was a man.

Dressed in rags and stoking a small campfire, he was talking to them in a low voice, but nobody could hear what he was saying.

"What the heck?" Brutus mumbled. "How is this guy out here living in the forest while everyone else who comes out here gets torn apart by a wild animal?"

"And who are all the people hanging out with that dude?" Devinon inched a little closer, using some bushes as cover. He still couldn't hear the man, nor could he see what anyone else was doing. "It's like everyone had come to listen to him speak. He must be pretty interesting or something."

"Why don't you go check it out?" Liandra suggested. "You know, sneak around, see what he's saying, and come back with your findings?"

"I don't understand," said Pylara. "It's just a guy and some other people at a campfire. What's the danger?"

"If you recall," Liandra replied, "our last encounter was supposed to be with sandwiches, but three sand witches tried to kill us and then three *actual* sandwiches also tried to kill us. Anything can be dangerous."

"And tasty," Brutus added.

"I guess that makes sense," Pylara agreed. "Sounds like a good idea, Devinon, so how about—"

Devinon had already disappeared. Pylara scanned the area and eventually found him sneaking into the camp, lurking along the perimeter, and making his way to the far side.

"Well," she whispered, "I guess we wait."

"Splitting up the party is always a bad idea," Brutus muttered. "Usually people get killed."

"I doubt we have to worry about that," Liandra chuckled.

"At worst, I think we'll just have to deal with clunky narration."

Devinon deftly made his way through the forest, keeping to the edge of the clearing and making sure to be as quiet as possible. From this distance, he could still hear the man talking but, as before, couldn't understand a word that was said. He didn't understand the need for all the subterfuge, but the possibility of loot drove him forward. If these people were so transfixed by this man's word, they wouldn't notice Devinon robbing them blind.

From here he could see the other side of the house which appeared as though it would collapse if someone sneezed near it.

"Well, hello," Devinon muttered, finding a gap in the wall. In his current position, he was obscured from everyone's view —including his own party's. "Time to see what's inside."

The absence of a door was no problem for Devinon, who swiftly slipped through the gap and into the house. "The only real danger here is probably tetanus. Or rat poop."

Once inside, he immediately regretted his decision. An overwhelming stench assaulted his nose and brought tears to his eyes. He tried holding his breath but that only helped for so long and resulted in him gasping for air afterward, which defeated the purpose of holding his breath in the first place.

"Why do you make me do these things?"

I have no idea what he was talking about. I never suggested he enter the house in the first place. Devinon was, in fact, driven by his own curiosity and, moreover, his undying greed. He should've known better than to think there would be anything worth stealing in a hovel in the middle of the forest.

"Fine," he sighed, inspecting the area. The house consisted of one simple room, a dirt floor, and many piles of discarded junk. He briefly sifted through a couple and found nothing of worth.

"Even if I *did* find something worth taking, I'm sure it would bring this lovely smell with it. As far as random encounters go, this one's a dud."

He slipped back outside and made a loop, reappearing suddenly back where the rest of the party stood, waiting.

"Can we just go?" he asked. "It's just a bunch of people listening to some dude around a campfire. I doubt the experience we'd get from slaughtering them all would even be worth the effort."

"Who said anything about slaughtering them all?" Liandra asked, appalled. "We're not killing anyone. If anything, we should speak with these people and see if they know anything about the wild boar in the area."

"Agreed," Pylara ... well, agreed. "And maybe discover how these people have all lived out here safely without being mauled by a rabid pork roast."

Throg licked his lips.

"Let's focus, guys," Liandra growled. "We'll just go talk to this guy and see what he knows. We've been cautious. Now it's time to act."

"Fine," Devinon relented. He burst into the clearing, followed by the rest of the party. "It's just a dude talking to some other dudes around a campfire."

"Hey, *we're* dudes!" Brutus exclaimed. "Well, dudes and dudettes. We'll fit right in. This should be the easiest encounter we've ever had!"

"And now you've jinxed us," Liandra growled. "These guys are all probably high-level wizards and warriors, and I bet they'll attack us. Thanks for that."

Everyone braced for combat, but none came. In fact, nobody in the camp even paid them any attention. The man kept speaking in his low, rumbling voice, and those who listened continued to ... well, listen.

The party stood just inside the clearing, unsure of what to

do next. Brutus cleared his throat loudly, hoping to grab someone's attention, but nobody noticed. Darwin's armor created enough noise to wake the dead but, apparently, it wasn't enough to disturb anyone in the clearing. Nobody was sure if the noise was intentional.

"So," Darwin began, "now what?"

"Huh," Devinon said, "I totally forgot you were here. Anyway, I bet I could take out probably five of them without anyone noticing. I mean, the way things are going, I doubt they'd notice if I killed every one of them!"

"We're not killing anyone," Liandra reiterated, trying to be stern and quiet at the same time.

"What if they attack us?" Brutus asked.

"Well, then, sure ... I guess we can. But I'd prefer *not* to kill anyone. Besides, it doesn't look like anyone's going to attack us."

"We've been wrong before," Pylara added.

"Let's just get closer and try to get their attention." Liandra advanced and motioned to the others to follow.

20

The party made no effort to be quiet. In fact, they spoke loudly and made as much noise as possible, pretending to laugh and have a basic conversation.

"So, I said to him," Devinon shouted, "That's not a bastard sword, that's a bastard's sword!"

Everyone burst out into laughter. Though Devinon knew it was fake, he didn't care—at least he thought the joke was humorous, and an audience pretending to laugh was better than no audience at all.

Neither the crowd of people nor the speaking man seemed to notice. They certainly didn't appear to be bothered by the party in the slightest bit.

"Seriously?" Devinon griped. "That was my best material!"

"I, for one, am shocked," Pylara said. "I can't believe that was your best material."

Everyone laughed and, this time, it was real—except Devinon's laughter, of course.

Again, no laughter arose from the strange crowd before

them. The party was probably a good twenty feet from the back row of the audience now, and still nobody moved.

"We could just kill them all, take their loot and move on," Devinon suggested.

"We are *not* doing that," Liandra scowled. "And would you keep it down? We don't need everyone thinking we're going to murder them all. And why does killing always seem to be your first idea?"

"Oh, you want me to keep threats quiet but bad jokes are fine?"

"I don't understand—"

"Liandra," Devinon found a rock and picked it up, "it doesn't matter what we say, these people aren't responding. Look—watch this."

He threw the rock, missing absolutely everything and everyone.

"Okay, wait," he said, finding another rock. "I mean, watch *this*."

He threw the next rock, this time hitting one of the audience members squarely on the back of the head. The person—man or woman, nobody could tell—made no move. It was as if they hadn't felt the rock at all.

Devinon frowned, confused. "I'm beginning to think we could murderate all of them and nobody would notice."

"I said we're not—"

"I know, I know. So, what do you suggest we do instead? The opposite of murder? I mean, what is that, anyway?"

Nobody had an answer. They all, in fact, simply stood there, dumbfounded, and waiting for someone else to propose a course of action.

"Maybe we could ask someone for directions?" Pylara suggested. "It's always a good ice breaker."

"I don't think conversation starters are our biggest problem,"

Liandra replied. The smoldering glow in her hair was intensifying —something Devinon always looked forward to. Where there was smoke, there was fire, and fire was certainly a better alternative to standing in a clearing and watching a bunch of deadbeats do absolutely nothing. "Wait," she continued, "where's Brutus?"

They looked around and soon spotted the priest seated on the ground amid the audience, intently listening to the low murmurings of the man at the center.

Pylara strained to hear the speech but, as before, couldn't understand what was being said. "Oh good. Maybe Brutus can shed some light on what this man's riveting words are."

"Or we could all just sit down and listen," Liandra suggested.

"Pfft," Devinon scoffed. "This is too much like school, and I didn't do my homework."

"There was no homework," Liandra quipped.

"It doesn't matter; it's not done. It was never done."

"You never even went to school, did you?"

"Nope. My education is experience."

"And murder?"

"Yeah, that too."

Liandra sighed, something she realized she did a lot with this group. Particularly frustrating was their current situation. How would they defeat a world-eating end boss if they couldn't figure out a simple lecture?

"Come on," she said, the reluctance in her voice painfully apparent. "Let's just sit down and listen to what this old guy has to say. Maybe it'll be useful. And, when he's done, we can ask him about the boar."

Liandra moved forward and, once she found an open space, sat cross-legged on the ground patiently, awaiting this man's wisdom.

"I specifically recall becoming an adventurer so I could avoid this type of thing," Devinon grumbled. Eventually, however, he too followed suit and sat next to Brutus. Pylara and Throg were close behind.

"So, anyway," the man said, "I was walking slowly down the road, minding my own business, when I came across a rock."

It was more than just a little intriguing, the fact they could all hear and understand this man clearly now that they were seated among the audience. Liandra marveled at the revelation but soon focused on the words he uttered.

"Now this rock was no ordinary rock. No, wait, it was an ordinary rock. It was as ordinary as the day was long which, it being the peak of summertime, each day was very long. Have I ever mentioned the day one summer I woke up before the sun and that day felt like several days? I swear it was the longest day you could possibly imagine, and I hadn't enough tasks to keep me occupied. So, what I ended up doing was taking a nap and, when I awoke later, I had no idea what day it actually was. I tell you, I was so disoriented and groggy I almost forgot to pee. But thankfully, I remembered, and it all turned out fine."

Liandra yawned.

"But then," he continued, "I realized I had nothing to eat in my house over there, so it was time to get hunting before the sun went down. And since I'd taken that nap, I literally had no idea how much sunlight was left. Now, in case you didn't know this already, hunting during the day and hunting during the night are vastly different, because you need to know what clothes to wear—it's of paramount importance!"

Liandra yawned again. This man's drivel was of no importance, yet she found herself unable to do anything but pay attention to his every word. Nothing he said could have been construed as useful but, whenever she tried to get up, she yawned, stretched, and remained seated.

"... so, I told her she could stay for dinner if she liked but, still again, she refused. I offered every reason for her to stay and enjoy a nice meal, but she kept telling me she had to go. It wasn't until later that night I discovered she was a tree branch. I'll never make that mistake again!"

As she stretched her neck and shoulders, Liandra forced herself to look around—an action that took monumental effort for some reason. Though the endeavor was brief because she didn't want to miss any of this man's oration, she couldn't help but notice those around her seemed ... odd. But surely it was nothing and she had already missed enough of the man's story.

"... and let me tell you, putting your hand down a random hole in the ground is *not* a wise thing to do! Fortunately, nothing happened but something very well *could* have happened, and then this story would have been completely different! But, as it is, this is how it ended. And that reminds me of the time I got lost in the woods. I mean, there have been many times, actually—one such time was just recently, actually —but this one particular time, let me tell you, it was *exactly* like all the other times. I'll now describe in great detail each encounter with me getting lost in the woods, point by point ..."

Liandra wanted to get up, but she felt fatigued, and standing wouldn't be worth the effort. At least, sitting here on the ground, she was comfortable and there was entertainment. There was really no reason to get up when she had everything she needed right where she sat.

But she caught another quick glimpse of the person to her left and her mind screamed, urging her to stand. For a brief moment, she came close to moving, but those thoughts faded, and she relaxed, having already long forgotten any past motivations.

The man continued droning on and, even though Liandra knew his stories were pointless and mundane, she couldn't help but want to know more. Her attention hung on every word. Her mind was enthralled by his proficient, riveting speech, and her body was firmly planted on the ground. She could listen to him speak forever and be happily satisfied. She was perfectly content to be here, in the moment.

Until Devinon appeared, sailing through the air, almost in slow-motion and she could do nothing but watch.

"Die, evil monster!" he yelled, planting two daggers in the old man's back ... multiple times ... with great aplomb. "I don't care about your rock or your branch or what clothes you're going to wear!"

The man gurgled and collapsed to the ground as Devinon continued driving his blades down onto him, shouting profanities and threats.

Liandra suddenly snapped out of whatever daze she'd been in. The sleepy haze lifted, and she looked around her, now noticing precisely what had felt wrong before.

Everyone around her—everyone in the audience—was a desiccated husk, staring intently at where the man had stood before Devinon assaulted him. How long had they been here, listening to this man's drivel? Were they even still alive?

Liandra jumped to her feet and saw the rest of the party do the same. "Devinon!" she screamed.

"Don't stop me! This guy deserves what he's getting!"

"I don't plan on stopping you! Keep going!"

The old man shrieked and flailed. No blood erupted from his body, however. Instead, plumes of dust arose with each dagger strike, wafting into the air and eventually dissipating.

The man's agonizing screams eventually turned to growls, then nefarious laughter as he threw Devinon off him and stood, brushing himself off.

"How dare you!" he shouted, pointing at the party as they grouped together. "You caused me to lose my place in the story! Now I'll have to start over and it's all your fault!"

"Let's get the fifteen-or-so Hells out of here before he

starts up again!" Pylara shouted. "No way am I sticking around to hear about his rock."

"Yeah, let's get out of here," Devinon said, already making a break for the tree line. Everyone else followed close behind, almost stumbling over one another, desperate to escape the danger as quickly as possible.

When they finally made it to the forest, they disappeared among the trees and never looked back.

21

xcept they actually *did* look back. Sure, I fibbed a little—all great storytellers do, because it creates tension and excitement. And it was far more dramatic to end the chapter that way, so stop judging me!

Anyway, once the party reached the edge of the forest, they paused to catch their breath and looked behind them, back into the clearing where the old man, as if nothing had happened, calmly mumbled incoherently to the audience of husks that stared on, completely riveted by his words.

"It's kind of sad," Pylara muttered, "how lonely he must be. All he wants to do is talk to people."

"And suck out their souls in the process," Liandra added. "That doesn't sound so sad to me. He kills people with boredom."

"Oh, now it makes sense!" Devinon laughed. "I'm surprised I didn't figure it out earlier."

"Figure what out?"

"He's a wild *bore*! Get it? Because he's boring? He's not a rabid pig!"

A hush fell over them.

"You know," Devinon continued, "just in case nobody realized the whole last bit was based on a terrible play on words ... it feels almost as if *someone's* not even trying anymore. It's really just lazy writing."

Pylara frowned, groaning. "Let's just get out of here and never speak of this again."

"I'm with branch lady," Devinon agreed.

"We shouldn't leave," Liandra argued. "That sad, boring old guy is going to continue killing people if we don't stop him."

"No way," Brutus disagreed. "No way am I going back there and listening to his rambling stories."

"Fine," Liandra acquiesced, apparently also not willing to brave the man's inane ramblings, "Let's leave. I don't like the idea of abandoning the innocent people, though."

"We can't be sure they're even alive anymore," Pylara argued.

"If they are," Brutus added, "I'd say hydration is their first concern."

"And if we rescue them," Devinon moaned, "then we'll have to explain things to them and help them back to town and that's just *so much work*. It's better if we just go. You know, better for us."

And so it was The Last Available headed out, disappearing into the grove of trees, away from the danger of eternal boredom and on toward an indeterminate amount of walking, trading one form of boredom for another. They valiantly retreated from confrontation, keenly aware that violence never solves anything, (shut it, Devinon) and left the boring little troll in peace to tell his long-winded tales to dried up, withered people for the remainder of eternity.

In the distance, they swore they could hear the man's ramblings, still tugging at their souls and senses of etiquette even though they were fairly certain they were far enough away so as to be unaffected. But the ear worm still bothered at them, nagging and niggling for attention and—

"Good lord, are you finished yet?" Liandra asked. "You're seriously just about as boring as that guy back there."

Fine. Whatever. Be that way.

The party traveled in silence for a while, hoping whatever they encountered next would be more exciting, less dangerous, and possibly fluffy.

"Hey, guys?" Pylara asked, breaking the silence. "Does it seem ... well, a little *too* quiet?"

"What do you mean?" Devinon asked. "I was rather enjoying it until you spoke up."

"I mean, there's something missing. I'm not used to it being this quiet lately."

"Maybe that old dude's verbal diarrhea's gotten to you. I think it's nice to be free of the constant prattling."

"I feel it, too," Liandra agreed. "It's like we're missing something or something's not quite right."

They stopped and looked at one another, obviously settling on the same suspicion but not being able to pinpoint exactly what was amiss.

"Darwin!" Liandra exclaimed.

"Who?" Devinon asked.

"The guy from Candyville! The dude who made so much noise when he walked, I couldn't hear myself think."

"Oh yeah!" Brutus laughed. "That guy! Where'd he go?"

"I guess we left him back in the clearing."

"I hate to ask this," Brutus groaned. "Do we ... do we want to go back and try to get him?"

"Absolutely not," Devinon interrupted, earning ashamed looks from virtually everyone except Throg who clearly wasn't paying attention. "We already agreed we weren't going back there. That guy knew the dangers and, anyway, he himself was pretty boring. He'll fit right in."

For a moment, everyone was quiet, and they looked uneasily at one another until they all silently came to agreement and nodded.

"So, let's stop making excuses to go back there." Devinon resumed walking.

"I mean," Liandra muttered, "rescuing a friend isn't really an excuse."

"Maybe," Brutus replied, "but we barely knew him, so was he really a friend? And, quite honestly, he tried too hard."

"More of an acquaintance," Liandra concurred.

"I'd say more of an escort mission, really," Devinon added. "And we all know those suck."

"The map!" Liandra exclaimed, interrupting Brutus's feeble attempt to make everyone feel more noble.

"What's it show?" Pylara asked, peeking over Liandra's shoulder.

"Nothing!"

"Nothing? Is that good?"

"No, I don't mean nothing. Well, not exactly. I mean there is no next step to get to Gobthorak's lair. The next step *is* Gobthorak's lair! Guys! We're almost there!"

Spontaneous cheers erupted from the group—even Throg who may or may not have understood why they were all so relieved.

"The bad news, however—"

"Wait wait wait." Devinon stopped Liandra, rudely interrupting. "You can't just say 'the bad news is' without saying what the good news is."

"But I just gave you the good news."

"Is it really good news though? I mean, yes, it's good that this long-ass quest is finally going to end, sure. But that same quest also ends with a world-eating mega super being which, if I'm being honest, doesn't really sound like good news to me."

It truly was a situation of mixed blessings, where the threat of certain death overshadowed the joy of reaching the end. Throg, however, continued cheering.

"Let's just keep moving," Liandra finally said, packing the map away and pushing through the underbrush. "This is what we were hired to do, so let's get it done. The world is depending on us to succeed."

"Oh," Brutus said, in a matter of fact tone, "certainly no pressure, there."

"Guys," Liandra continued, "we were *chosen* for this! This is our moment!"

"Yeah," Pylara replied, "we were. But only because we're the last hope. We aren't the right heroes for this job, we were simply the last available. We're no saviors. We're just meat to throw at Gobthorak."

"That's not true."

"Yes, it is true." Pylara sat on a fallen tree and fidgeted with her mighty branch. "Everyone else before us failed, and they were far better equipped to handle this threat. They were seasoned adventurers who probably worked as a cohesive team, and they all perished. If they couldn't do it, what chance do we have?"

Liandra's hair pulsed orange and red. She didn't appear angry and seemed to be mulling over Pylara's words. "It's true," she finally relented. "It's true that those before us all failed, waves crashing against rocks and failing to make it to shore. So many adventurers before us met their untimely deaths—probably terrible, brutal deaths."

"This is possibly the worst pep talk I've ever heard," Brutus quipped, followed by nervous laughter "Way to really rile us up."

"Ah, but you haven't let me finish."

"Oh boy," Devinon sneered, "I can't wait to hear what's next."

"My point is, yeah, we're it—we're the last hope, and not

because we're mighty, but because we're still here. We *are* The Last Available. But where others failed we will succeed. How many of those poor souls sitting in the clearing could be adventurers who came before us? How many fell to the Sand Witches before we defeated them?"

Throg burped and rubbed his belly.

"We don't even know how many made it this far! It's quite possible we're the first group to get here, and we owe it to the world to do our best to make sure it sees many more sunrises."

The looks on everyone's faces slowly turned from sadness and despair to hope—cautious hope, to be sure. After all, they still had to face off against the Eater of Worlds and defeat him and, really, this was a complete unknown since nobody had any information on him. It would absolutely be their most difficult task yet.

"Oh, shut it. We were having a moment before you interrupted me."

My apologies.

"Anyway, as I was saying, *we can do this*. We have our wits, and we have our skills."

"And we have our weapons," Pylara added, hefting her log high into the air.

"We have everything we need and if we throw it all at this Gobthorak guy, there's no reason we can't win."

"You're right!" Pylara shouted. "Let's march in there and save the world!"

They cheered and, for the first time ever, it felt as though they were truly a team with unlimited potential. They could do this. They *would* do this. The world was depending on them, and they would not let it down. Of course, it wouldn't matter to them if they did because they'd be dead and wouldn't know what came after, but the stakes were still super high, I assure you. Like, really really high.

"Let us be off, then!" Pylara motioned forward with her

tree branch. "Onward, to Gobthorak's lair where we will defeat him and save the world!"

"And hopefully get paid a whole lot of coin when this is over." Devinon rubbed his hands together and chuckled.

"And maybe," Pylara added, "get Liam brought back to life."

"I mean," Devinon grinned, "let's not rush ourselves. One thing at a time."

And so it was, the party of brave adventurers continued their travels through the forest until they breached the tree line and gazed upon the most wondrous sunset. I'm pretty sure it was a sunset, but I really haven't been keeping track of the flow of time—so let's just go with sunset. It was definitely a sunset.

And as the sun burned in the sky so, too, did their newfound courage burn within them. Of course, the burning sun was actually setting, so that would mean its light was fading, so maybe their courage was fading too? Damn, metaphors are hard. Or is it an analogy? I get the two mixed up. No, metaphor. The sun is definitely a metaphor.

Whatever. Look, the sun was setting, the adventurers were courageous, and they were heading toward Gobthorak's lair—that's all you really need to know, okay? So just work with me here. The important part was they were getting close, and they were ready to kick some world-eater ass!

"Cripes," Liandra growled, "are you done already? We've been staring at this sunset for ten minutes and I think I'm getting a sunburn."

22

"Well," Liandra muttered, "here we are."

The party stood in front of the entrance to Gobthorak's lair, in awe of the two massive iron doors that barred their passage. Set into the cliff wall, they were anything but ornate, but they appeared to serve their purpose just as well.

"So, uh," Devinon stammered, "how big is this dude anyway?"

"I'd guess at least ten feet tall," Brutus replied. "He *is* the eater of worlds, after all. I reckon he'd need to be pretty tall to do that."

"That seems pretty arbitrary—ten feet." Devinon laughed and threw a rock at the door. It bounced harmlessly off and clattered on the rocky ground. "Is that, like, a prerequisite they ask you in an interview to make sure you're worthy?"

"Eaters must be this tall to devour a world," Brutus laughed, holding his hand out above his head as if measuring his height.

"I guess I'll need a stool to be able to reach his ass so I can kick it."

Brutus laughed some more. "You probably need a stool to kick anyone's ass, actually."

"Are you two done?" Liandra asked.

Devinon scratched his chin, desperately trying to think of another gag. "Yeah, I guess so," he said. "So, how do we get in?"

Throg knocked on one of the doors.

"Right," Devinon scoffed, "because it'd be that easy. Hey, Gobthorak, can we come in pretty please?"

To everyone's surprise, the doors slowly opened, the grinding and squeaking of metal on metal piercing their ears. They watched and waited for what felt like hours as the doors took their sweet time opening until, finally, they stopped and the chilly air of the passage beyond gripped them.

"Knocking polite way," Throg said.

"Well then," Liandra said, her hair glowing brightly, "onward."

A torrent of chilly, damp air wafted over them as they cautiously filed in, weapons drawn and eyes darting about. The cavern itself was spacious with the ceiling being barely visible in the dim light.

"Do you think he's expecting us?" Devinon asked, pointing to the already burning torches on the walls spaced neatly every fifteen or so feet. "It seems a waste of torches to just have these burning nonstop all the time."

"Dungeons are really super wasteful, aren't they?" Brutus added, shaking his head. "This Gobthorak guy must be pretty well off to be able to afford so many torches and keep them lit."

"Ooh!" Devinon shouted. "That means he's probably got some wicked loot we can scrounge!"

The two high-fived while Liandra rubbed her forehead in frustration. "They're probably magically lit," she said, inspecting one. "Nobody would just have torches burning constantly for no reason unless ... well, unless they have a constant stream of adventurers invading.”

“But why, then, would Gobthorak make his lair so accommodating?” Pylara asked. “Come on in,” she said in a haughty voice, “I’ve been expecting you. Travel down my well-lit corridors and, oh, watch your step! Make yourselves at home before we try to kill each other.”

“It doesn’t matter,” Liandra growled. “What matters is we push further in, find him, and put an end to his evil. Be glad the torches are lit so we’re not stumbling over our own feet.”

“Don’t you have some kind of light spell you could use if we needed it?”

Liandra looked at Pylara who, in turn, nodded knowingly. Any light spell Liandra may or may not have would involve fire and probably explosions. She should’ve known.

The cave path sloped gently downward and angled to the right—a positive sign for adventurers wanting to delve into a dungeon. It was common knowledge that the treasure was more valuable the further down an adventurer went. Look it up—it was in all the instruction manuals. But they soon came to a split with one path to the right, the other to the left. It was their biggest dilemma yet.

“So,” Pylara said, keeping her voice hushed so as not to disturb any monsters nearby. “Which way do we go? And is anyone drawing a map so we don’t get lost?”

“A map?” Devinon laughed. “Nobody draws maps anymore.”

“Well, okay, smarty pants. How do you suggest we keep track of where we are then?”

“Just push Tab for a mini map.”

Pylara had no answer because she didn’t in the least bit understand the response. “Fine ... whatever. So which way are we going then?”

“Let’s just go right,” Brutus said, pointing onward. “We

don't know what's down either path so why overthink it?"

Liandra clapped Brutus on the back and smiled. "That's maybe the most logical thing you've ever said. Yes, let's just take the right path and see where it leads us."

And, so, that's precisely what they did. And when they discovered a massive, impassable pit filled with sword-wielding snakes and fire-breathing rocks, they decided to turn around and take the left passage instead.

"Never mind, Brutus," Liandra said, "that was a terrible idea. You don't get to decide things anymore."

"How was I supposed to know there were sword-snakes that way? There could have just as easily been snakes *without* swords instead!"

"Because that would've been *so* much better."

"I'm just saying ... I made a decision instead of standing around, picking our noses."

"Throg hate snakes."

"So, now we go left," Liandra continued, stomping down the left path. Come on, we're wasting time."

Her hair was a lovely shade of pissed off. Fortunately, it was radiating its own light so, even though there were plentiful torches, the added illumination was convenient.

"If we irritate her just a little bit more," Devinon whispered to Brutus, "we can probably get a really good tan."

The path ended abruptly in an empty, circular room with no exits.

"Whatever dungeon designer Gobthorak hired for his lair obviously had no idea what they were doing," Brutus said. "I hope he didn't pay them much. But at least there are no snakes or swords ... or snakes *with* swords in this room."

Liandra shot Brutus a look that aroused fear in the very core of his being. "Devinon, can't you search for secret doors or something?"

"Wait," Devinon replied, "hold up, there. Just because I

occasionally pilfer a few items and sneak around and, yes, *sometimes* stab people in the back to take their loot, you just *assume* I can find concealed doors and passageways? Isn't that a little stereotypical?"

The party fell silent with nobody sure what to say.

"You assume a lot about me having only known me for a few weeks. Oh, Devinon can do that because he's a thief and all thieves are the same! I am seriously insulted by your judgment."

"Well," Liandra retorted, "can you, or can't you? Surely, you're useful for something, and this may as well be it."

"Oh, no I totally can. I just don't appreciate your snap judgments."

"You ... don't appreciate me asking you to do something you have skill in?"

"Can't *you* just blow the crap out of the walls with fire instead?"

"Are you going to help or not?"

"Okay, fine. You guys just sit and have morning tea while ol' Devinon here does all the work. Don't mind me, I'm just saving the world and stuff."

"You're laying it on a little thick, don't you think?" Brutus laughed.

"Is it working?"

"Not really."

Devinon frowned. "Damn."

Devinon proceeded to inspect the wall, beginning at the entrance. He slowly worked his way around, running his hands over the surface and scrutinizing every inch, squinting, and sometimes licking the stone.

The party watched, largely confused, as he did his thing and made small talk or stared in random directions.

"This is the part they don't tell you about," Brutus muttered.

Pylara sat, inspecting a rock she found on the floor. "What's that?" she asked.

"The boring parts. All you hear about is the fighting, valiant victory, and treasure. Nobody tells you about the parts where you sit on your asses waiting for something to happen while you watch a kid molest the wall."

"Could you all keep it down?" Devinon growled.

"Are we disturbing your work?" Pylara chuckled.

"No. But if I have to be miserable then you guys should be miserable, too."

"Well, what do we do if you don't find anything?"

"Not my problem."

Pylara frowned and flicked a bug off her tree branch. "Aren't you supposed to be skillful at lots of things? Surely you can think of something."

"What'd you guys do, read my class description in a book? Just let me do my job and you do yours—whatever that is. Dungeon delving isn't all combat and explosions and fun things like that."

"That's the truth," Brutus griped. If he shined his shield any more than it already was there would be nothing left of it.

"Besides, I found a door."

Devinon pressed his hand against a rock and the wall slid open to reveal a passage beyond. "Voila," he said, motioning to his discovery. "But there's no way Gobthorak could fit through this if he's as big as the tunnels would suggest."

Instead of the usual spacious tunnel, this passage was much smaller and cramped. As with all other tunnels, flaming torches lining the wall cast flickering light.

"I'm tellin' ya," Brutus muttered, "this guy's torch bill ..."

"Focus, guys," Liandra commanded, stepping through the open door. Her hands were out in front of her, ready to cast a spell should she need to. "Now let's go."

"Yes, m'lady," Devinon said, bowing deeply and

exaggerating every movement.

This particular passage twisted around several curves until it, too, opened into a room much like the previous circular room, except this one was full of goblins.

"Well," Devinon whispered as they all stopped at the entrance. "I guess we have to kill them all to advance past this room."

"I'm not so sure about that," Pylara countered, pointing to the many goblins sleeping peacefully. "I think they're just camping here. Look—they have tents and smoldering campfires. I don't believe they mean us any harm—"

"I think Pylara's right," Liandra agreed. "They don't even have any weapons. In fact, judging from their belongings, they look like one or more families. Maybe we can learn from them and gain valuable information about this place?"

"But why are they even here?" Brutus added. "Are they just hanging out in Gobthorak's dungeon for fun?"

"Maybe," Liandra posited, "it's safer in here than it is outside? After all, most creatures just want to go about their lives. We call them monsters, but they're often just misunderstood."

"That makes sense," Brutus agreed. "I see just one problem."

"What's that?"

"All done!" Devinon shouted. He stood amidst many dead goblins, motioning for the party to move into the room.

"Son of a bitch," Liandra growled.

"Yeah ..." Brutus said.

Pylara, Brutus and Liandra gave Devinon dirty looks. Even Throg looked perplexed, but that wasn't unusual for his normal state at any given moment.

"What?"

"Nothing," Liandra said. "Never mind. Let's just keep moving."

23

hat in the fifteen-or-so Hells is this?" Liandra asked as the passage behind them sealed itself.

"Should we move closer?" Pylara squinted, inspecting the room. "I mean, this could be a trap."

"Hey, Devinon," Liandra said, "you can search for traps, right?"

"Ugh." Devinon rolled his eyes and sighed. "Yes, I can search for traps. Do I *want* to search for traps? That's the question, isn't it?"

"Would you rather slay harmless goblin families in their sleep like a coward?" Pylara asked disapprovingly.

"Well, yeah," Devinon responded. "Obviously—they're going to have loot. Traps just try to kill you and they explode and stuff. Goblins don't explode ... well, usually. There was this one time—"

"And he missed the point." Pylara sighed. "Just go search for traps or something while we wait over here ... out of any kind of blast radius that may or may not occur."

"I appreciate your confidence in my ability," Devinon sneered as he got to work.

The room was simple and sparse, with the only object being a table in the center. As with the last room, there were no visible exits, and the entrance had already sealed itself. Devinon made sure to search for hidden doors as well as traps but there was no reason to let the party know of his hard work. They would never appreciate it.

Besides, they appeared to be having fun, talking and carrying on in the corner of the room while they all huddled behind Brutus' shield. He briefly considered, if he found a trap, setting it off just to see what they would do. But then they'd just question his ability and give him grief over it for as long as they remained together. No, it was far easier to just do his job and get through this as quickly as possible.

"Hello," he mumbled, "what is this?"

As he brushed his hand over the wall he felt an anomaly —a bit of stone that jutted ever so slightly out of the otherwise uniform surface. Upon further inspection, he discovered it was a button and, without a second thought, he immediately pressed it—because that's what buttons are for.

The grinding of stone on stone indicated he had made something happen, but as he scrutinized the wall before him, he couldn't see any immediate effect. So, he waited, hoping something would present itself.

He didn't have long to wait. At his feet, a hidden compartment in the floor revealed itself, the cover sliding back under the wall. He waited until it was fully exposed before bending down to inspect the contents. It was odd that the grinding stone noise continued even after the compartment finished opening, but he paid it no mind. Whoever designed this dungeon had probably cut corners.

"Obviously not Dwarven stonework," he muttered as he reached into the container and pulled out a large wadded up pile of white cloth. He then held it in front of him and inspected it, running his hands through it and moving it around in all directions, looking for any hint of purpose.

"What in the fifteen-or-so Hells is this garbage?" he mumbled, still scrutinizing the bundle of cloth. "This is possibly the lamest dungeon I've ever heard of."

The moment he felt a hand on his shoulder he spun around with a dagger in one hand.

"Devinon," Pylara said with a dire look on her face. "What are you doing, fooling around over here? We need to get out of here now!"

"What are you talking about? I'm not *fooling around* as you put it. I found this cloth and—"

"Who cares about some cloth? Have you not noticed?"

"Noticed what?"

Pylara motioned to the wall with her hefty tree branch and Devinon immediately recognized the reason the stone grinding sound hadn't stopped.

The walls were closing in on them!

"Well crap," he sighed. "But if they began moving when I found this fabric, then the two must be related."

He moved to the center of the room and set the cloth on the table, spreading it out.

"Devinon!" Liandra yelled. "Get away from there!"

"What? Why? It's just a piece of cloth. Will it harm me?" He laughed and made no immediate attempt to move away.

"Devinon! That's a fitted sheet!"

"Oh, son of a bitch!" he yelled, diving backward and cowering in the corner with the rest of them. "I could have died!"

"That was a close one!" Brutus agreed. "This dungeon's not fooling around."

"So," Devinon wheezed, "you don't think we have to fold it ... do you?"

"I think that's exactly what we have to do," Liandra

replied, obviously inspecting the fitted sheet from afar. "Or these walls are going to crush us."

"What a cunning, deadly trap!" Brutus shrieked.

"We don't have much time," Pylara added. "We need to get this done quickly."

"But this is impossible," Devinon whined. "Nobody can fold a fitted sheet. And what even is the point anyway? Whoever designed this dungeon is a nefarious, evil person ... who I'd really like to meet someday. You know, if we survive."

"You know what?" Liandra said, approaching the sheet on the table. "Screw this. Fitted sheets deserve to die!"

Jets of fire exploded from her fingertips and engulfed the sheet in a torrent of flames. Acrid smoke billowed from the table, assaulting their noses and bringing tears to their eyes. When she finished, the table was no more.

But the fitted sheet remained. Unscathed and pristine, it now lay on the stone floor, daring them to fold it. If a sheet could actually dare anyone to do anything. But it can't, can it? I mean, it's just a sheet. I don't know how these things work.

"Well now what?" Brutus asked, his voice shaky.

Pylara boldly approached it, never taking her eyes off the cloth. "We obviously must fold it," she said, kneeling and making an attempt.

Everyone else watched in horror as she fumbled with the corners, pausing many times to inspect the mess that she ultimately created.

They all winced and collapsed to the floor as pain wracked their bodies for what seemed like an eternity but was probably only four or five seconds.

"Apparently that wasn't good enough," Pylara said, gasping for breath as the pain subsided. "And the punishment is severe."

"So we either die by getting crushed or we die by whatever that was," Devinon replied. "Brilliant. So, who's next?"

Nobody made any immediate move to step forward as the walls continued slowly closing in.

"Do you think we only get one attempt each?" Liandra asked.

Pylara shrugged and moved to try again but was violently forced backward the moment she touched the sheet. "My guess is, yes," she growled.

"I hate this place," Brutus griped as he reluctantly stepped up to make his attempt. "This is absolutely the worst," he continued before even touching the fabric.

His attempt was less than stellar, ending with him wadding the sheet up in a ball and throwing it on the ground, resulting in the same painful punishment as before.

"You didn't even try," Liandra said, scowling at him.

"I did try!" he shouted. "Everyone knows this is impossible! Nobody folds fitted sheets anyway! I told my mother over and over, but did she ever listen? No. She only ever glared at me and told me I didn't get dinner until I folded the sheet! I don't want to fold the sheet, Mommy! You're mean!"

The party remained silent, looking at one another and trying not to acknowledge what just happened. But they couldn't ignore the walls which were getting ever closer. The room was now about half its original size.

"Okay ... so, um, who's next?" Liandra asked. "Preferably someone without a dark fitted sheet-related past maybe?"

Brutus sobbed quietly.

"Brutus," Devinon said, "can't you pray to the goddess of fitted sheets or whatever for help?"

Brutus sobbed not-so-quietly.

"I don't think I can take a whole lot more if we keep failing," Liandra said. "If I had any way to measure my health, I'd say I'm at about half."

"You're a little over half health," Devinon retorted.

"How do you know?"

"Your health bar." He pointed above Liandra's head.

Liandra tried desperately to figure out what he was talking about but couldn't see any health bar as he had specified.

"You guys seriously can't see that?"

Everyone shook their heads except Brutus who was still trying to regain his composure.

"Whatever," he sighed. "Who's next?"

Throg courageously stepped forward.

"No!" they all shouted in unison, obviously not trusting an orc to do something so delicate as fold a fitted sheet. But when Throg neither looked back nor stopped his advance, they all braced for the pain they knew would soon follow, closing their eyes and wincing.

For what seemed like years, they waited. Until Throg grunted and the grinding of stone on stone ceased.

"Throg finished."

They slowly opened their eyes to see what appeared to be a perfectly folded fitted sheet and a proud, beaming orc.

"What?" Pylara gasped.

"I don't ..." Liandra stammered, "what just happened?"

The stone on the wall across the room slid open to reveal a passage beyond.

"Right now," Devinon said, hustling toward the other side, "I don't really care. Let's just get out of here before this room forces us to give a cat a bath or something worse."

"What's worse than giving a cat a bath?" Brutus asked, afraid of the answer.

"I don't really want to find out. That's why we're leaving."

Apparently, the very thought of dealing with a cat was enough to make Throg bolt across the room and exit well ahead of anyone else.

24

he party cautiously made their way through the narrow tunnel which, conveniently, was still lit by torches. The dungeon may have been trying to kill them, but it also apparently wished for them to die in a brightly lit environment—possibly so they could adequately witness their own deaths. That's pretty morbid when you think about it, though. I mean, what kind of a jerk would do such a thing?

Gobthorak, apparently. They were learning much about their foe and he was apparently more nefarious and dastardly than they at first thought.

And his monthly light bill was probably outrageous. He singlehandedly kept torch makers in business, apparently.

"Wait," Liandra said, holding out her arm to try to keep anyone from advancing. Nobody got the hint, and she was forced to keep walking with them. "What's that sound?"

"I don't know," Pylara responded, straining to hear, "but it's coming from up ahead."

"I guess we'll find out soon enough," Devinon added. His voice was almost cheerful, as if he believed the worst was behind them. He might have been right. After all, evil fitted linens are super dangerous. But he also might have been wrong.

His suspicions were confirmed the moment he stepped out of the passage and into the next room.

"Well," Devinon said, "this is pretty terrible."

The sound they'd heard was that of spewing fire. Nonstop spewing fire, constantly streaming out from holes in the walls and floor.

"Can we just leave?" Pylara asked.

The room before them was not so much a room as it was a pit—a pit filled with spikes and lava and more spikes and more lava. Spanning across the pit was a narrow stone bridge. Of course, that sounds bad but not *that* bad, right? Oh, no, it was worse. Fire spewed randomly from the sides of the room and tiny blades shot out of the ceiling.

"Does this just go all the time?" Liandra asked. "Just … nonstop fire and blades? That seems really wasteful. I mean, how often do adventurers even come here anyway?"

"Gobthorak," Brutus replied, "Waster Of Fire. This all seems really excessive."

"And really hot," Devinon added, "and really dangerous and painful."

"Yeah, those as well."

Devinon frowned, feeling the heat from the fire ahead. "And what kind of lazy-ass eater of worlds just sits in his lair and lets all his traps do the work anyway?"

"It's totally elitist," Brutus agreed.

"Not only that," Pylara added, "it eliminates many henchman jobs. How many minions go hungry because of Gobthorak's selfishness?"

"Exactly!" Devinon motioned to the myriad of hazards that lay ahead. "It's absurd!"

"You're stalling, aren't you?" Liandra asked.

"Yes I am."

"Well, these hazards aren't going to disarm themselves so …"

"Is that all I am to you? Devinon, the trap disarm … guy or something?"

"Well, not exactly," Liandra replied, "but seeing as how you're the only one of us qualified to do the job, then yes."

"Oh yeah? Well, what about Throg?"

"Wait," Liandra said, perplexed, "what do you mean?"

"I mean … Throg could probably smash it all or something."

"Or eat it," Brutus added, snickering.

"Uh, or that," Liandra agreed.

"Why don't we just throw the bard's corpse in there?"

"What good would that do?"

"Probably none, but the carnage would be exquisite. And since he's an ex-minstrel, nobody would have to feel guilty!"

Everyone, including Throg, looked at Devinon disapprovingly.

"Fine," Devinon pouted, arms crossed in front of him. "Once again, Devinon will save the day so everyone else doesn't get chopped up and cooked."

"You're just bitter because there's no loot involved," Pylara retorted.

"It's like you know me or something. But if there *is* any loot—"

"Just go already!" they all shouted in unison.

Devinon grunted and moved forward, observing the gouts of fire and projectile blades covering every inch of the narrow stone walkway that spanned the lava-filled pit. He walked to the edge of the platform where it met the bridge and observed, seeking out any pattern in the obstacles' behavior.

Unfortunately, there was no pattern.

"And you couldn't have told me that before I stood here like a doofus, watching and waiting, could you?"

Hey, I'm the narrator. I do what I want. I'm building tension.

Devinon shrugged and sighed, deciding it was better to just trudge forward with reckless abandon than to finesse his way through the room. He took it at a run, sliding under the first jets of flame, then leaping forward to avoid the flying blades.

Rolling to his feet, he was nearly cooked by more fire and even some lava that erupted from the pit below. He moved just in time as the lava landed on the bridge, melting a small section of it.

"I bet ol' Gobthorak will be none too happy about that," he laughed. "Good. Screw that guy. And look at me! I'm wearing boots in Gobthorak's home and getting dirt everywhere!"

Devinon's mirth was rudely interrupted when tiny knives launched from one of the walls. He moved quickly, avoiding the fire nearby, but several blades tore through his cloak, nearly cutting his leg.

"Damn it," he muttered. "I hate this place."

Once he'd made it to the halfway point, a small door opened on the opposite wall and goblins flooded into the room. Carrying crude knives, clubs, and even rocks, they charged onto the bridge to attack Devinon.

And, in an instant, every one of them was cut down and incinerated, their mangled bodies tumbling into the lava.

"I see *someone* didn't really think this through very well, did they?" Devinon laughed, quickly dodging more fire that came from the ceiling and avoiding yet more blades.

Liandra grimaced, watching the multitude of slain goblins plummet into the lava. "Were they just waiting all this time, doing nothing until that door opened?"

"If Gobthorak can afford to be this wasteful," Devinon muttered to himself, "then he must have some excellent loot."

With a few more evasive maneuvers, Devinon finally reached the opposite side of the room, leaping off the bridge and landing on the ground as the blades and fire continued to fly behind him. He waved to the rest of the party who waved back.

The button was easy to see—a large, red circular button affixed to the wall with a sign that said "Deactivate." Devinon pressed it and the knives and fire instantly ceased while a door opened on the wall in front of him. The text of the sign changed to "Activate."

"Come across!" he shouted, motioning for the rest of the group to meet up with him. As they made their way across the room, Devinon briefly considered pushing the button again but realized they could be useful to get through the rest of the dungeon and, thus, waited until they were safely across before pushing it again.

"Why reactivate the hazards?" Pylara asked.

"It's what a polite houseguest would do," Devinon grinned. "Leave only footprints, am I right?"

"That's for nature," Liandra said, "not for a trap-filled dungeon."

"I was really just hoping more of those unfortunate goblins would come streaming out of somewhere and we could all watch the carnage together—you know, kind of like a teambuilding exercise."

"You're a sick individual," Pylara sighed, "you know, that don't you?"

Devinon grinned. "It's one of my more redeeming qualities."

"Sometimes," Brutus laughed, "I'm intensely curious about your less redeeming qualities."

"Well, I—"

"No, Devinon, maybe not *that* curious."

"Besides," Throg said, "that not how you build team. Teambuilding about working together, not watching goblins explode."

"Well," Liandra retorted, "the orc has given us *actual* words of wisdom. It seems to me it's time for this adventure to wrap up, because we've now seen it all."

Liandra was right and, with that, the party hurried through the dungeon and found Gobthorak. They slew him with ease, ending his reign of fear and eternal hunger, and becoming the world's greatest heroes. They were lauded for generations and had many statues erected in their honor. They even got a permanent ten percent discount on all seasonal items at a well-known store that sells scary seasonal décor.

"Really?" Devinon asked.

Ha ha, no. In fact, the party had only scratched the surface of Gobthorak's dungeon. They were merely beginning their dangerous delve into the depths of mayhem and carnage that were so brutal they could drive adventurers mad before obliterating them.

They could also make them very thirsty, for there were no drinking fountains to be found ... anywhere!

"Well, nuts," Devinon said.

"I guess we continue through there." Liandra pointed to a now open passageway ahead of them.

"When did that open up?" Brutus asked.

I'm pretty sure I told you about it.

"No, I don't think you did, weird voice."

I definitely did.

"We would've seen it and been all like 'sweet! Let's go through there, ol' chums!' but it wasn't there until now."

It doesn't matter when it appeared. The important thing is, it's there now and you should go through it.

"Fine," Brutus pouted, "but we're going through because we *want* to, not because you told us to."

Throg, apparently bored, maybe tired, but probably just hungry, grew impatient and made his way into the passage. The rest of the party soon followed, nobody too eager to find out what lie in wait for them.

25

iandra was first through the door, and she waited by it as the rest of the party scurried through. Pylara was the last through the door and Liandra slammed it shut and slid the bar in place, leaning against it and closing her eyes.

For a moment, nobody spoke as they all stopped to catch their breath and process what just happened.

"Wow!" Brutus said, gasping for air. "I don't know how we made it out of that one alive!"

"We are quite fortunate," Liandra agreed. "This dungeon is huge. How long has it been since we entered?"

"It's been a while," Pylara said, visibly counting on her fingers. "This place seems to distort time somehow. It seems like it's been weeks."

"I'm pretty sure," Devinon added, "nobody would believe us if we told them about all the strange and dangerous adventures we've had since the goblin explosion room!"

"I bet you're right," Pylara agreed. "Maybe one day we'll be able to tell the tale—possibly in a serialized fashion—but, right now, nobody wants to hear about it. Besides, it would take far too long to recount everything."

Liandra nodded. "Also, Uni the eight-legged unicorn, I don't think we need you anymore."

"Okay!" the multicolored, many-legged unicorn said cheerfully. "Then I guess I'll be going! And you know what I always say!"

"Sparkle on!" the party all shouted at once as the magical animal winked out of existence.

"I'm going to miss her," Brutus said.

Liandra put a hand on his shoulder. "We all will, Brutus. She's been an important part of our team for so long, now, it's difficult to imagine going on without her."

"Hey," Devinon giggled, "remember when Throg got turned into a frog?"

Everyone laughed except Throg.

"He was pretty adorable," Pylara cooed, "what with his little froggy axe. But it's a good thing we found the antidote ... though I'm really unsure why anyone would have one in a dungeon if the goal was to stop adventurers by turning them into frogs."

"Flies taste terrible," Throg grunted.

"Speaking of adventurers," Devinon chuckled, "remember that room stuffed full of dead adventurers?"

"Oh yeah!" Brutus laughed. "I still wish I knew how they all died. There weren't even any hazards or monsters in that room."

"Dead adventurer storage?" Throg asked He had that glint in his eye—the look everyone recognized. He was remembering that room fondly, probably because he devoured several of the bodies while he thought no one was looking. There was a standing nonverbal agreement among the party members to never speak of it.

Before them lay a small, empty chamber that led into a dark tunnel.

"Maybe this is it?" Devinon asked, hopeful. "Maybe this is the tunnel that leads to the final boss fight? We could be on the cusp of greatness, about to slay the big bad guy and save the world! Suck it, Gobthorak!"

Filled with confidence and bravado, Devinon courageously led the way into the dark tunnel, guided by the light from Liandra's smoldering locks. He held his daggers high, almost marching forward into the unknown, ready to end this and save everyone.

Well, yeah, there was that, but there would also be treasure and, let's be honest, this is Devinon we're talking about.

Throg sallied forth, excited for whatever lay ahead and ready to do battle with Gobthorak, for he had never tasted a god-like almighty ... you know what, never mind. You get the point.

Pylara gripped her tree branch. A battle-hardened, finely honed instrument of destruction, it would serve her well in the coming battle. Long had it vanquished many a squirrel. Both rat and mole had fallen to its greatness. It would perform admirably this day.

Brutus trembled, holding his shield in front of him, praying to whatever god or goddess he chose to follow that day. Some would call it cowering, but others would call it hiding—at least, according to him. If Gobthorak couldn't see what was behind the shield, then he had the element of surprise.

Liandra couldn't be bothered with outward appearances and braggadocio. She was busy going over all the hot, fiery spells she would lob at Gobthorak, daydreaming about turning him to ash and ridding the world of the ultimate evil.

"Remember that genie?" Devinon asked.

"Absolutely," Pylara responded. "Remember when he said he'd grant us one wish?"

"Aye."

"And remember when you wished he'd just shut up and stop singing?"

"Oh yeah!" Devinon laughed. "Well, that wasn't my point but that was indeed good times. Anyway, do you suppose we could've wished him to return the ex-minstrel back to being alive?"

"I definitely think that would have worked," Liandra growled. "Too bad we didn't have more than one wish. Also, too bad you couldn't keep your mouth shut."

"You have to admit he was a terrible singer. I did us all a favor."

"A bigger favor would have been to return Liam to life."

"Well, yeah, but then he'd probably sing too. And that would've sucked even more."

The rest of the party reluctantly nodded in silent agreement.

"So," Pylara said, eager to change the subject, "what's our plan for when we arrive?"

"The plan is, I shove my daggers in Gobthorak's ugly face, we take his treasure, and then we all have pie."

"Don't you think it'll be a bit more complex than that?"

"Not really. Daggers simplify everything. You really only have two options—stab or no stab."

"Why does that actually make some modicum of sense?" Brutus asked.

"Because it doesn't make *any* sense!" Liandra argued. The embers in her hair blazed for a moment before dying down again. "You can't just walk up to such a powerful being and stab it in the face. Such a thing would require at least a natural 20, maybe two or three. Critical hits don't just grow on trees, you know."

"Well, yeah," Devinon agreed. He held up one of his daggers in the dim light, examining it as someone would admire a fine gem or a tasty taco, if such things existed. "Fortunately, I'm really lucky and highly skilled. This won't be a problem, I assure you." He made stabbing motions with the blade.

"Where did all this courage come from all of a sudden?"

"Liandra, we've made it! This is the lead up to the final fight! We've come much farther than anyone else. This is our destiny—we were meant for this!"

"I'd like to point out," Pylara interrupted, "that we're alive largely because we've simply managed to avoid death, not because we've courageously vanquished every foe. These two concepts are not the same."

"Well, yeah ... okay, I'll give you that."

"So ... by that logic, it stands to reason that we shall beat Gobthorak by ... running away." Brutus suggested.

"That makes no sense," Liandra scoffed.

"Exactly," Pylara agreed. "Which means we'll actually have to fight him, and we're not really that good at fighting."

"We'll figure it out!" Brutus exclaimed courageously while still hiding behind his shield. "The truth lies somewhere in between."

"I guess we *have* made it this far," Liandra agreed, running a hand through her hair. "And nobody else has—even the most seasoned adventurers have perished."

"Perhaps they killed all the really horrible stuff for us?" Devinon posited.

While Liandra didn't like that idea, it wasn't out of the question. Had anyone actually made it to Gobthorak, or had they all died before reaching the journey's end? It was entirely possible. After all, nobody had been able to even describe the hulking beast. In fact, just calling him a hulking beast was an assumption, as was calling him a "him."

She started to feel the excitement within her and became giddy with anticipation. They could do this. They really *could* do this. Sure, it was apparent they'd had help but, really, who vanquishes world-ending evils without help? That's a part of the power of good, right? Good has allies and friends and fortune on its side and those are all crucial pieces of the puzzle.

Yes, it all began to make sense. Success was success no matter how one looked at it. And they had absolutely been successful. What adventuring party doesn't have their mishaps and near-death situations? Their little band of heroes was no different from any others except for the fact that they'd delved further into Gobthorak's lair than anyone else.

"Guys," she muttered, "I really think we *can* do this."

"Heck yeah we can!" Pylara agreed, hefting her branch in the air.

"Do you see that up ahead?" Liandra pointed to a faint light in the distance.

"It looks like the end of the tunnel," Devinon replied.

"Indeed," Liandra agreed. "Which means we're probably close! Last Available, it's time to get serious. Gobthorak dies this day!"

"Hear, hear!" Brutus shouted, clattering his longsword against his shield.

"We're coming for you, Gobthorak!" Pylara yelled.

With that, they all charged down the tunnel shouting and screaming, until they emerged from the tunnel and onto a ledge, barely managing to stop in time and avoid falling into the abyss below.

"Well, shit," Devinon muttered.

26

"Well, this is fantastic," Brutus whined, his voice echoing throughout the vast, empty chasm before them. "Where are we supposed to go from here?"

"It seems to me," Liandra replied, "the only way to go is down ... really fast."

"There's only one problem with that—the ground."

"If there even is any," Devinon added. "I don't know if bottomless pits exist but this one looks like a pretty good candidate for that description. Here, give me a rock or something."

The party looked around but there were no rocks to be found—no debris, no junk, no random baubles to toss into the pit. Everyone just sort of stood around and shrugged.

"Brutus, give me your sword."

"Why?"

"I want to drop it down the pit."

"No way! Why don't you drop one of your daggers down the pit?"

"How dare you! I would never part with one of my children! And what kind of a monster would even suggest that?"

"You've got serious problems, man."

"Wait!" Devinon exclaimed, "I've got an idea! Pylara, let me have one of Liam's fingers!"

Pylara briefly considered arguing but not only would she most likely lose the debate, she really couldn't think of an adequate reason to resist. Still, she hesitated.

"Seriously." Devinon shook his head in dismay. "He wasn't a very good bard and he's an even worse corpse. At least let him be useful."

While nobody wanted to agree with such a rude statement, everyone found they couldn't really disagree, either. And, while they knew they should have felt bad about this, it was obvious they were just tired and simply wanted to be done with it all.

Sighing, Pylara reached into her backpack and rummaged around until she found what she needed. There was a sickening snap as she produced another Liam finger for Devinon.

Devinon dropped the digit down the pit and listened carefully for it to hit the ground below, somewhere in the dark.

He waited for several moments, as did his companions. No one made a sound. Even Throg's stomach complied.

"Son of a bitch," Devinon whispered.

"It really *is* bottomless," Liandra added, conjuring a ball of fire, and tossing it into the pit. "Maybe *this* will ... shed some light on the situation."

"Okay," Brutus replied, "I'll admit—that was a pretty good joke. Well done."

Again, the group was silent as they watched the flickering

fireball descend into the depths of the pit. It got smaller as it fell and its light grew dimmer until, eventually, they could no longer see it.

"It's either an extremely deep pit," Brutus concluded, "or it truly *is* bottomless. Maybe one of us should jump in?"

"That's, like, the *worst* idea I think I've ever heard!" Pylara laughed. "Why would we do that?"

"Because whoever jumps in can report back!"

"And how exactly would we do that, genius?"

"I don't know." Brutus looked as if he was reconsidering the notion. "I was just trying to come up with a reasonable idea—it's more than anyone else is doing."

"That's about the *worst* idea I've heard," Devinon laughed. "And I, myself, have come up with some super bad ideas in the past! And, in the present, too, actually ... and most likely in the future."

"Well, does anyone have any better ideas?" The frustration in Brutus's voice was palpable as he desperately tried to formulate a new, less ridiculous idea.

In true party fashion, nobody had any better ideas, of course. This wasn't a big surprise and was actually, in fact, expected.

"Well, then," Brutus finally said, "now what?"

"We can't just stand around." Liandra inspected the circumference of the pit which was, unfortunately, much too large for them to traverse by any mundane means. "Bottomless or not, it really doesn't matter. The depth of the pit doesn't change our goal of getting across."

"Well, yeah," Devinon replied. "But it absolutely matters whether we fall for eternity or eventually splatter on the ground really hard. While I prefer neither option, if I'm going to hit the ground, I'd at least like to see it coming. There's nothing worse than a surprise of that magnitude."

"We could run away," Throg suggested.

"And how would *that* get us across the pit?"

The orc shrugged. "It work before."

The entire party nodded and grunted, recalling their spotty history. And though it was an accurate assessment, running away would not help them in this situation.

Just then, there was a low rumbling sound and the ground quivered. The group immediately stumbled away from the pit as the shaking intensified and the rumbling got louder. And just when they thought they could take no more, it ended and a finger popped out of the pit, landing at their feet.

"What just happened?" Devinon asked, nudging the familiar finger with his feet. It was indeed Liam's finger—that much was clear—but what kind of a pit threw things *out* of it.

"Did ..." Liandra stammered, "did the pit just barf on us?"

"*Doch norak v'susistrus galfinor.*"

It was a low, guttural voice that emanated from the dark depths, and it settled in their ears, causing every fiber to vibrate in kind. They looked at one another, speechless, and all took another step back from the chasm.

"Um," Liandra said uneasily, "what?"

Several moments of silence resulted, followed finally by the same voice.

"*Doch norak v'susistrus galfinor.*"

"Does anyone understand what is being said?" she asked. Everyone shook their heads.

"I think we all only speak the Common Tongue," Devinon replied. "Well, except Throg who probably speaks Orcish as well."

"Nope," Throg responded, "only Common."

"Huh." Devinon smirked. "I should be surprised, but I'm really not."

"We don't understand what you are saying!" Liandra

shouted into the darkness, speaking slowly as if that would help a pit understand their language. "We only know the Common Tongue!"

There were, again, several moments of relative silence until the voice finally responded.

"I said, stop throwing your trash down my mouth."

Everyone gasped in unison, looking at one another with both confusion and a sort of surprised glee.

"Wait," Liandra replied, "your ... mouth?"

Again, there were a few moments of silence before a response came. I'll just ask you to assume there was a lag in between each communication instead of telling you because I'm sure that would get old really quickly, and nobody wants that.

"And what adventuring party doesn't know other languages. Did you sleep through adventurer school or something? But, yes, my mouth. I don't want your musician fingers and I *certainly* don't wish you to throw fire down my gullet. Not only does it taste terrible, but it's super rude."

"So," Devinon said, approaching the edge of the chasm, "you're not a bottomless pit, then? But you must be pretty deep."

"I'm not a pit at all!" the voice growled. "Well, yes and no. But, yes, I'm very long. Do you know the amount of energy it takes to vomit something up?"

"Um, no," Devinon replied.

"Well, it's a lot. And it's not pleasant. Have you ever seen a giraffe throw up?"

"That's also a no."

"It takes, like, five minutes! And I'm sure it's not pleasant. So, in conclusion, don't throw your crap down here."

"Oh, I get it!" Devinon exclaimed. "Is that why it takes so long for you to talk?"

"Yes, that's why it takes so long for me to talk!" the voice responded in a sarcastic tone. "I had to say something because not only do I not want your refuse, but your constant bickering up there is really annoying. If I weren't a pit, I'd probably kill myself just listening to it. If I could throw myself down an even bigger pit, I would."

"Okay, okay," Pylara interrupted, "we get the point. We really just want to get to the other side of you, so can you tell us how to do that?"

"What do I look like, a trap designer? No. I'm a friggin' pit. What the fifteen-or-so Hells do *I* know about getting across a pit?"

"Actually," Liandra said, "being a pit, I would think you'd be the expert on that subject."

"Well, I'm not the expert on that!" the voice said, mocking her. "I'm the expert on falling and dying when you reach the end, not on avoiding falling and dying when you reach the end."

"My apologies. It's just that ... well, we haven't met many pits so we're not knowledgeable on the subject. Do you, have a name by chance?"

"I do, thanks for asking. But to pronounce it in the Common Tongue is simply to scream."

"Huh, that makes sense," Devinon mused.

"So, instead, you can call me Kevin."

"It's nice to meet you, Kevin," Liandra said as graciously as she could.

"Whatever."

"It's nice meeting you," Pylara added, "but we still need to traverse you."

"Oh, but of course you do. No one ever stays to hang out with a chasm. They all just want to get across it as if it's just a meaningless hazard!"

"But," Devinon replied, "I mean, you *are* just—"

Pylara jabbed him with her elbow and frowned. "Don't piss off the chasm," she mouthed.

"But you know what?" Kevin continued. "I simply *cannot* sit here and listen to your inane ramblings for one more minute, so I will help you cross as long as you promise never to come back and *absolutely* never to throw bard fingers down my mouth again."

"Or what?" Devinon quipped. "You'll yell at us some more?"

"Hey kid," Kevin replied.

"I'm not a kid!"

"Whatever. Anyway, you ever smell the breath of a really long pit at the bottom of which reside innumerable corpses and garbage?"

"Uh, no. But what does that have to do with—"

"I think he's threatening to burp on us," Liandra said.

"Oh. So ... no thank you. We promise never to return then, oh benevolent hole in the ground!"

"If you're going to fight Gobthorak," Kevin chuckled, "then I believe you."

"So ... how do we get across you then?" Devinon inspected the area and there truly was no way around or across. If Kevin knew of a way, it was not obvious.

"Oh," the chasm replied, chuckling, "you're going to love it!"

"Really?" Brutus asked, ever hopeful.

"Nope. You most certainly are *not* going to love it."

"Great," Devinon groused, "I knew that would be the answer. Of all the talking pits in the world, we had to encounter the sarcastic pit."

"We're all sarcastic pits."

"Really?"

"I have no idea," Kevin laughed. "I'm a hole in the ground. I don't get out much."

"Okay, so," Liandra interrupted, "what is the method with which we can cross you?"

"I'm going to have to barf you out."

"Did he just say 'barf us out'?" Brutus asked.

"I can't say I didn't see that coming," Devinon sighed.

27

"Why did we agree to this again?" Liandra shouted.

"This was a bad idea!" Devinon screamed.

"Whee!" Throg laughed.

The five party members tumbled out of control, having agreed to let Kevin "hork its wad" as Brutus so eloquently put it, and now found themselves descending the mostly dark pit, regretting this—possibly the worst decision they had ever made. Also, quite possibly the last decision they ever made.

"So, how long do you think we have to fall?" Liandra asked.

"How should I know?" Devinon sneered, "this is my first time falling down a stinky, sentient pit!"

"It *does* indeed smell rather foul in here," Brutus noted, as if nobody else had experienced the aromas. "So, I truly hope this will all be over soon."

"Oh sure," Devinon replied, "any minute now. I can feel it."

"Really?"

"No."

"Well then, what do you suggest we do?"

"We go that way." Devinon pointed down but he wasn't sure Brutus could see his overly flourished, sarcastic movements in the dim light of Liandra's hair. "And we go really fast."

"Well thank you for that wisdom, genius."

"You're welcome, though I'm not sure what you expected because we WILLINGLY JUMPED DOWN A HOLE IN THE GROUND LIKE A BUNCH OF FOOLS!"

"Would you two stop bickering like children already?" Liandra shouted. "It's not helping."

"But is it really hurting?" Devinon laughed.

"It *is* hurting ... my ears," Pylara added.

"Whee!" Throg squealed.

"Can't we just gloss over this part?" Devinon asked. "You know, like we did with the traveling and a bunch of the dungeon?"

No, no we cannot. To gloss over "the part with the pit" would be a disservice and we just can't do it. I've got my reasons and I'm bound by my own arrangements, so just fall and scream or whatever and it'll get resolved in due time. Just be patient. Besides, I spent a lot of money on this pit.

"Yes," Kevin agreed, "just be patient." This statement was followed by disturbing laughter.

"I think," Brutus posited, "it's quite possible we made the wrong decision."

"You think?" Pylara growled. "And whose idea was it?" She glared at Devinon who probably couldn't see her but also probably somehow felt her gaze.

"That was a whole chapter ago. I can't be expected to remember such things," Devinon replied. "Besides, I'm not sure anyone actually made the decision. It just sort of happened."

"If we all become stains on the ground," Liandra growled, "I'm coming back to haunt the living crap out of all of you."

"Can a ghost ... haunt other ghosts?" Devinon asked.

"I don't think so," Pylara replied. "If it's all ghosts then it's less haunting and more hanging out, I think."

"If you lie flat and spread out your arms and legs, you'll fall slower!" Brutus suggested, doing just that. He had his shield out like a parachute. He was not, however, falling any slower than anyone else. "In fact, you can probably fly!" he added, totally not flying.

"You know, if Liandra knew any useful spells, we probably could've teleported across and been just fine!"

"I hate you, Devinon." Liandra resisted the urge to cook the little bastard with a fireball right then and there. She debated it for several moments, though. "Besides, I don't recall seeing a door anywhere and there was no floor! Where would we teleport to?"

"I don't know!" Devinon shouted. "Because there was no way to find out without a spell to teleport us in the first place!"

"That doesn't make any sense!"

"Your face doesn't make any sense!"

"I *do* have a spell that can teleport you ... into the afterlife if you'd prefer."

This appeared to be all that was needed to end the asinine argument and they fell in silence for a spell, trying not to focus on the terrible stench of ... well, whatever it truly was. Nobody wanted to think about what exactly could produce such an odoriferous concoction. It was, however, probably the smell of the last group of adventurers who thought it was a fantastic idea to hurl themselves down a dark, sentient, talking pit.

"So, guys?" Brutus asked.

"What is it, Brutus?" Pylara said. The tone in her voice conveyed great disappointment that someone broke the peaceful silence.

"I was thinking. What if the exit we're looking for is at the *bottom* of this pit? Or what if we're actually falling up instead of down? Or what if we're not falling at all and this is just an elaborate illusion meant to test us somehow?"

Nobody knew how to respond to that kind of flawed logic.

"What if," he continued, we indeed aren't falling but, instead, the terrain around us is moving. Whoa ... that's really disorienting if you think about it."

"Well," Liandra responded, "that's not a good sign."

"What's not a good sign?" Pylara asked.

"The holy man's got pit madness."

"Pit madness?"

"It's a condition of confusion and dementia related to falling down long, dark, vacuous areas."

"Did you just make that up?" Devinon scoffed.

"I most certainly did not."

"Because it sounds made up."

"She's right," Liandra argued. "It's a real condition. I read about it as a side effect produced by a certain class of spells. It was text included in the book as a precaution."

"It just sounds ... oddly specific is all."

"Devinon, are you accusing me of making up a mental condition?"

"I mean ... maybe? It sounds made up. And why don't the rest of us have it? Besides, you don't even cast spells that would cause such a condition so how can you really be an expert on it? If I need someone to give me advice on how to stop, drop, and roll when I'm on fire, I'll look you up."

"I have the ability to understand concepts that don't relate to fire. It's called learning and critical thinking, but I doubt you'd know anything about that because it doesn't involve thieving and stabbing."

"I'm sorry, I wasn't paying attention until I heard the words 'thieving and stabbing.' But that did catch my interest."

"What else could you possibly have to pay attention to?" Pylara asked.

"Plenty of things. Complex things. Things you definitely wouldn't understand."

"You're a funny kid," she snorted, "but not 'ha ha' funny —more like 'might tell a joke, might stab me in the face' funny."

"Funny you should mention that," Devinon laughed. "That was my slogan when I tried to run for a council seat in Baranston. I should've won, too."

"With a slogan like that, how could you lose?" Pylara replied sarcastically.

"Right? Everyone found out I murdered my competition and, get this, they wanted to throw me in the dungeon instead!"

"Sounds to me like a bunch of ungrateful people," Brutus laughed, obviously being facetious.

"Whee!" Throg continued.

"So, how long do you think we've been falling?" Pylara asked.

"I guess that depends on how fast the reader can read." Devinon quipped.

Nobody knew how to respond to this, so they all remained quiet again. For a few moments, blissful silence reigned—well, except for Throg who appeared to be having the time of his life, laughing and carrying on.

"So, whose idea was this again?" Pylara asked, finally breaking the silence. "Because I'm starting to have regrets."

"It was Liandra's idea," Devinon snorted. "This must be her idea of a good time."

"Hardly," Liandra replied, sneering. "There would be more fire involved. Besides, it was Kevin's idea, remember?"

"Well," Pylara continued, "I'm not going to lie—I'm not liking this plan anymore."

"Which part isn't living up to your expectations?" Devinon joked. "The falling or the ... falling?"

"I'd like to point out," Brutus interrupted, "that the splatting when we eventually hit the ground should probably be your main concern."

"Oh, yes, that *is* a concern of course but, honestly, I'm bored and stuck here with you guys and have nothing to do and nothing to steal."

"This really is the worst pit ever," Brutus agreed. "As far as pits go, it's rather lackluster. Not that I expected full amenities or anything, but at least the smell could be better."

"Thanks for reminding me," Devinon growled.

"Oh, for pit's sake," Kevin piped up, his irritation obviously apparent. "Do you guys ever stop bickering?"

"Not really," Devinon replied.

"Nope," Brutus agreed.

"You know, I *was* actually going to eat you because you were foolish enough to jump down a pit at the first recommendation but now, I'm not even sure I want to. You'd all probably give me indigestion."

"Wait," Liandra said, "you were going to *eat* us? You lied to us?"

"Well, yeah. Why is this so surprising? I'm a hazard in a dungeon! And, as much as life is boring and lonely, I have to eat sometimes. I mean, no hard feelings, but I get hungry."

"You betrayed us! How could you?"

"I recommend not enthusiastically leaping into strange pits," Kevin continued. "Ooh, you know what? Those are words of wisdom that should go on one of those inspirational paintings."

"If you had a body, I would burn it to cinders."

"Hey now, there's no need to get angry. I told you it wasn't personal. And, besides, I've decided *not* to eat you, remember?"

"Yeah, but only because you think we're not tasty!" Devinon shouted angrily. "That's insulting!"

"Right?" Brutus agreed. "Are we not good enough for you? I bet we're scrumptious!"

"It *does* seem pretty judgmental," Pylara added, "to assume we're not delicious without any proof. You're jumping to conclusions without any fact-based evidence."

"I don't have to eat a dog turd to fully understand that they're not tasty," Kevin laughed. "Intuition is a handy thing."

"Did he just call us dog turds?" Brutus whispered.

"I think he did," Pylara muttered.

"Are you guys actually trying to convince a dungeon hazard to eat us?" Liandra asked. "Because I'd rather not."

"I said I *was* going to eat you. I've changed my mind, so just cool your fireballs already."

"Fine," Devinon pouted, "so what's going to happen, then?"

"This."

There was no period when their momentum slowed down —no gentle shift in direction and no warning whatsoever. There was first a terrible sound, as if Kevin had been storing up one mighty belch for the ages. This immediately coincided with the adventurers being catapulted upward at great speed and with great force.

And it was accompanied by an even worse aroma than before.

Everyone screamed and flailed as they sailed and tumbled uncontrollably through the air, faster than they had fallen.

"That's the worst odor I've ever smelled!" Pylara shouted, trying not to vomit. The sounds coming from her companions indicated they were probably attempting the same colossal feat.

"Did he just burp us out?" Devinon asked.

"Sort of," Kevin replied. "Pits only have one giant hole …"

"I'm sorry I asked!"

"I, too, am sorry you asked," Pylara replied.

"Of all the encounters we've had on this journey," Brutus added, "this might be the worst."

"I think you're forgetting the musical episode," Liandra retorted.

"I stand corrected. *Second* worst."

"I wish I could say it's been fun," Kevin said, "but you really are the worst sort of mean, bickering, petty imbeciles and I'm quite happy to be rid of you. So, I bid you goodbye, and mind the bump."

"What bump?" Devinon asked.

They briefly found themselves back on the surface with the room's ceiling approaching quickly. As they all braced for impact, they sailed through the ceiling and tumbled out of a wall in a new room, landing in a tangled heap on the ground.

"Is everyone all right?" Liandra asked, struggling to stand.

"I can still smell it," Pylara whined, dusting herself off. "That smell is stuck in my nose. I shall never be rid of it!"

"It's the worst!" Brutus exclaimed, trying to clean the smell off himself with his hands.

"We here," Throg said, pointing ahead of them.

"They stood on a plush red carpet in a spacious, grandiose room, brightly illuminated by torches on pedestals and on the walls. And there, high upon a dais of marble, was an ornate throne fashioned from bones, weapons, and clothing. If the sight hadn't been so appalling, the party might have appreciated the quality craftsmanship that went into such a piece of furniture but, no, they were too busy being cowards.

"Hey," Devinon said, "have a little sympathy. We just got almost eaten and then burped out by a pit, okay?"

"I think we were deuced out, actually," Brutus argued.

"Let's not speak of that again," Liandra grumbled," ever. Anyway, we have more important things ahead of us."

"If this is Gobthorak's throne," Brutus said, "then where's Gobthorak?"

"Do not be so quick to charge headlong into your own demise," a deep, rumbling voice said. "It'll happen soon enough."

28

ou guys smell terrible," the voice said.

"Thanks for noticing," Liandra sneered. "How about you show yourself so we can skip the parlaying and get down to the combat."

"Oh, so you're rollplayers and not roleplayers?" the voice laughed.

They all looked at one another, confused and unsure of what do to.

"It's a play on words!"

"I don't get it," Devinon said, shaking his head.

"I guess it loses something in translation from text to speech. I guarantee you'd laugh if you saw it written down. Trust me."

"Whatever," Liandra said, her patience wearing thin. "Can you just come out here so we can get this over with? We've had a long day."

"Fine. Behold the grandiose glory of Gobthorak, Eater of Worlds and Bane of all Existence!"

Everyone drew their weapons and prepared for the fight of their lives, expecting a grand entrance from their final foe. A small door on the side wall opened and Gobthorak stepped through.

Instead of some hulking, drooling, fearsome monster, Gobthorak was small, gaunt, and green but looked otherwise human. He shut the door behind him and entered the room, nearly tripping over something on the ground.

"Oh, wow, I haven't cleaned in a while," he said meekly. "I apologize for my messy throne room." He picked up whatever object he found on the ground and threw it behind the throne. He then struggled to climb onto his mighty chair.

"Do you need some help, little guy?" Devinon snickered. "Maybe a booster seat?"

"Shut up," Gobthorak growled, finally making himself comfortable in the chair which now eclipsed him. "So anyway, what in the fifteen-or-so Hells do you want?"

"Oh, hi there," Liandra said, "is your daddy home? We're here to see Gobthorak."

"I *am* Gobthorak!" he shouted, adjusting himself as he sank into the throne.

"Would you like a phone book or something to sit on?" Pylara laughed.

"What's a phone book?" Gobthorak asked.

"Oh, wait, those don't exist here, do they?" she laughed some more.

"No, they do. I was being sarcastic because nobody uses them anymore. What are you, two-hundred years old? Can I get you adventurers some hard candy?"

Everyone in the party remained silent but nodded as they acknowledged the sick burn.

"See? I can be a jerk too," Gobthorak hissed.

"So," Devinon laughed, "this is you?"

"What do you mean by that?"

"You're Gobthorak, Eater of Worlds, Bane of Existence?"

"The very one."

"Huh," Brutus said, rubbing his chin thoughtfully.

"Wait, what do you mean, 'huh'?" Gobthorak stood from his throne of skulls and stretched.

"Well, I mean, we've all heard so much about you and, now that we're here, standing before you, it's all a little ..."

"Well, go on. A little what?"

"Lame," Devinon added.

"Underwhelming," Pylara chuckled.

Gobthorak looked at them all, confused, but said nothing, presumably waiting for more information. It was a very unheroic, awkward moment, for sure. But, then, that pretty much summed up this entire group anyway.

"Yeah, lame," Devinon continued. "Not as lame as, I don't know, raisins, but I guess we just expected more. You're ... you're just a dude."

"A dude whose ass we're going to kick," Brutus laughed. "I mean, any one of us could pound you into goo with our eyes closed."

"What's wrong with raisins?" Liandra muttered.

"Well, what in the fifteen-or-so Hells did you expect?" Gobthorak sounded moderately perturbed which, given his diminutive stature, came across as utterly adorable.

"I mean, something way scarier," Brutus snorted.

"Yeah, scarier," Throg agreed. "Like big rat or something."

Devinon stifled a laugh. "I dunno, something with fifteen eyes and lots of tentacles and claws and teeth and maybe action missiles which definitely don't exist so *of course* I mean fireballs. Yeah, fireballs. Or maybe, like, just a big monster with twenty butts or something. And, not that I want to criticize or anything, but all you've got is a throne of skulls that you probably bought from a local merchant."

"I did not *buy* this throne."

"Right," Pylara giggled.

"These are *real* skulls! This throne is fashioned from all the foes I have vanquished in combat!"

Pylara snickered some more, trying to hold it in and failing. "Vanquished foes? Were they made of plastic?"

"These are real!"

"Fake," Pylara laughed.

"Real! Do you know how difficult it is to get them to match up size-wise and then fit just perfectly for sitting? It took me years to—oh you know what? Screw it. I have nothing to prove to you."

Gobthorak folded his arms across his chest and scowled at the party.

"Okay, whatever," Liandra grumbled. "Fine, your throne is gorgeous and I'm sure the screams of your many fallen foes will echo through this chamber forever. None of this matters, because we're here to stop you."

"Stop me from what?"

"From destroying the world, of course. Eating it or whatever it is you're going to do."

"Wait, what? Why would you think that?"

"Because, genius," Devinon spouted, "you're the 'Eater of Worlds' and we're here to stop you from, you know, eating our world!"

Gobthorak relaxed and chuckled, apparently having forgotten the insults they had slung at him. "You're all not very bright, are you? I'm not going to eat this world!"

"Wait, what?" Liandra stepped in front of the rest of the group, her hair smoldering. "We were told you had awakened and were going to devour our world."

Gobthorak laughed some more which was worrisome, because it was a combination laugh of "that's so funny" and "you guys are so foolish I am going to toy with you before I destroy you."

Maybe a little fart joke-related laughter in there as well.

"I would be a fool to eat this world."

"Why's that?" Devinon inquired. "Would it upset your stomach?"

"Because I live here! This is where I keep all my stuff! I have this kickass throne and this awesome lair with traps and hazards and stuff! Not to mention it has not one but *two* bathrooms!"

"What stuff do you have besides the phony throney over there?" Devinon asked.

"Shut up! I have stuff! Lots of it! I have *way* more stuff than you have, I bet. I keep it in other rooms, of course. I like to keep my throne room tidy."

Liandra was both bored and annoyed. "Okay, fine." This whole quest had been for nothing and standing around here wasn't making things better. "I'm sure you've got plenty of stuff and your throne is magnificent. Since you aren't going to end us and everything in this world, we'll bid you good day and leave you alone. It's a long journey back and I'm over all this."

"Oh, so the thing about that is," Gobthorak laughed, "I'm actually pretty hungry. And since you're here, it would be a shame not to just eat you. Otherwise, I have to go looking for something to eat and, frankly, delivery is just so much easier than going out to eat."

"Good luck with that, slim," Devinon cackled, drawing his daggers. "Okay, so who wants first crack at the pipsqueak?"

"What was your suggestion? Fifteen eyes, tentacles, claws, teeth, and fireballs?"

"I mean," Brutus said," it still sounds pretty lame."

Before Brutus could argue further, Gobthorak exploded into a hulking, green, teeth-filled monster with fifteen eyes and several massive tentacles. "Is this to your liking?" it asked, its voice booming and low, shaking the entire cavern.

"More or less," Devinon muttered, now terrified.

"I prefer the twenty butts," Brutus muttered.

"Hey wait," Throg said. "Where fireballs?"

"Dammit Throg!" Pylara smacked the orc upside the head.

"Oh, right. I nearly forgot." Several of Gobthorak's eyes ignited in an infernal blaze and each one expelled a ball of fire that exploded on the ground around them.

"You had to ask!" Devinon shouted.

"You're one to talk," Liandra replied, scolding him. "You're the one who suggested this in the first place! I would've preferred something like puppies!"

"Yeah," Devinon mumbled, "probably scary-ass puppies with multiple heads that shoot death rays or something."

"Stop giving him ideas!"

"Can you grow horns?" Devinon asked.

Gobthorak obliged, sprouting several horns from his mottled green head. "Easy," he sneered.

"Ooh!" Brutus shouted gleefully, "what about claws?"

The horns shrunk back into Gobthorak's flesh, replaced by several large, crab-like claws that emerged from different places on his body.

"I was thinking arms with claws at the end, but I guess a claw coming right out of your head is cool," Brutus muttered, somewhat disappointed.

"Can you turn into a book?" Liandra asked.

"Why would I want to turn into a book?" Gobthorak asked, puzzled.

Liandra shrugged, lacking an adequate retort.

"Because then you'd be moderately useful," Brutus laughed.

"Oh wait!" Pylara said, "how about—"

"Enough!" Gobthorak shouted, obviously annoyed. The claws disappeared, returning him to his former appearance. "I grow tired of this nonsense! You have invaded my sanctum and—"

"I mean," Devinon interrupted, "let's call it what it is. It's a cave, man."

"It doesn't matter! You aren't welcome here and I'm hungry, so this all works out quite well. So now, my friends, I guess this is goodbye." Gobthorak slowly advanced on the party, swiping at them with his tentacles as they backed up, looking furiously for an escape.

"Now just hold on there," spoke a voice from behind Gobthorak.

29

"Wait, what?" Gobthorak asked, his face painted with confusion. "Who in the fifteen-or-so Hells are you?" he continued, turning to face the small group of people filtering into the throne room.

"We can't let you eat these people," the voice continued. The group walked toward the party, passing Gobthorak who could do nothing but watch, dumbfounded.

"And just why can't I eat them? They broke into my home and trashed the place, then they made fun of my appearance. Not only do they deserve their fates, but I also haven't had breakfast yet.

"It's, like, two in the afternoon, dude," Devinon said, but backed down after Gobthorak shot him a dirty look.

As the group of people got closer, everyone began to recognize them, and they all felt a warm kinship with their possible saviors as they stood side by side in the face of certain doom.

"We will *not* allow you to eat these people," the man said. Devinon immediately recognized him—Darwin Goodblood, the armor-clad knight they met in Candyville. He was a bit surprised he didn't hear the man coming.

"Indeed," another man said. "The warrior is correct. You cannot have them."

It was the man from Duskenheim—the man they procured the map from. Devinon scoured his brain to remember the man's name. Ah, yes, Brisket.

His name totally wasn't Brisket; it was Briskel, but whatever. Devinon didn't care.

"And who will stop me?" Gobthorak laughed. "You?" he pointed to Briskel. "I eat dog turds like you for snacks!"

"You eat dog turds for snacks?" Pylara asked, trying not to laugh. "Do you at least dip them in a sauce or something?"

"You know what I meant! And, in case you didn't, I was saying that this little group of people over here has no better chances of defeating me than you do. Just to be clear, I'm going to destroy you all. Wait, how did you all even get in here?"

"Oh," Briskel said, "the back door. We used the key under the 'Please Die' mat."

"Oh, for Gamchakara's sake, now I have to change the locks. Thanks a lot for that."

"♫ It's not our fault your security measures are so lax, ♫" a woman sang.

The entire party cringed as several others sang harmony— at least, that's what they assumed it was supposed to be. It sounded more like a wounded gortog ... if such a thing existed in this realm.

"♫ But surely a better lock would discourage attacks! ♫" they continued.

Gobthorak growled and screamed. "Knock off the singing!" he shouted and, to show he meant business, scooped up and ate one of the singers. "Ugh, they even *taste* off-key, if such a thing is even possible."

"They're bad enough that I'd believe it," Devinon whispered to Brutus.

"Anyway," Gobthorak continued, "I was aiming for a light breakfast but, as any of my friends will tell you, I won't turn down extra free food!"

"You have friends?" Liandra asked, surprised. "Like, there are other world-eating creatures out there? This is fascinating!"

"There are none so grandiose as me," Gobthorak replied, huffing. "I am the sole eater of worlds. Most of them just eat, like, entire continents or mountains or something. And, besides, there are far fewer of them around these days."

"Why's that?"

"I sort of ... ate them."

"Do you just eat everything then?"

"Well, yeah. I mean, no, I didn't eat *them*. Of course I didn't, that would be silly! But no, seriously, I ate them. Yes, I eat everything—especially sarcastic, self-centered little twits like yourselves."

"Perhaps a bargain can be reached?" Briskel asked, stepping forward with his hands raised. "I think our goal and your goal are essentially the same."

"Wait a minute," Gobthorak said, holding up a finger—a finger that wasn't there a moment ago. He then scratched his oozing, shape-shifting head. "I thought you were here to save these losers."

Everyone in the group laughed in unison while the party swapped confused and worried glances, unsure what to make of the situation. Devinon considered simply fleeing but was also morbidly curious about the newest developments.

"♪ Save them?" a man sang.

"Oh no," Briskel laughed. "No, we're not here to save them! That's hilarious!" The group all shared a hearty laugh while Liandra and the rest of the party looked on. Worry slowly crept into their faces.

"No, we're not here to *save* them!" Briskel continued. "We're here for revenge!"

The group's laughter stopped suddenly and the happiness on their faces turned to hostile anger as they all glared at the group of adventurers.

"They deserve what's coming to them," Briskel growled, wringing his hands together.

"Well, this is a shock," Devinon whispered. "He seemed like such a nice, helpful man. What did we ever do to him?"

"These jerks ignored my child's cries after he fell down a well!"

"Oh yeah," Devinon muttered, "that *did* happen."

"And that's not the worst of it," Briskel continued.

"I mean," Devinon said, "to be fair, who falls down wells anymore? That's why there's always a sign posted that says 'do not fall down this well you damn kids' or something like that. Not that I read signs."

"I have to side with the kid on this one," Gobthorak said, his voice booming through the great cavern. "Your kid doesn't sound very bright."

Devinon couldn't see the exact dirty look Briskel shot at Gobthorak, but it must have been something because the Eater of Worlds recoiled slightly before regaining his composure.

"They ate my friends," a familiar voice shrieked before someone held up a hot dog.

"No way!" Pylara exclaimed. "How did you get here?"

"We sandwiches are powerful," the hot dog replied.

"You're not even a sandwich," Devinon scoffed, turning his nose up.

"Not only did they eat my friends," the hot dog continued, "but they keep belittling my status as a sandwich!"

"They left me for dead in a forest filled with boring, droning awful things!" Darwin shouted.

"Now come on," Liandra countered, "we didn't leave you, we just ... couldn't find you!"

"Did you try looking for me?"

"Well, no ..."

"Now that's just terrible," Gobthorak said, wagging a finger at the adventurers. "And I have opinions about the hot dog/sandwich debate, but we can cover that later. So far, however, I'm not convinced."

"♫ They left us to die in a music-filled hellshole of a city!" a man sang ... poorly. "♫ Doomed to sing ourselves to death!"

"There was nothing we could do!" Brutus pleaded. "We couldn't lift the curse."

"♫ So, instead, you took the source of the curse to another town, thereby cursing them!"

"Uh, yes," Brutus stammered, "we did indeed do that. And now that you put it that way, it does sound sort of bad."

There came a low rumbling sound from a pile of rocks that, upon further inspection, wasn't a pile of rocks at all. It was the rock monster!

"Oh, you too?" Devinon shouted, exasperated. "And you're pissed off because, what, I touched you?"

The rock monster nodded.

"I swear I didn't see the 'do not touch the rock monster' sign!"

"Oh man, you touched him even though there was a sign asking you not to?" Gobthorak frowned. "That's cold, man."

"This doesn't appear to be going well for us," Liandra whispered. "We might want to look for an easy exit."

"They're so entitled, they thought I should give them my wares for free!"

"They stole a book from my shop!"

"They blew up my uncle's house, along with all his rats!"

In unison, the party slowly inched their way along the wall, hoping to find this "back door" everyone supposedly used to get in.

"They destroyed my dusk machine!"

"They robbed me!"

"They robbed *me* too!"

"Excuse us," Liandra said, trying to sneak past the group.

"They wouldn't shut up when I was trying to eat them!" Kevin shouted from the previous room.

"Hey, so, we're just going to let you guys all sort out your differences and come to some kind of agreement," Devinon said, following Liandra's lead. "When you've come to a consensus, then let us know."

"Don't interrupt us!" a woman shouted, scolding Devinon. "Like I was saying, they robbed us too!"

"Okay, now," Gobthorak said, trying to defuse the tension, "it indeed sounds as if you're owed some kind of retribution, so let's come up with a solution that works for us all."

"Maybe we can split them? We get to kill three of them and you get two!"

"Now I don't think that's fair. I should get three and you should get two!"

"Hey, wait," Briskel shouted, motioning around them. "Where did they go?"

They all scoured the chamber, desperate to find the adventurers but the party had long escaped out the back door, fled the area, and didn't stop running until they were clear of all danger.

"That was close!" Brutus said in between gasps as he tried to catch his breath.

"Yeah," Devinon panted, "we almost saved the world!"

"The word 'almost' being key here," Liandra added.

"What good is saving a world that doesn't want you in it?" Devinon asked.

Liandra knew she could argue with Devinon about that very subject and get nowhere so she decided not to even try. Instead, she rolled her eyes and looked behind them. They were safe and, no, the world was not ending.

So, while they didn't actively save the world from any threat, it appeared they were the only adventurers skilled enough to discover there was no threat in the first place. Where all others had perished, they came through like a shining beacon of heroism, not having to face a real threat but also confirming the world's safety.

They would eventually return to me for their well-deserved rewards and revel in their tales of courage and skill, even if they were really just lying to themselves. They would gather at the circular table in the taproom of the Inn of the Scorned Woman and gorge themselves on a victory feast, drinking enough ale to kill your average ox—but not the really good, above-average ox. Let me tell you, that ox can drink *anyone* under the table. I don't know where he puts it.

But, yes, they would celebrate heartily one day when they made it back to Ralph's Keep. Today would not be that day, however, nor tomorrow—because traveling takes a while and they had gone far. But many more obstacles stood in their way —some deadly, some just mere annoyances. But, when you're as inept as they were, all obstacles were hazardous.

"Are you done yet?" Devinon asked.

Fine. Whatever.

These adventures, however, are best left for another time. For we have run out of pages in this book, and it is definitely past my bedtime.

COMING SOON

Mage Breaker Eight Bullets
August 2024

ABOUT THE AUTHOR

Sean R. Frazier lives in Missouri with his wife and two daughters. He also shares the house with two dogs and three cats. He is the award-winning author of the Forgotten Years fantasy saga. That award was a participation trophy from his elementary school soccer team. When not scribing important tomes, Sean enjoys reading, playing guitar, running, playing tabletop and video games, 3d printing oddities, and he recently picked up archery. He's decent, but don't call him Hawkeye just yet.

www.ingramcontent.com/pod-product-compliance
Lightning Source LLC
Chambersburg PA
CBHW020749190726
48285CB00006B/1953